The Widow Darcy Journals, Book 1

First Kiss

First Kiss

By

R. ELIZABETH CARPENTER

THE GOLDEN EAGLE PRESS

www.thegoldeneaglepress.com
@widowdarcy

This book in all formats is a work of fiction. Names, characters, places and incidents are either a product of the author's imagination or are used fictitiously and invented for the dramatic purposes only; any resemblance to actual persons, living or dead, businesses, or events are coincidental and not intended to reflect any actual or real character, history, product or entity.

For Jim. I wish you could be here to see this.

Acknowledgements

This book is a product of many years of studying, writing, learning about the craft of writing, and growing an intimate relationship with my muse. While traversing this path, I have needed and received the enthusiastic and loving support of so many people along the way. I would like to thank each and every person who has said an encouraging word and held me up on my journey.

First, I must whisper to the heavens my undying gratitude to my wonderful departed husband, Jim, for his unwavering, devotion to me and my work. He spent his entire adult life happily, proudly encouraging and supporting me through every laborious, discouraging, excruciating step. He never waivered in his faith in me or his belief in my talent. If it weren't for him, I never would have had the courage to pursue my dreams with the tenacity and persistence that he afforded me. It was in his loving eyes that I saw the potentiality of my own best self.

Next, I thank my son, Jonathon, for his lifelong support of his mother's passion and life's work. He was born the son of a writer, grew up in the writer's household, and was cradled in the arms of creative pursuit. He probably thought every mom spent hours making up stories and writing them down. Then again, perhaps he never noticed because his father was always there to duel with light sabers while momma was in her studio writing.

Thank you, Michael Korda—In 1976, you were the very first editor to reject my novel, *The Burglary*, which you did with the kindest letter telling me you saw something in my writing and advising me to work at my craft and grow. Your letter became the terra firma upon which my fragile self-belief rested all these years. Thank you so much for that generous mentoring of a neophyte author.

To Sharon DeVita, my lifelong and dearest friend with whom I share this vibrant, life-giving need to put words to paper. We've raised our kids together, clung to each other along the path of sorrows, and celebrated the ecstasy of our characters coming to life. No one understands the way you do. Thank you for this treasured and irreplaceable gift we share.

∽

First Readers

To Nancy, the very first reader of this book, my heartfelt, deepest gratitude. You entered Darcy's world and lived it with such authentic enthusiasm and passion, you convinced me of its right to live; you shored up my tattered ego; you encouraged me to transcend my highest personal heights and to never give up. You gave me hope for this book, hope for these characters, renewed hope for my future. Your excitement gave me the courage to pursue my dreams again.

To Mary, award winning English and ESL teacher extraordinaire—thank you so much for your incredible enthusiasm and unending support. I knew these characters were alive and vital when you got so mad at some of them! And then you helped me see through your intelligent, incisive eyes the beauty of my work, a rare and priceless view for a writer.

To George, the very first male reader, my Irish twin, who has read nearly everything I've ever written—your calls to me as you were reading to share specific passages and laugh with me over the funniest parts—thank you for your objective eye and loving encouragement, every step of my long path. When you read the book a second time, and kept calling me to talk about it, I knew: I think I've got something here!

Editorial

Thank you to Clare Moen for her excellent and expert copyediting of this manuscript. Your poet's eye and editorial expertise made all the difference.

∽

Art

Deepest and warmest thanks to Rajesh Maurya from New Delhi, India, the gifted and versatile graphic artist for this book. You listened to my vision and gave life to exactly the cover ambiance and diagrams I asked for. Your designs are gorgeous; your vision the perfect balance between art and function. Thank you for your patient, always generous partnering on this project.

❦

Most of all, to Thomas, my wonderful, loving groom—you fill my life with love, music, and joy. When I enter a room, my eyes seek only thou.

Prologue

Dearest Sean, my sweetest Paco,

Yesterday I had a session with Trudy. I expressed just one tiny fraction of my despair and depression, and suddenly she became aware of my feelings and started running all these diagnostic questions by me. I realized she was alarmed—so I pulled back.

She expressed surprise at my depressed hopelessness—"But you've been dealing with reality so well. You know Sean isn't coming back. ..." She studied me. "You are doing everything you need to, to move on. You know Sean is not coming back. ..."

I just looked her square in the eye, unblinking. In that moment, I couldn't believe she was saying this to me; I couldn't believe that after three years of grief counseling with me she had so little comprehension of how I feel.

She repeated, "I mean, you know he's not really ever coming back."

And I said, "But Trudy, of course I expect him to come back!"

And then you know what she did? She glossed over the moment and made excuses for me. "But you're dealing with life (meaning reality). You're taking care of Jaime (not incapacitated)."

She was concentrating on my actions, i.e., dealing with the emergencies—the day-to-day needs and Jaime's needs—not me, not my devastation, not my hopelessness, not my despair or my depression. In fact, I realize now that's what she does in session; she allows me to dwell on my actions—what I need to do—instead of how I feel.

I asked her if it was abnormal for me to still be wearing my wedding ring, and she said another weird thing. "Well, you know you're not married anymore. In session, you're talking about the pain of being single, the pain of doing everything alone."

I looked at her incredulously. "What are you talking about? Of course I'm still married! I'm still completely committed to my love, to our relationship!"

To which she replied, "You are no longer in a relationship with Sean." But she spoke with discomfort and pressed to gloss over the subject, to move on. She did not stay in the authentic moment.

Sean, I was shocked and dismayed to hear her assumptions and the shallow way she evaluated me, the unbelievably superficial way she viewed me.

How could she say I was no longer married? How could she say there is no more relationship? Is she in la-la land? After all this time, does she have no idea what my world is really like? What my experience is? If I weren't in a relationship with you, I wouldn't be in pain. If I weren't still married to you, I would be actively seeking a new mate—I could no more do that right now than I could eat a slab of beef.

It's not over 'til I'm done. Maybe never. I don't know. All I know is today, the pain I feel today.

For three years, I have confided in this woman more than any other living person. I thought she understood the underlying torment and grief and mourning that I was going through at the least. I thought she, of all people, appreciated the overwhelming despair I have to overcome in order to even get out of bed each and every morning.

But she hasn't a clue.

Yesterday I realized how she uses behavior to judge health or stasis or growth or stability. Yet behavior is a very bad basis of measurement. Only at the most extreme side of an emotional continuum does behavior become altered or impaired. We all do our best to at least give the appearance of coping.

I think of myself as disabled by what I am going through. Yet, for all the trauma, all the pain, look at all I am able to accomplish to the eye of the outsider. I have gone back to school, getting straight As, I am managing my finances, I am renovating the house, I am raising our son. So what? That says nothing about how I feel inside. It says nothing of my despair. It says nothing about how much I love you.

It is only Jaime that keeps me alive. I do all this work—all this life's work—for Jaime, to help him through, to give him stability in a time of chaos, to give him something to live for (which I don't feel for myself), to give him a future to strive for, to give him love and comfort—the very things I have lost forever.

She asked me questions about suicide—have I ever considered suicide? Have I ever taken steps toward suicide? The regular assessment questions I know she must ask a patient she is concerned about.

And I felt nothing but disdain. How could she be so off base—of course I'm thinking about suicide on some level during this. After twenty-one years, I've lost my soul mate. There's nothing to live for without you, Sean. That's the very definition of losing your other half, for god's sake.

Don't they get it? That's the nature of despair. *All is lost.* There is nothing left. That doesn't mean I can't find joy in the moment, or remodel my house, or take care of my child or take care of business. Are they all morons? Do they *none* of them understand what's happened to me or what was happening to me the last two years of our marriage as you were disintegrating before my very eyes, though I didn't know why? Even if they didn't understand back then, wouldn't my grief tell them now?

She says, "Suicide is a temporary solution to a temporary problem."

What a crock of shit. It can also be a permanent solution to a *permanent* problem like the permanent loss of a love.

It is a legitimate decision to decide life is not worth living without your soul mate. I think many people make that decision without committing the actual act of suicide. Hell, lots of people give up and live life as if they *are* dead their whole lives. It would have been more courageous to kill themselves in the first place.

Oh yes, I *fully* know (on one level) that you are gone. You are never coming back. But on another level you could come back at any time because I still love you and I haven't changed.

You could come back because you are still very much alive within me. Nothing is changed inside. I still talk to you, argue with you, and rage against you, and I still feel you every single moment of every single fucking day. That's why you could come back.

People are not one-dimensional. People do not live on one plane. How could she not know? How could she be so stupid?

Yes, I work toward tomorrow: I plan, I work, I change my surroundings—so what? Don't they understand this is all meaningless? The outside is a shell. The outside is superficial. The outside is an appearance like Plato's shadow on the cave wall. It isn't real. What is real is what is on the inside. If she really wanted to know what was on the inside, she would know because I haven't hidden my pain. I have expressed it quite precisely and candidly. But apparently, she has judged me on my capacity to act, to behave in certain ways. I feel nothing but contempt for that. It's so superficial, and it does anger me because it is so dehumanizing to me—it's so invalidating of my true experience, my true self.

If I say there is nothing to live for, then I should be classified as suicidal? Because I *feel* there is nothing to live for, that means I am suicidal?

No, it means I am grieving. I am in mourning. I am suffering a loss of a part of myself.

"... And you shall become as one."

What do they think that means? It's a psychic union. If one person dies, the other is left *maimed* for life.

I am bleeding; I am in unbearable pain. I feel no hope, no desire to go on. I feel your absence every single moment through every single cell of my body, my mind, and my spirit. That is reality for me. It is relentless. There is no getting away from such despair.

But within this despair, I have to make choices. I don't know how the choices will affect the pain tomorrow because I'm still in it today. The nature of my choices is that they surround the caretaking of Jaime. I can't imagine having any reason to live at all if it weren't for him. He is my *raison pour la vie*. I hope I'm in a better place in two years when he leaves for college, because I will be in big trouble if I'm not.

I feel betrayed by Trudy. I feel as if she's only there as long as I perform correctly according to her behavioral codes. She's in the end truly a behaviorist! It's disgusting.

I am *not* the sum of my behaviors. I am so much more than my behaviors—in fact my behaviors *mask* who I truly am.

If I can suffer and bleed as much as I do and still carry on, I should be applauded, not judged badly or *assessed* or diagnosed as not doing well. Now I feel as if I have to hide my experience, not represent it authentically and spontaneously. What good is therapy if one cannot be real and authentic?

Paco, I feel so isolated and alone. I mean, at first I was so alone because of losing you. And then I became even more alone because society grew tired of my plight; people no longer wanted to hear about it. On top of that, it is our son's job—our son, the one reason I do have to be alive—it's his job right now to separate from me emotionally so he can grow up and become a healthy adult. And now I am even *more* alone because the one person I *pay* to understand understands so little and on such a superficial level. I feel so betrayed. So abandoned on every level. I'm so alone.

I've made a decision, my dearest Sean. I am not going to depend on anyone to validate me anymore. I am going to depend on *me* to get me through this. I feel as if I'm on a journey where no woman has ever gone before. Yet it must be the journey of a million other women. I can't be the only person who's ever felt this way. But I may well be one of the few who decides to trust in herself.

Ever since the night you died, Paco, I've had the feeling I was on a distinct path, that I was being guided every step of the way. Maybe the angels lead my way. Or maybe it's you.

From now on, I will trust my own experience as natural and correct. I will trust myself to go in the right direction. The hell with the world. From this moment on, I am the lone traveler. And the universe is my course.

Love you forever,
Darcy aka Your Berry
P.S. Where **Are** You?

Chapter 1

November 14, 1998

Dear Sean,

I'm in a 747 right this minute flying east, across the Atlantic, away from my life, away from our Chicago home, and, Paco, it feels as if I'm going so very far away from you.

Eddie came to send me off at the international terminal at O'Hare. I'm only going to be away for five weeks, yet he kissed me goodbye as if I were never coming back. It was one of those intense and emotional big sister/younger brother moments Eddie and I have. He looked at me with admiration and said I had guts, but he was wrong. Sean, I am so scared I can hardly think. I'm breathing as if I've just run a 10K. You know how it gets when you're scared—your brain goes all fuzzy and you just can't think. I don't know what I'm doing flying off to Spain like this—I don't even speak Spanish that well.

How did I get myself into this? What has come over me? One moment I'm a middle-aged widow going to school so I can get on my feet and support our son, and the next I'm flying off to Madrid for a course I'd never heard of until two weeks ago. When a friend at school told me about this English teaching course and suggested I might want to go, I heard myself say, "Yes!" before she could finish the sentence. Much to my own amazement, I meant it. I really wanted to go. What the class was about was not important. I wanted to go to Spain. And now here I am, just two short weeks later, all alone, on a flight to Madrid, about to begin god knows what kind of adventure. Me, a forty-five-year-old. Oh my god, what have I done? What's gotten into me? Whatever it is, I think I like it.

The flight is fine so far, but you know how I am about flying. I got my beloved window seat so I could "will" the plane up into the skies, and I am sitting next to this Spaniard named Enrique who is very handsome and friendly. That's helpful. He speaks English pretty well. He has eagerly offered to tell me anything I want to know about Spain. I thought perhaps he would take it back if he knew what I really wanted to know—I am curious about Spanish men.

I am finding myself thinking salacious thoughts about men more and more often in the last few months. They sneak up on me and burst into my consciousness before I have a chance to censor them. I know you of all people would approve—you! You've been scolding me all along—I've heard you sweet Paco, I've heard you, but I'm doing the best I can and I just haven't been ready. It's only you I want, Paco. Only you. Where have you gone? I just wish I knew. I just wish I understood better. I'm so scared all the time still. I've never in my entire adult life been alone. We did everything together, my soul mate, my sweet wonderful you. When will the fear go away?

I notice the fear in the pit of my stomach goes away when I listen to Enrique speak. He is centered and confident and seems very happy to be alive. Earlier, he proudly told me about Spain's new democratic government. He's very excited to live in a democracy. He made me forget the fear I'd been feeling in my gut all day. For that I was grateful. He's sleeping right now. It's the middle of the night, the cabin is lit in muted shades of soft darkness, and we still aren't even halfway across the Atlantic. The view outside the plane is inscrutable inky blackness interrupted only by the red blinking lights out on the wing. Frightening inky blackness, just like my life has been without you by my side.

Remember when we traveled overseas together on our honeymoon, Paco? Our first exciting adventure together, the first of many to come. But

I'm scared to go to a foreign country all by myself. In fact, at this moment I'm convinced I've lost all sanity. But this man nestled so close beside me makes me think about Spain and the unknown worlds that lie across the Atlantic. He reminds me of all the brave humans who have crossed this very ocean over the centuries and all the hardships they endured. They had far fewer comforts and much less knowledge about what would greet them at the end of their journey than I—though I'm not very sure about what awaits me, either.

Yesterday, Walter Smith, the head administrator of the English Language Academy (the ELA) in Madrid, emailed me and said that I would be sharing an apartment with a British man named Christopher St. George and an American woman named Cindy Sorenson from New York. I thought this was a strange development. To be rooming with an unknown man feels weird. I guess I assumed women would room with women. Eddie, always the suspicious cop, thought it highly irregular. Though he rarely expresses his emotions, I can always feel them in his lapses, in his brooding silences. He was silent when he heard this news.

When Walter told me about this English guy, I was thinking, what would have happened to this Cindy woman had I not been able to come? Would they have had her living with a strange man all by herself? That seems a bit ... dangerous to me, a bit risky. I mean, I know I'm a different generation than the twenty-year-olds whom I go to graduate school with and I'm more conservative in my outlook, but I'm starting to wonder about this school. What kind of an outfit is this, anyway? How do I know it's on the up and up? After all, I got the information off of the Internet. Good grief. And look at me, I'm just wondering about it now! This is so unlike me, to run off without double checking my research thoroughly. Oh well, it's like this bumpy airplane ride: It started out smooth enough and then hit air pockets—the only thing to do is hold on for dear life and enjoy the ride. I guess I can always hop onto a plane back home if it doesn't work out.

The other thing Enrique reminds me of is how beautiful—no, how exquisite—life can be. I can't resist glancing at him while he sleeps so peacefully. This man is gorgeous, with lovely caramel brown eyes and a *joie de vivre* and an innocence that I have not seen in an adult face in a very long time. I'm wondering, will I find many people such as this in Spain? If so, it could be marvelous, indeed.

It's been so long since I've felt real joy, so long since I've really lived. Fun to me is getting to bed by 10:30 and hearing David Letterman's Top Ten without the interruption of a house full of six-foot, hulking teenaged boys playing death metal in the living room beneath me. Fun to me became getting through a Friday and Saturday night without a phone call from the police. Fun to me has become the peace and quiet of having the house all to myself. That is one of the reasons this trip appealed to me. Jaime's in his first semester of college, way off in California, and there was no reason for me not to just take off and go, for the first time in five years, no reason for me not to spontaneously do something crazy, just because it piqued my fancy.

I wonder what this trip will bring. Five weeks away from home in a foreign country is a long time. Long enough for a few adventures, I think. I don't want to get my hopes up for too much sightseeing in case the course is difficult. I'm going to Spain to get certified to teach English as a second language to adults. I don't want to get sidetracked by traveling too much. I've emailed with my new roommate a couple of times and Cindy is planning to travel to Italy several times to visit her fiancé on weekends. She thinks the course will be a breeze. She thinks European schools are a joke next to American schools.

I have a feeling it's going to be harder than she thinks.

∽

November 22, 1998

Holy shit, Paco, they've paired us with a maniac! My new roommate Cindy met me at the Madrid airport and we took a cab to the apartment together. We got along instantly, Paco. I like her. But our other roommate—he answered the door in a toga! Actually he was half undressed with a blanket wrapped around his naked torso like a toga. With a cigarette dangling between his fingers. My first reaction was, Woa! What do we have here? Oh yeah, this is going to be interesting. My second reaction was alarm when we walked in the front door.

He did agree to carry our suitcases up the fourth floor walk-up when asked. But when we got to the apartment—ye gods! There was a mountain of empty beer cans and wine bottles and open garbage teetering next to the front door. That was just the beginning.

The tiny kitchen was so filthy I couldn't believe someone would actually cook fresh food in there. Cindy took one look and said, "This is disgusting. I'm not living in a dump like this." There were no light bulbs in fixtures, no sheets or linens of any kind, including pillows, and no heat. Paco, there's no central heat here. And it's cold. Last night it went into the thirties. There is a washing machine in the bathroom though. Thank god I thought to pack my own sheets, a blanket, and of course I always bring my own pillow (such a middle-aged woman after all). For all the airline people who laughed at me carrying my flower pillow on board, ha.

Within the first hour, this Christopher guy, though very cute and appealing in a boyish kind of way, was talking about his late-night adventures in Spanish bars. He's already talked about sex and drugs and a host of weird people he's met here in Madrid, and he's only been in town for three days!

As soon as Cindy said she wouldn't live in such a dump, Christopher ran to the kitchen and started cleaning. "Don't leave! I'll clean it. I'll clean it. It's not my fault. It was the bloke who lived here before me. He was an absolute pig," he declared in over-dramatized British outrage. In a half-hour, the kitchen was spotless. I thought it was quite funny and endearing. He didn't want to lose his "Americans." That's what he calls us, Paco, his Americans. So cute.

Cindy was not amused or convinced this was a habitat in which she wanted to live. Christopher, reading her reaction with pinpoint accuracy, begged her to give him a chance. He didn't want to lose all the comforts he would automatically inherit living with two women. Comforts like cooking and cleaning and some semblance of domestic order, to name a few. When he looked at Cindy, I knew there were some other comforts he wouldn't mind acquiring. She is a drop-dead gorgeous blonde.

But, Sean, I have a bad feeling about this place. About this guy. He's a little too loose. He chain-smokes. And I don't believe his protestations about the alcohol. There are entirely too many empty bottles in this apartment. When he went to get changed, he came out in his boxers. We haven't been in the apartment for two hours and he is already parading around half-naked. Look, it's not as if I've never seen a man in boxers before, though as I recall you never wore a thing beneath your jeans … but the fact that he has no sense of etiquette is alarming. I have no idea how old he is, though he can't be older than twenty-five or -six. I'm sorry, but after seeing a man in his skivvies, it's impossible to think of him as a boy. So, I find that I am in a foreign country with a boy-man who has no boundaries. Charming.

᠗

November 23, 1998

I like Christopher. He's cute as a button, with his scruffy longish brown hair, charming as a child with his unself-conscious chatting, and he's funny as hell. He's that kind of boy-man who simply wins you over with his engaging personality. You can't help but like him even when he's being annoying. As soon as he told me he'd been a philosophy major at Edinburgh University, I knew I was lost. Paco, a philosopher. Just like you. What are the chances? In those first few minutes we were alone (Cindy went off to make phone calls or something), we sat and talked about serious things, matters of substance, and I instantly felt as if I were waking up inside. Talking with a man is intoxicating—something I've missed so much since you left. But there was also this physicality, this energy that immediately seemed to explode between us. Within the first half-hour, I was touching him (his arms in talking gestures—and he accepted my touch), something I just don't ordinarily do. In spite of his peccadilloes, there's something about him that I find very attractive.

Still, and maybe because I am attracted to him, I knew within the first hour I could not live with him. It's not that I don't think he's a nice guy. It's just his lifestyle that I can't live with. He's incorrigible—he smokes nonstop, even after promising not to. He drinks incessantly, just as I had feared. And he has friends ringing our doorbell at all hours of the night. After all the alcohol he consumes, he doesn't even hear the doorbell ring. Tonight I just ignored it, though my bedroom is located right next to the front door. I'm not opening the door to any more of his strange menagerie of friends in the middle of the night with him passed out down the hall. Forget it.

Last night he and Cindy went for a sightseeing walk. I was too jet-lagged to go. Some guy came to the door and put a key in the lock! I was lying in the bedroom, so I heard it immediately. I had bolted the door before retiring, so he couldn't get it open. He started banging on the door and shouting. The whole building reverberated with the noise and the pounding. I thought, what kind of a man creates such a ruckus? I knew Christopher was expecting a friend who had one of our keys, which we needed by today, so when he identified himself as Christopher's friend, I did open the door, but with trepidation. He burst in the doorway as if he owned the place. Not even as much as a "pardon me." I told him Christopher wasn't home. Apparently he didn't believe me. He pushed past me with a snarl—"Who are YOU, then?"—and proceeded to march into the apartment, inspecting every room along the hallway.

"I'm Darcy," I introduced myself as I followed behind. "Darcy McMahon. I'm here to take the English course."

"I'm Dylan. Here for the course, then? That's a mistake. Massive mistake to be sure."

Massive mistake? Completely shocked the shit out of me! Then he proceeded to tell me how impossible the course was. I listened without reacting. When his words didn't have the effect he was anticipating, he told me that since he'd had to withdraw from the course once because it was too hard, I definitely couldn't be smart enough to pass.

Can you believe it? He doesn't even know me! The arrogance. The stupidity. If someone that stupid thinks he's smart enough to pass on a second try, I think I'll take my chances on a first. In fact, I am grateful to this crazy Englishman named Dylan. He has inspired my competitive nature to kick in. Because of the physical hardships, I was already wavering about whether to stay. But now I am determined to give the course my best effort.

But get this, Paco, when all those arguments didn't send me scurrying to pack my bags, Dylan then proceeded to tell me how dangerous Madrid is. "You're going to get mugged here, you know. Everyone gets mugged here, so get used to the idea."

That was most alarming. But before this guy had left, he'd told me all about his family, his two stepmothers, his father's sex life, and his own sex life. I'm thinking, this guy is a nutball! He was talking about really inappropriate things, and he had a weird look in his eyes as if he were on something. I was hearing warning bells about him the whole time he stayed. I couldn't wait for him to leave. In fact, I made sure I was closest to the exit at all times. I don't want to be alone with him again.

By the time Christopher and Cindy returned to the apartment, I was unnerved. I told Christopher what Dylan had said, and he was outraged. "I can't believe Dylan said such things. What's got into him? It's not true, any of it. What did you say to him to make him behave so badly? He's really a nice person."

"Me? I didn't say a thing to him!" I couldn't believe Christopher was so vigorously defending someone he'd just met himself. "He just kept saying horrible things about me getting mugged. Are you sure Madrid is safe?"

"Of course 'tis. I never heard such a thing," insisted Christopher in his deep, melodious British tone. He was gurgling the last words in the back of his throat in the most appealing way.

Even before Dylan's remarks, I was already uncomfortable in this neighborhood. The littered streets are lined with boarded-up apartment buildings tagged with colorful Spanish words and designs. They look like gang signs to me, which I find disconcerting. And by now, I've discovered we're almost a half an hour away from the school via the subway. I know I'm going to need to travel late at night by myself on the subway, and I'm very uneasy about that prospect. Just what I need—to walk foreign, gang-infested city streets late at night alone. I wouldn't do that at home!

"We'll ride on the tube together," Christopher reassures me when I express my misgivings. He is acting as if we are old friends and he would be devastated if I left. But I know he and Cindy are both in their mid-twenties, and younger people don't have any loyalty to schedules. I need to feel safe wherever I'm going to stay. Safe enough to travel on my own. Because I know I am on my own in this city. I've been through too much in the last five years to delude myself into depending on the generosity of others. Especially the unreliable generosity of well-meaning children. And besides, to need them is to become disappointed when they aren't there for me. And I don't need any new disappointments—I still haven't survived the disappointment of losing you. ...

Paco, as I locked the flimsy lock on my bedroom door tonight, my second night in Madrid, I was worried. And I'm having trouble sleeping tonight. Am I afraid of what an inebriated, unpredictable Brit might do in the middle of the night? Or am I just apprehensive about the uncertainty of this strange, new city? Or is it because it's twenty-eight degrees with no heat? Or could it be because we live over a noisy block of bars and restaurants? It's past 2:00 a.m., and the noise is still going on. Music, singing, large groups of drunken people yelling and speaking strange words and expressions in the street below, bottles being dumped into garbage cans in the alley beyond, *ad infinitum*. I have never heard such a noisy place as this Madrid. I'm going to have to find a new place to live. Fast.

 ❦

November 24, 1998

When I awoke this morning, I had a fever and the chills and I couldn't stop shaking. Oh my god, there is no way I can study under these conditions. I realized I had to let Christopher and Cindy know right away that I'm planning to find a new place. I was worried about Cindy being there without me—she's an adult, and I realize she isn't my responsibility, but I feel that just by virtue of my age I should look out for her. From what I can see, she has very little common sense about her own personal security, surprising since she's from New York City. She took off alone with Christopher within the first two hours we were here in Madrid, before we had any idea what kind of guy he is. She has exhibited zero caution in this foreign environment that I can see.

So, I told them first thing this morning. They were upset when I told them I had to move. I told them both, "Besides the physical hardships in this place, we have different lifestyles that aren't compatible." I told Christopher privately, "I like you a lot, Christopher. And I think we could be good friends. But if we lived together, we would hate each other by the end of the course. We will be better friends if I move out." He looked at me, unsure whether what I had said was a compliment or an insult. He was unconvinced. But it was true. Even as I said those words to him I felt this little pang of sadness about not living with him—I am drawn to him; I don't know why. Probably because he reminds me of you a bit. I know I will be giving something up by leaving, a quality and quantity of interaction with Christopher. But regardless, I know I need to live in a different environment. Really, in life as well as here, I'm on my own now, Paco. And I know I need to pay attention to my needs and take care of myself. No one else will.

Both Cindy and Christopher could see how ill I was, so they didn't argue with me this morning. They were disappointed, which made me feel some pangs of regret, but after forty-five years of living, I have a pretty good idea what my survival needs are. And a dormitory lifestyle is not on my list of survivable environments.

Spain is not turning out to be the marvelous place I was hoping it would be. It is, in fact, for me, a really difficult place in which to live. The people don't take for granted a standard of living anything close to ours in the States, which I knew before coming, but somehow the living it is different than the thinking it. Such fundamental things as *heat* are not readily available to me in thirty-degree weather. I'm having trouble finding acceptable vegetarian food. This is definitely a meat-eating culture. Just finding food alone is difficult. Finding stores and restaurants open is a problem because the language is a definite barrier to understanding how things work, and you don't know the words to form the questions to even ask once in a store or a restaurant. And all the foods are so different; I don't even know what's in front of me on a menu in a restaurant.

Also, I have limited access to a telephone. Well, actually I found one a couple of blocks away and called your sister, but it was very difficult negotiating the telephone system in Spanish; I nearly gave up. I'm glad I persevered because Anne gave me moral support. She said I should stay here at least until I've seen the school. Though I did note after my descriptions of Christopher and the apartment, she only hesitantly encouraged me.

Oh, and I don't have a typewriter for my assignments, or even an English-Spanish dictionary, which I didn't think to bring. And of course, at the bookstores here, the dictionaries are *Spanish-English.* I didn't bring any books at all. Not even a notebook to take notes. Everything happened so fast, I guess I didn't plan very well.

But of course, worst of all, I don't have you to encourage and comfort me when I'm afraid. I just can't get used to that, Paco. The void. I will never get used to the void.

I feel deprived on so many levels. Inside I am feeling this incredible mixture of eager anticipation and trembling fear. This is scary. But it's also exciting, exotic, and new. I just keep reminding myself that there is no immediate danger to me and so everything is okay right now. Are you watching out for me up there? Or are you completely gone?

༄

We took the subway to school. It felt as if it took hours because I was so sick I could barely sit up—I was feverish and dizzy. The train was unbelievably clean, and the people looked just like ordinary middle- to upper-middle-class people on their way to work, very polite, very well dressed. I kept thinking if I weren't surrounded by Spanish advertising banners and if I didn't hear them speaking in Spanish, I could easily think they were Americans. Well, actually, Americans wouldn't look or act so nice.

When we got to the school, Walter hadn't arrived yet. We waited in the lobby where everyone congregates, students and teachers alike—and they all smoke. First thing in the morning and the air is thick with billowing smoke. I can't get away from it. My lungs are burning. I can't breath. This is intolerable for me. It never occurred to me to inquire about a smoke-free environment. It's something we Americans now take for granted.

Finally Walter arrived and introduced himself to me. He has honey-colored hair and speaks with a smooth English accent. He asked me how I was, and I said, "Not so good." When I told him I was sick and why, he didn't seem to want to know about it. I found his lack of concern troubling. I had expected him to take responsibility for our welfare since he is the liaison between the school and the foreign students. So then I requested he find me a new place to live. "You said if I didn't like the apartment you would find me something else," I reminded him. He agreed to call a woman who lived nearby and ask if I could rent out a room in her apartment. I was placated. At least long enough to go to our first class.

The English Language Academy is located on the third floor of a six-floor office building directly facing the Plaza de Castillo in the center of the financial district of Madrid, a bustling and crowded part of town. The plaza is the second-largest plaza in the city with eight busy streets feeding into the roundabout, which, like all the roundabouts in this city, has a huge sculpted water fountain landscaped with colorful flower gardens in the center. The school itself is nondescript. Small and cramped, a run-down urban office building retrofitted into a school. Like any urban school for that matter.

Cindy, Christopher, and I followed Walter's directions through the smoky haze into a small classroom with windows facing the plaza. We chose desks opposite one another, Christopher and Cindy on the far side of the room. The other students wandered in and each said hello. There are nine of us in all. Five men and four women. A small class. Cozy. Our desks are arranged in a circle like this:

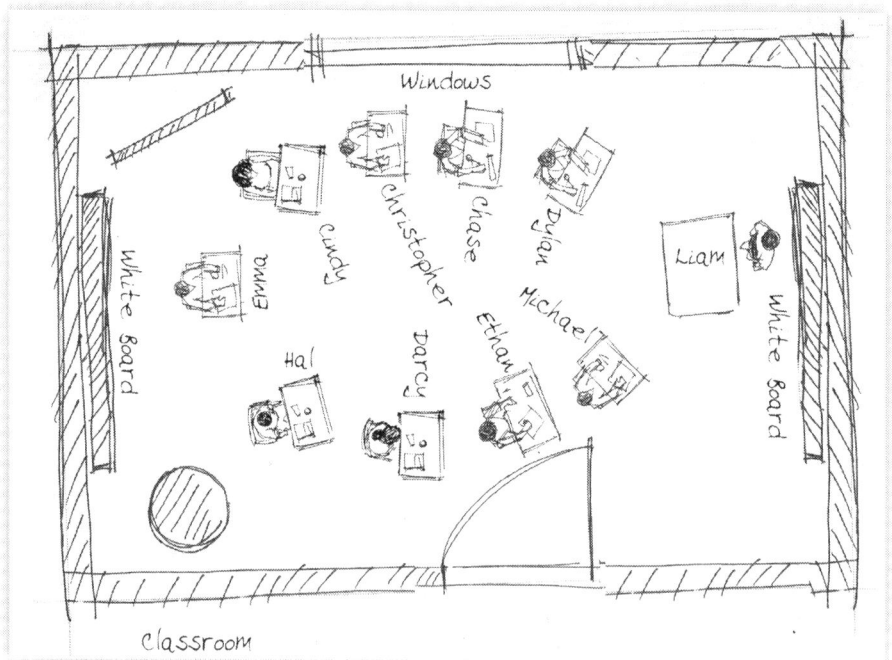

CLASSROOM

When the teacher arrived, he introduced himself as Liam O'Shaunessy. He is as Irish as the grass is green. He is gorgeous. I'm feeling distracted from feeling lousy already. Liam asked each of us to introduce ourselves, especially the new Americans. So Cindy and I went first and told a little about ourselves. Cindy told us about growing up in Brooklyn and studying theatre at NYU. She has a dramatic way of gesturing and enunciates her words in an affected manner. She has an airy little laugh that bubbles up from her diaphragm. The men are spellbound.

Then it was my turn. "Hi, I'm Darcy McMahon. I come from a suburb of Chicago where I'm a graduate student in writing." Someone asked if I'd ever written a book. Without thinking, I said, "Yes, seven of them. Novels." There was a moment of utter silence in the room. When I looked around, all eyes were upon me with stunned expressions, even the teacher. It made me feel so uncomfortable. I have a big mouth. I wish I'd kept that to myself. I hadn't thought about the inequity that piece of information might create between us. But it was too late now. The discomfort was palpable.

The men introduced themselves one by one. The first was a redhead named Ethan from London. To my untutored ear, his accent was not refined, but musical all the same. He was quiet and didn't say much. I remember last night Christopher made fun of him for being so quiet, but he looks nice enough to me. You were always the quiet one, Paco, and I fell in love with you, so as far as I'm concerned, the quiet ones are the gems.

The next was Dylan, whom unfortunately I had already met. Dylan said he was from the Northwest, whatever that meant. He mumbled and spoke in a low tone so he could barely be heard and he had to be told to repeat what he was saying several times. Very different from the sharp voice of bravado aimed at frightening me off last night. Next to Dylan was a man who identified himself as Hal from Wales. His face reddened as he spoke; he seemed embarrassed and self-conscious but quite sweet. Next, a blond-haired Scot named Chase Mackenzie. He was very handsome and refined in his speech, though his accent was definitely different than the English accents so far. I don't know why, but he seemed out of place in the class, like he would feel more comfortable in a boardroom than a classroom. Then, a blue-eyed, brunette woman spoke up in a sweetly sensual, melodious English accent, "Hello, I am Emma May. I'm from Leicester, a leafy suburb, quite charming and quaint, but very boring and quiet, really, nothing like Madrid." She tilted her head and smiled suggestively to the guys who snickered as if they were all in on a private joke. I thought, ooo, she will be interesting. Last was a jet-black-haired Asian woman from the Philippines who introduced herself as "Michael. I am a woman." Then she laughed nervously; her eyes crinkled as she laughed. I thought she must have weird parents who had wanted a boy. When she entered the classroom, I noticed her hair, long and straight, brushed her flat derriere. It was gorgeous. Once the introductions were finished, Liam welcomed Cindy and me to the class. Then he began the day's lesson: grammar.

The class was incredible! Liam's lecture on grammar absolutely captivated me. I was actually excited, trembling inside with the dynamics of a brand-new perspective on English that I heretofore had not known existed. This is unbelievable. Liam is the most awesome teacher I've ever had. He knows so much about grammar and the English language. Though sick as a dog when it started, I was mesmerized throughout most of the class and forgot how I was feeling. We didn't get out until four in the afternoon, which Liam says is earlier than usual. And we have so much homework, not just what was assigned today. Cindy and I have four assignments the others have already done over the weekend. I cannot wait to dive into this new subject.

But earlier, Walter had called me into his office during a coffee break and told me the room down the street was available for me to rent. During the mid-day break, I went around the corner from school, literally only four doors away, and met the landlady, Inés. Inés looks to be about thirty-five with medium-length, wavy brown hair; she seemed very pleased to have found a renter for her extra room. We spoke in broken English and Spanish, giggling at our awkwardness, but managed to communicate pretty well. She gave me a tour of the apartment, showing me the kitchen, bathroom, and my room. The room is small and dark with one permanently shuttered window, but perfectly acceptable for my purposes. Most of the room space is taken up with a single-size trundle bed. Next to the bed, there is a desk adjacent to a wall lined with off-white shutters. I spied a wardrobe and a two-shelved bookcase along the near wall, plenty of space for my clothes and supplies. I will be comfortable here; most importantly, I will feel safe. My new home away from home.

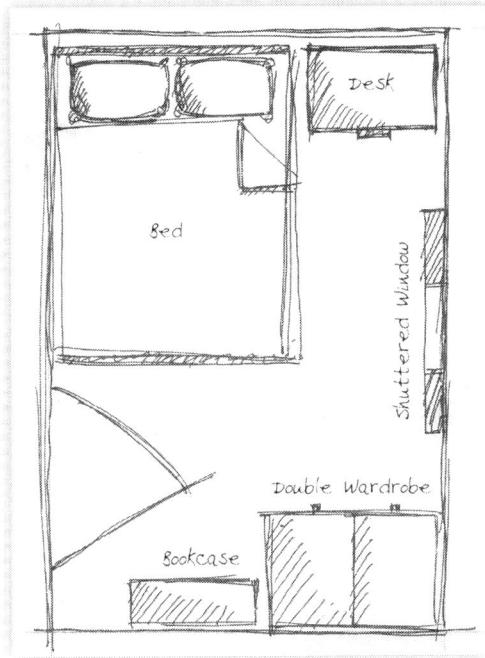

MY ROOM

So, studying grammar will have to wait a bit. I have to use the extra time off this evening to get back to the apartment on Calle Ancora, pack up all my belongings, and move all the way back here to the Plaza de Castilla. I'm off to do so right now with Christopher and Cindy.

∽

It took hours. When we got to Ancora, there still wasn't any heat—well, there were two old portable heaters, but one of them had once exploded and caused a fire in the apartment, so everyone was afraid to turn either of them on. One of the things I was afraid of last night was that an inebriated Christopher would decide he didn't care and turn the remaining heater on and start a fire in the middle of the night. And there was no back entryway.

Anyway, Cindy was beside herself about the heat. She went down the street and called Walter at home. She demanded he move her and Christopher to a youth hostel for the night until new heaters were purchased. I mean, she was ranting and raving and crying. Last night she woke up in the middle of the night and started screaming about how cold she was! She woke me up with her screaming down the hall after I had just gotten to sleep. And then, of course, I couldn't get back to sleep. I'm too old for this kind of youthful insensitivity. I'm too old for all this shit. What am I doing here? Why didn't you hit me with a bolt of lightning or something and stop me from coming?

I waited for Cindy to get packed, which took her ages because of her complaining and bitching. Christopher just packed his backpack and was ready to leave in five minutes flat. While we were waiting for Cindy to finish packing, Christopher was working in the kitchen. He loves to cook. He whipped up some calamari right there as we chatted. Very impressive. It's fun to talk to a man about cooking.

We used to cook together all the time, remember Paco? Our kitchen was a family kitchen in which everyone participated. So homey. So lovely. Miss you. Miss you so much. …

Being there in Christopher's kitchen, laughing and talking, felt unbelievably natural to me. At one point, I told him what a nice person he was. He whirled around upon me suddenly and replied in a low, rather gurgly, lilting British voice, "You don't know anything about me. You have no idea if I'm nice or not." His undertone sent goose bumps tripping up and down my spine.

Even as I acknowledged to myself that he was right, I looked into his scowling hazel eyes and told him, "Yes, I do. I'll trust my judgment on this. You're a nice guy." He turned back to his cooking without accepting my pronouncement. Now, that makes me uneasy.

When it was time to leave, we started out in the same cab. Cindy wanted to go to a part of town she called *Sol*. She and Christopher had gone there yesterday, and she was in love with it. Christopher gave the driver instructions in pretty comfortable Spanish. I was relieved to be with someone who could communicate well. However, minutes later, only several blocks from Ancora, Christopher realized he'd forgotten his wallet. Cindy said we should drive around and wait for him. But he insisted that the cab stop and that he and Cindy go back to the apartment to retrieve his wallet and proceed to Sol alone. Since he was going to stay with Cindy at the youth hostel, they left together. The whole incident was bizarre and of course left me in full red alert alarm.

Suddenly, I was alone with a Spanish cabdriver going god knows where in this completely unfamiliar city.

I continued on in the cab alone. What choice did I have? The cab driver immediately turned in his seat and asked me what was going on. I knew this by his questioning tone, not by his words. I told him, *"No sé,"* in answer to his question. And then I said, *"Mis amigos son locos!"* We both laughed, and I thought, okay, I *can* do this. Thank god for my sense of humor—it translates into any language.

This really was my first moment in the city alone. And I was afraid.

Here's the thing about me. I'm not afraid of everything. But I do feel especially vulnerable since you have gone. When you are married, especially for a long time, you come to take for granted the protection your marriage affords you in the world. To be on my own is often unnerving and frightening to me. You married me when I was nineteen and I always knew you would be there for me. I could count on you watching out for me, protecting me, and I you. That's one of the perks of being married. Now, after twenty-one years of comfort and security with you, I am on my own. But it doesn't stop me from doing what I want to do. I just do it anyway. So, I was afraid. I've spent a lot of time being afraid since you died. But the fear wouldn't have stopped me from doing what I wanted to do. I don't regret coming because of the fear. I just wonder when, oh when, it will go away.

I decided to look out the window and enjoy the beautiful white architectural facades along the Spanish *calles* we were speeding through. Different multicolored lights bathed the beautiful Spanish architectural walls of each building we passed. The colored lights turned the ordinarily white facades of each building into magical, dancing, colorful Madrigal characters.

The cab driver asked me a question in Spanish. I understood he was asking me about my friends again. *"¿Que pasó?"* What happened? Were they coming back? I was able to tell him that I was going alone. Apparently, I know just enough Spanish to stumble through a conversation.

The city is so beautiful. In broken Spanish, I told the driver how beautiful the city was. *"¡La ciudad es muy hermosa!"* The driver became very animated and excited. I had to tell him to slow down and to say things simply because my Spanish was very poor—I haven't spoken Spanish since I was in high school. (Was it *ser* or *estar*, *tu* or *usted*???) But I could make out what the driver was saying. "*¿Te gustan los hombres?*" He was asking me if I liked men! "*Sí,*" I answered automatically. He asked if I was married, and I answered yes again. I was wearing my wedding ring, which I wear now when I need the security of a wedding ring. I have just recently taken my wedding ring off, Paco, because you are gone. I am alone. I'm just trying on the single life. But I still retreat to the married symbol when I feel the need. One of the few perks of the widow's position.

I told him again my friends were *locos*. He told me all Spaniards were *locos*! He told me all about Spanish men and what they liked—drinking, cigarettes, women, and fun. He asked me if I wanted to go out for a drink! At that point, after getting over the initial disbelief that he would ask that, I became concerned about where he was actually driving me. I wouldn't know if he weren't taking the right route. Suddenly, I thought with alarm that I wouldn't know if this were a legitimate taxi. Christopher had lunged into the street and hailed a passing cab.

But soon after, I spied the already familiar Puerta de Europa, its two leaning high-rise towers forming a steel arch over the avenue, and we drove around the Plaza de Castillo roundabout adjacent to my new street, Calle Bravo Murillo. The driver pulled up in front of my new building and helped me with my suitcases to the ornately scrolled wrought-iron-and-gold-leaf front door. His expression was one of regret, but he didn't confront me on my refusal. That was quite enough of an adventure for me on the first day.

I rang the landlady's doorbell with a goofy grin of female satisfaction on my lips. Paco, my first invitation for a drink! Well, well.

¡Hola, España!

Chapter 2

November 25, 1998

Dear Sean,

Our average day begins each morning at 10:00 with grammar, language, and teaching lessons led by Liam. In the afternoon, we are given time for teacher planning (TP). This is when we work together in our teacher groups to prepare our lessons and write our lesson plans. We don't break for lunch until 2:30. At 4:00 p.m., teacher practice begins—real live Spanish-speaking ESL students arrive, and we actually teach the classes until 7:00 p.m.

Today Liam split us into two groups. I'm assigned to Team B with Chase, Ethan, and Michael. Cindy and Christopher are on Team A with Hal, Emma, and Dylan. I feel terrible that I've been separated from Cindy and Christopher—I really want to be with them. We already feel like we know each other; we'd make such a good team. Oh, well. Maybe I'm better off not being distracted by Christopher. I don't dislike anyone in our group, but I'm not sure how well my group will work together. Cindy is openly unhappy about our being separated. She whines about it, even in front of her new teammates. I'm embarrassed for them. They are obviously thrilled she is on their team, and she is behaving with zero graciousness under the circumstances.

Liam gives us time to meet in our groups for the first time and prepare our first lessons. I have to deliver my first lesson on Friday; it is just a ten-minute grammar element lesson. Chase and Ethan each have their first 75-minute lessons tomorrow. I am stunned that they have to do so much work first time out. They have to research their topics and create four components to the lesson: a listening module, a spoken module, a reading module, and a writing module; in addition, they must gather and make all their materials, write a formal lesson plan, and create their class notes and handouts for the students—and it all must be timed to last no more than 75 minutes. It doesn't seem fair.

Chase is not happy about the inequity. He tells us he went to Liam to complain and got nowhere. His attitude is pretty amazing. Even though he is angry and worried about how it will affect his grade, he's accepting the teacher's refusal to change it almost impassively. It's like two opposing natures struggling at once. Yet he simply accepted the verdict of his teacher with no anger or will to rebel. Very unusual. To my American mind.

So anyway, we went into a planning room alone, the four of us, to start working on our assigned lessons.

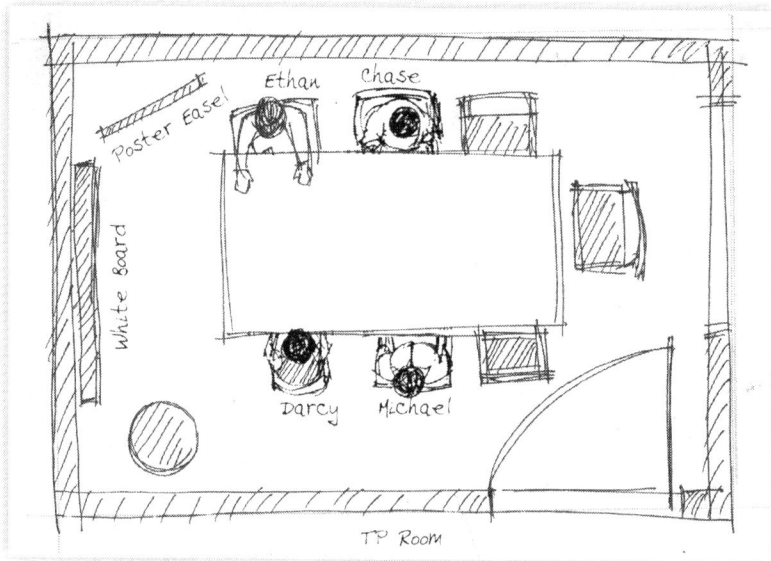

TP ROOM

Ethan's first assignment is to make a recording, for his spoken module, of all the teammates introducing themselves and telling "what sports I love and play." Listening to native English speakers talking naturally is one of the four language skills associated with learning English.

I'm thinking, oh no, how embarrassing for me because I don't do sports. By now, you know, I've already established myself as the "mom," the helper of everyone, the joker, and the support system for everyone. I feel comfy in this role with them all (except for Christopher, whom for some insane reason I persist in looking to expand roles with). But to have to discuss sports in front of Ethan and Chase (who is an absolute sports nut) has me mortified. Somehow I remembered playing field hockey in high school and loving it—I thought for sure no one would know what it was and that it would get a pass on obscurity alone. I've never met a soul at home who ever played field hockey.

Ethan speaks into the tape first—he reports being a marathon runner and a weight lifter (which is amazing to me because he is so very tall and has a wiry physique). Then it was my turn. I spoke with my back to everyone and talked about field hockey, basketball, and mountain hiking. I ended with a comment about Long's Peak in Colorado and how beautiful climbing mountains is. When I finished, Chase jumped up with the "thumbs up" sign and a very enthusiastic congratulations—"Great job, Darcy!"—with this incredible "ahr" sound in the back of his throat that makes me smile inside. Then he went next.

He told the students how he had been *the* champion field hockey player representing Great Britain on the European team, when he was 15—woa. I just about died on the spot! Then he went on to tell how he's organizing the field hockey team for Greece for the next summer Olympics. Then he went on to tell how he's a mountaineer. And about all the mountains he's climbed! I was *so* embarrassed, but also absolutely *freaked* that I had thought to include a sport from my high school years that he *happened* to be a star at. What are the chances of that kind of co-incidence happening?

Afterwards, I felt some kind of recognition from Chase. A kinship exists between mountain-climbers. If you've never climbed a mountain, you don't know what a spiritual experience it is, how absolutely awesome it is—now I know that he knows, and he knows I do—something we share. It's kind of a nice feeling, but I feel bad about my being in such bad physical shape now. After five years of grieving, I've put on weight and let myself get out of shape.

I'm feeling very self-conscious about that at this moment. I'm feeling ashamed of my body and exposed before him as an imposter. I certainly don't look like a mountain-climber anymore. But I do feel an acceptance from him that wasn't there before the taping. That's nice.

൪

November 26, 1998

Today in TP I found out much more about Chase. He had his first 75-minute lesson to give today and chatted nervously to me all afternoon in the TP room. His full name is Chase Campbell Mackenzie, and he's the great grandson of a military officer who was knighted for his service to his country during a war of some sort. Chase was born in Scotland, though he was sent to boarding school in England. His father sounds like he's an influential man in his own right, a man who sounds like a rebel and scofflaw. I think that's one of the things I like most about Chase—he has this sense of naughtiness and adventure—he isn't a rebel like Christopher, more like very determined to do things his own way and completely confident of his right to do so. He is an inheritor of a throne, the son of an upper-class family who has been born and bred to a certain station, a station that, though he's been groomed for it and bears it in the very stature of his magnificent male body, he rejects—a rejection which seems from what he's told me so far to have brought him closer to his father and more at odds with his mother.

He is a stunning and beautiful figure of a man; he wears a presence much larger than his actual size. He stands a little over six feet tall, the perfect height for a man—imposing but not overwhelming. But it's the way he holds his body that is most impressive. He stands with a casually regal posture, the stance of a man who owns his world, who is born to the knowledge he is privileged and unquestioningly accepts his good fortune as deserved. His fair hair is swept back across the crown of his head and feathered at the sides. His legs are long as tomorrow; his waist is high. His lips are full and sensuous, with deep dimples on either side. His eyes, oh his dark blue eyes, beckon and pull while teasing and laughing. His nose is substantial and prominent on his face like that of a magnificent thoroughbred stallion. He is athletic and handsome with his blond hair and blue eyes—so handsome—he is sport-minded, a jock, a man's man. Not really the kind of guy I'm attracted to. Too conventional. Someone to look at and enjoy, but not to take very seriously.

I know it sounds like an exaggeration, but he looks like a Greek god. For that reason, I dismissed him as inconsequential. Okay, I admit it—I don't think much of gorgeous men, except that they're fun to look at—is this sexist enough? In my experience, they are not very interesting people—like gorgeous women, their time is spent in the zone of the physical—a zone that bores me easily. I do, however, have to acknowledge his physical beauty. I acknowledge it and enjoy it fully. But that's the end of it. It's a peripheral interest, not one of substance. It takes a lot more than physical beauty to attract me.

Besides, I'm already entranced and completely turned on by Christopher, who attracted me first with his intelligence, then with his sense of outrage toward the world. (I'll always love the rebel.) By the time I attended the first class, I had known Christopher for only two days and was immediately aware of this amazingly strong attraction between us. I feel this attraction, but I don't fear him. I feel this singular blanket of protection from him, even when Cindy told me two days ago that he'd threatened her. I thought he would never touch me in harm, not just because I'm not young and gorgeous like Cindy, but because of something else, this bond that is already forming between us that I can't explain just yet.

Today I am not feeling well for the fourth day in a row. Yet I am hungry because I can't find any decent food. I am not a happy camper. The only thing outside my physical discomfort that registers is this relentlessly growing interest I am feeling for Christopher—this is so nutty. What is happening to me?

But Christopher is rarely around now. During every break he and Dylan disappear—I assume they are doing drugs. But all the Brits, including Emma, disappeared at break this morning, too. I couldn't believe it when they all returned with alcohol on their breath. The classroom reeked of alcohol! I was thinking, how completely unprofessional. These people want to be teachers? And I was thinking, what kind of people run out for drinks on a twenty-minute coffee break? It's mind-boggling to me. But they all did it. And no one seemed to care. I'm just trying to keep an open mind. This trip is not about me superimposing my values on people from other cultures. I'm going to try to stay neutral about things like this and just watch. I didn't come here to stay within my own culture.

The funniest thing happened today—an event that may define my standing in the group, especially with Chase—it came out in TP that I had believed Ethan in his narrative about being a marathon man. Ethan and Chase laughed their heads off about my gullibility, and of course I played into it with genuine expressions of surprise (actually I was totally shocked that he had *lied*). The possibility had never occurred to me.

Chase could not *believe* I really fell for it—it was beyond his comprehension, and in some perverse way, it endeared me to him. I think it's going to be a turning point between us; afterwards we started to relax together, to let loose and have fun. We laughed throughout TP. It feels a bit like it used to with one of my earliest boyfriends who started out as a big brother/friend kind of guy—Chase is feeling a little like a big brother/friend—my sparring partner, my bad boy in arms. I encourage his naughtiness, needle him relentlessly, push him beyond his own naughty proclivities. And he loves it.

∽

Tonight I decided to taste the *vino tinto* for the first time. It was a special night—tomorrow is a short class day and we were in a party mood. In hindsight, I think I decided to test the waters for a few reasons: First, the pressure on me to drink here is enormous. The guys hate that I am drinking *agua mineral*. They say it's a disgrace—actually, Chase said that. Christopher gurgled something about it making everyone else "look bad." I'm impressed that they know enough to know they look bad. The second reason is simply that I feel safe with all these men. Pure and simple. There isn't one of them who wouldn't have watched out for me if I needed watching—well, all except Dylan, whom I'm still leery of. The third reason is Chase. He is beginning to feel like a safety net to me. Last night in a bar he questioned me about your death; the protectiveness and caring in his eyes was profound. I'm not used to seeing those emotions in a man's eyes anymore. More and more, I just feel I can trust him. He is a strong man, not so much physically, but of mind and spirit. He is sharp, intelligent, and spirited and has a highly developed sense of integrity and a quick wit.

When Hal asked me what I was drinking, I shouted, *"Vino tinto!"* to everyone's delight and whooping cheers. And so tonight I had my second glass of *vino tinto*. And a rowdy night it was. We were close to completing the first week of the course, and everyone was in a mood to party.

We were seated like this at two square tables pushed together:

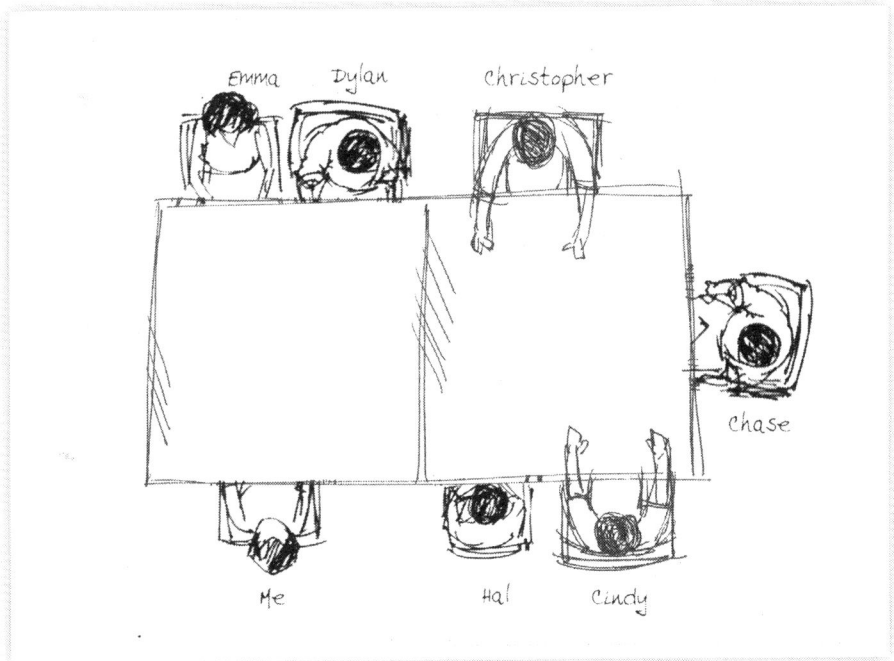

RESTAURANT SEATING

Chase was in an especially lively mood. He'd put away several beers already, plus he had two American girls at his mercy—he was relentless. He completely lampooned us for every conceivable weakness, including our language, our politicians (with Clinton's Lewinsky, it is not a good time to be abroad), and our money (our money!) Our sports, our winning the

Revolutionary War (!), our being "number one"—which he is most caustic about—he balls his right hand into a fist and thumps it over his heart two times, holds out his index finger high into the air, and says, "Darcy, we're number one!" with total sarcasm.

And Cindy played right into his tirade with her ignorance of world politics, the British culture, and all of history, both American and British. Younger Americans have not been educated to know much about the outside world, and tonight it was pretty embarrassingly obvious. ("Who's King George?" She asked with a blink. "I thought you have a queen.")

"Oh dear Gawd, no, Cindy, no," drawled Emma leaning across the table toward a genuinely confused Cindy.

"HeLLOOOOOO!" cried an offended and outraged Chase. "Who is George? Cindy, what was the Revolutionary War? HeLLOOOO!" This egged him on and on. "Cindy, who invented the light bulb? Who is Billy Connolly? Who invented golf? Who invented the computer? You don't KNOW?" He turned to me, irate. "Do you Americans think you are the only country on the planet? Oh! Oh! Darcy, what is football? Yeah? We're number one!" He thumped his heart again and put his finger up. "We're number one. We're the world champions! HeLLOOOO. ... Who else in the world plays American football?" He arched his brow. No one. It was an exhausting tirade that entertained the Brits at our expense. It was an eye-opener for me: I never knew the British were so angry at us and for such silly little things. I never knew the British were so sensitive about the inequalities between our countries. I never knew the Brits were simmering so across the pond. But then I'm an ignorant and completely insulated American girl who has never been abroad and socialized with Brits in a bar before. It was awkward to be the brunt of such an emotional attack, but it was also interesting to me, informative, and I paid attention to all the areas of his outrage, almost like a bystander watching from the outside. I wanted to know more.

Soon, I didn't fight back; I just let him rip. And rip he did, for hours. He knew about our culture because he had worked in the States for three years during the summer. But they all knew our culture, it seemed. And the comparison between what they knew about us and what we didn't know about them was downright embarrassing. It was his point really, and I had no defense for my ignorance. And well, Cindy's ignorance was unbelievable, really. She was so ignorant, she didn't know enough to feel self-conscious or embarrassed.

Once he got weary of his tirade, Chase told us he'd been a cop in Scotland, a fact that did not go unnoticed, though he didn't expand on it tonight. And he talked about sports *ad nauseum*. Sports, sports, sports. It is an amazing passion with him. Every sport on the planet he knows, loves, and keeps abreast of. The very definition of a fanatic.

I have to say that it was the fact he had been a police officer that instantly confirms my ease with Chase. Eddie is a cop, and so I instantly feel at ease with Chase for this. I knew before that he was a good man. And now I know he's familiar with danger and protecting. That has an enormous effect on me. I remember looking at him and thinking, "He is reliable," with an inner sigh of relief. Just a brief thought, but so reassuring. I have no idea why. Except that I am weary of always having to be on guard to defend myself, my life, my son. Chase immediately feels like an oasis to me.

Then the funniest thing happened in the bar. I started envisioning Chase in a redcoat uniform. It was a very strange vision. I wonder if any of his ancestors fought in the Revolutionary War. It's kind of a disturbing image, Chase in a redcoat uniform with a musket perched on his broad shoulder … and the image appeared to me several times during his monologues tonight. I thought, if he only knew what I'm thinking right now—the thought made me giggle to myself. Ridiculous imagination I have.

Once the novelty of Chase's attack wore off, I became more interested and preoccupied with Christopher. First he sat across from me, but when Dylan and Emma left, he came and sat next to me. He got drunk and started talking trash—about body decorating ("Do you have any tattoos, Darcy?") and then body piercing ("Do you have any body parts pierced, Darcy?"). Chase scowled at him when the piercing came up—it was a bit uncomfortable when he started talking about nipples and penises. Then he propositioned me!

His eyes met mine and in a flash of drunken insight (for he was roaring drunk by now) he saw something that led him to say out loud, so everyone could hear, "Is it possible?" He searched my eyes and said, "Could we? Would you like to?" I was mortified. Absolutely mortified. He was too drunk to know the accuracy of what he'd noticed—my attraction—but to think it was there and noticeable on any level simply embarrassed the shit out of me.

Everyone was listening, and, earlier, I had noticed Ethan watching me intently all the while Christopher and I flirted (we're always flirting—it's the way we relate to each other). Ethan didn't observe dispassionately. His eyes spoke of disapproval. It unnerved me and made me think I should stop and be more cautious in my behavior.

Christopher reached across the table, put his hand on my arm, and said, "Can I ask you a question?"

I looked down at my glass of wine. "Don't go there," I replied softly, self-consciously. My cheeks were burning.

"Don't go there?" he repeated loudly.

"Don't go there!"

"Don't go there," he muttered and let it go, joining the conversation between Hal and Ethan about American soul music in the fifties. Ethan adores soul music, knows everything about it.

I am beginning to understand that if there is one thing I can count on Christopher for, it's inappropriacy.

Ethan, in his cool, all-knowing appraisal, was not happy with me. I could feel it. His blue and gigantic eyes watched me like a hawk throughout the evening. I think he sees and observes more of me and about me than anyone else—he isn't personally involved with me very much, but we are on the same team and work together every day. He has been free to watch, which he does. Very quietly. I think I was the only one aware of his intelligent appraisals of everyone. It's the quiet ones you have to watch out for. I don't know why I cared tonight, but Ethan's potential disapproval stung. There were moments beneath his persistent stare I felt shame. He never spoke a word. He didn't have to. Like Dr. T.J. Eckleburg over the Valley of Ashes in East Egg, he was an all-knowing god. I knew what my transgressions were—I knew what lust for Christopher burned in my heart. And so did Ethan. I'm convinced.

Paco, I can't even believe these sexual feelings. I cannot believe what's happening to me. My cheeks are hot and red again tonight. I don't remember this ever happening to me before. Ever. What is it? What's happening to me?

❦

November 27, 1998

I think they consider me the queen of the group—they make me feel like a goddess of sorts. From the very beginning, they have regarded me with an awe that completely surprised me once I noticed it for what it was. I think it was my fiction writing that first day that totally wowed them. Last night, Christopher said, "I'm 23 (oh my, yes, 23!), and I've done nothing with my life." In his drunken state, Christopher went on a campaign to find out what I had done or accomplished in my life by the time I was 23. "Look how much you did before you were 23," he exclaimed with distress. "You even gave birth to a child!"

What*ever*. Nothing I can do to help him out there. If he lived to be 123, he wasn't going to have accomplished *that*!

But from the moment I told them about the seven novels, they were acutely attuned to my literacy. They pick up on and react to every single unusual word in my vocabulary, my personal lexicon—and as I'm discovering, there are a few special vocabulary words that I have been known to use casually. At first, it embarrassed me greatly, and I wanted to hide—I felt exposed as an imposter—after all I am *not* yet published. But now, I am coming to understand it is a great compliment—that they revere me for my talents, for my uniqueness. It fills me with warmth and awe that they are a witness to part of the real me and that it pleased them so. In class, they repeat words I say naturally that are unusual to their ears. They laugh and kid me, and at first I would stare at them silently, unsure how to respond to their mockery, but now the insecurity has changed to this delicious warmth that engulfs me in big bear hugs and makes me laugh along with them. They make me feel appreciated.

Today in class, we each had to give a mini-lesson, our first attempt at teaching to a language principle, a part of speech, or a grammatical form. I gave a presentational story about a girl who "mustn't do" all sorts of things, a lesson on the verb form "must do". Well, in my absolute terror at being in front of the class for the first time, I forgot my script and reverted to my own impromptu language—big mistake. I thought I'd done a good job—big mistake. Afterwards, during feedback, someone said—oh, it must have been Chase—"Darcy, 'much to her *chagrin*'?" And everyone burst out laughing!

Christopher yelled out, "Chagrin—I love that word. Darcy, it was brilliant. Absolutely BRILLIANT!" He spoke to me with such reverence and respect, and I saw it shining in all of their eyes. I realized then that they *liked* me for my language. I realized then my complete, irrevocable status in the group. It wasn't the word "chagrin" that had given me the status; it was a status I had been endowed with earlier by unconscious collective agreement and recognition of some qualities, a conglomerate—heretofore unspoken—of qualities they love in me. I've never been revered before, never been adored. Except by you, Paco. Except by you.

It's very special. I like it.

❧

Last night was a physical disaster for me. Staying in the smoky bar for so long left me unable to breathe and coughing all night long. Once again, I got no sleep. It's been four nights without sleep. It isn't worth it for me to do that again. I've made a pact with myself not to go to any more bars with the guys. Construction in Spain is nothing like we are used to back home. I can see outside through cracks in the wall even here. As I sit at my desk in the new apartment writing this, I can feel the cold air wafting past me. I am still freezing. And there's been no time to find a grocery store, so all I've had to eat today was a fish filet from the Burger King down the street. I feel so sick. I can't survive on this kind of greasy, unhealthy food. If I get sick, I won't be able to finish the course, and, after all, that is why I'm here. I am becoming so distracted by the men; more and more I'm finding I have to remind myself of the fact that I am here first and foremost to finish the course.

❧

Today, after class, when everyone decided to go to a bar, I declined. Chase stepped forward and said, "But, Darcy, why not? You must go. You can't leave us now." I felt uncomfortable to have to explain a physical limitation to Chase of all people—the guy with the fewest physical limitations of all—I wasn't even sure whether he would understand. At the least, I thought it would be a turnoff—make him dismiss me and walk away. I explained what had happened after last night. Instantly, he responded, "Then we'll find a different bar." Definitive. Resolute. Executive decision.

He walked off. And within minutes he returned; he'd found a suitable bar down the street with an open wall that allowed the smoke to escape out into the street. How could I argue with that? For a moment I felt guilty for making them move, but I got over it. ...

Tonight I really relaxed. I had two glasses of wine in the bar and another at dinner, and I let my hair down. Once again, in the bar, the topic of my being a widow came up. Christopher asked about your death. I decided to reveal a little more about myself under his questioning and told them about how your death had affected me. They listened silently. I explained how we'd been soul mates for so many years and how devastated Jaime and I were. I told them in a general way about the progression of my grieving, how it incapacitated me for so long. I told them about my commitment to raising Jaime, how it was the absolute worst time for a young man to lose his father. I told them about how I made Jaime my number-one priority and some of the troubles he had put me through, including middle-of-the-night trips to the police station and battles over rules. You could have heard a pin drop. I didn't feel comfortable with their sorrow for me—it was so intense—their "aws" and "ohs" were so heartfelt. I really want to relate to them in the here and now, not as a widow, but they have insistently demanded to know more.

"It's been really hard, but I've come out of it on the other side now. Jaime has gone off to school, and now it's my time. I'm ready to explore life again."

Hal sighed and said, "That's beautiful, Darcy," lifting his glass of beer over the center of the table. "Cheers," they all saluted, and I joined in. The bar rang out with the clinking of glasses.

Christopher piped in with his low drawl, "But you're awfully hard on Jaime, you know. You shouldn't tell him what to do so much."

And all my classmates joined in with a chorus of agreement, even Cindy and Emma. We argued the pros and cons of parental rules with lots of laughter, innuendoes, and kidding. "Darcy!" Chase called my name and said, "What would you do if Jaime wanted to bring a girl home?" Everyone grew quiet to hear my response.

"That would be wonderful," I said. "Jaime doesn't tell me anything about girls, so I'd love to meet his dates."

"No, no! I mean, if he wanted to bring her home to stay? Would you let her stay, Darcy?"

"Of course she could stay. That would be great."

"No, no! Stay the night, I mean."

Of course, I'd had a few and I was not getting this at all. "Yeah, sure. She could stay the night."

"Could she stay in Jaime's room, then?"

"What!" I cried in dismay. "Absolutely not!" I decreed over their laughter and jeers. "Over my dead body!"

"But, Darcy, he's old enough to sleep with girls, you know." Chase said this as if he were informing me of something very upsetting but inevitable.

"That's fine; I mean, I hope he chooses not to." They hooted and laughed at me. "Let me put it this way," I added. "I hope some day to meet and hold my grandchildren; I don't want to hear them being made."

Hal choked on his beer, while the others guffawed at my candid declaration. Chase was chanting, "You go, girl!"

They let the subject of my loss go that night as they were distracted by sexual banter then, but they are all very curious and I know the subject will come up again over the next four weeks. I will probably reveal a little more if they ask again. The atmosphere of caring collectively emanates so intensively from them, I am feeling uncharacteristically free to say whatever I want.

Tonight, the knowledge of my widowhood and my commitment to Jaime made a profound impact on the group. I could feel their respect, like an extra presence in the room, take root and grow right before my very eyes. Their protectiveness toward me grew as well. And the acceptance is making me feel freer than I've ever felt in a group before. That combined with the *vino* made me deliriously lightheaded. As the night progressed, I threw sexual innuendoes around like stardust. And they loved it. Especially Chase, who egged me on with glee. He is bad. I think the guys couldn't really believe they could be so free with me. I'm sure it was as novel for them as it was for me. It's a mutually freeing discovery.

Somehow we got to talking about speaking a second language—I know, we were discussing the assignment we have to do in which we have to linguistically compare two languages. Cindy chose Italian because her fiancé is Italian and could help her this weekend when he comes to visit. Chase had chosen French, and Christopher had chosen German. Emma chose Russian. Out of nowhere, I heard myself lament that I didn't speak a second language, but that once, I had awoken from surgery speaking Spanish pretty fluently. I was interested in the phenomenon of waking up from surgery speaking in tongues. My classmates instantly jumped on the fact that I had had surgery. Uh oh …

"You've had surgery?" Chase asked immediately. I keep forgetting how young they are in comparison to me. When you're having fun with people, you don't think about your age.

"Uh hmmm," I confirmed with a loose nod.

"What for?" Christopher asked.

Uh oh. It was when I had my first son, Ryan, in the hospital, and I had told them I have one son—but I'd already told them Jaime was born at home. I stared at him. A very uncomfortable few seconds ticked by until I decided, what the hell. Why not tell this too? "I was having a baby," I answered vaguely.

Everyone started talking and asking questions at once. Emma called out to me, "But you had a midwife with Jaime at home. Why were you in the hospital? Did something go wrong?"

"Jaime was my second baby," I answered.

For a moment no one said a word. They were stunned. Chase piped up, "But didn't you say you have one child?"

I could feel my cheeks getting red. I lowered my gaze to the *vino tinto* in front of me. "One child who lives with me. I have one son I gave up for adoption."

Once again, Chase was apologetic. "You don't have to talk about it if you don't want to," he reassured me, but it was clear he was *dying* to know more.

"It's okay."

"How old were you?" he asked immediately. There was no doubt about what he wanted to know.

"I was eighteen." I proceeded to tell them snippets of the story. I have to say I was surprised at how uncomfortable I felt. Now that I was in the thick of it, explaining my behavior, I was embarrassed. I didn't really want them to know this about me. It's from my past, a past I have recovered from, a past I've earned the right to correct and not talk about. Fortunately, Cindy stood to put on her coat and interrupted me.

She had to leave to meet Vincenzo, her fiancé, at the airport tonight. "Why don't we all meet tomorrow night for drinks and dinner?" suggested Chase. Everyone, including Cindy, loved the idea.

So tomorrow we're all meeting beneath the *"El Caballero"* statue in Sol. It should be fun.

I hope we get to have paella!

Chapter 3

November 28, 1998

Sean,

Well, tonight we met at El Caballero in Sol at 10:00 o'clock. I was there first, an hour early. I was nervous about missing everyone, and the plaza was *so* crowded—to me, 10:00 is late—I can't believe the thousands of people out this late, whole families strolling leisurely along (this is my first real weekend in Madrid). The plaza is in the shape of a semicircle, with maybe eight streets feeding into it, four of them open to cars, including one that bisects the central length of the plaza, the others intersecting it along the length. There is a statue of King Carlos III on a rearing horse (El Caballero, C) in the center and a fountain (F) on either side of the statue. Near the fountain on the left is a fanciful bronze sculpture of a bear (B) eating *madroño* fruit from a strawberry tree.

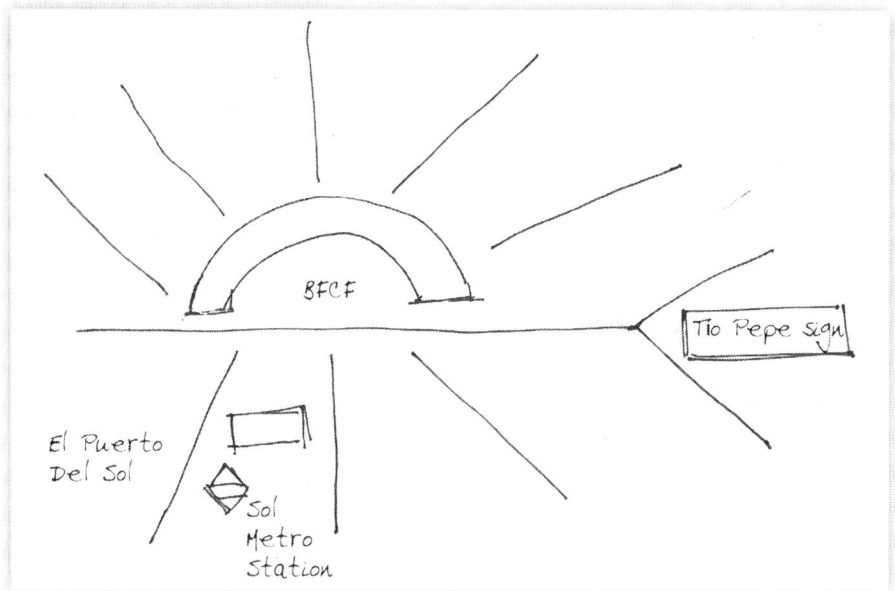

PLAZA DE EL PUERTO DEL SOL

Many of the surrounding Spanish buildings are brightly lit with strings of lights for the upcoming Christmas celebrations. Spain is a largely Catholic country, and Catholic holidays are huge cultural events here. There is a festive atmosphere in the plaza tonight. I don't know if it's always this way or if it's because of the holiday season. I suspect it's always this way.

On one of the pedestrian streets, I found Ecuadorian street musicians playing—the music was wonderful, haunting and ethereal. It moved me deeply, and I was transported for a time to the mountains and thin air. I haven't been moved by music in a very long time. I haven't been *moved* in a long time.

Hal was the first to arrive. We stood near a twinkling fountain and talked, a little self-consciously at first, until Christopher arrived. He was wearing brown corduroys and a huge, baggy wool sweater. As soon as he greeted me, Christopher leaned in close and said, "Oh, you're wearing makeup, aren't you?" When I confirmed the fact, he said in his gurgling way, "It's very nice. Rather brings out your inner beauty or … something. …" He turned and took several steps away.

I was insulted. I turned to Hal. "My inner beauty?"

"I think you look beautiful tonight, Darcy," Hal said, as if on cue. He is such a sweet man, so gentle and peaceful. … His complexion is soft and pink. He has an angelic air about him that makes him seem vulnerable. Makes you want to protect him from any unpleasantries in life.

"Thank you, Hal," I replied, and then I called out to Christopher, who had wandered over to the base of the statue, "I'm going to take that as a compliment, Christopher," which made Hal laugh. I have discovered in the past few days that Hal has a wonderful sense of humor, very dry and subtle. And he does brilliant impressions.

"But it is a compliment," he objected. "You look very nice tonight."

Our eyes met through the carnival night air. "Thank you," I said softly. Hal shifted uncomfortably as if he felt like an outsider, so I turned to say something to him. But just then Cindy and Vincenzo arrived. They were adorable together, all kissey and cuddly. Vincenzo calls Cindy "Cinzia" in his debonair Italian accent. Though we've only known each other a few days, I felt happy to see my classmate so absolutely in love. Finally, fifteen minutes late, Chase arrived. He is staying with friends somewhere nearby. I was actually surprised he wanted to spend his Saturday evening with us. I would have thought someone like him would have more interesting things to do on a Saturday evening, like Ethan, Dylan, Michael, and Emma, who all have other plans this evening.

After taking group pictures, Chase led us beneath this Tío Pepe sign (some kind of alcohol, Spanish beer I think) to a medieval, narrow, winding cobblestone street to the right. He seemed to know exactly where he was going by way of all the little side streets, and he led us through a labyrinth of ancient cobblestone back alleyways in Madrid's old city center. I was utterly lost within minutes. But excited to be having a new adventure. It occurred to me I didn't have to worry about not knowing where we were because Chase was there. He'd get me back when I needed to go. I knew I could count on that. What a nice feeling. For once I could relax and not depend only on my own wits.

We found a restaurant with an enormous steel pan of steaming paella right inside the front door. Once inside, we were seated with a Danish couple and their three-year-old son named Lars who were just finishing their meal. Eleven p.m.! We were seated at two adjacent tables that were pulled together.

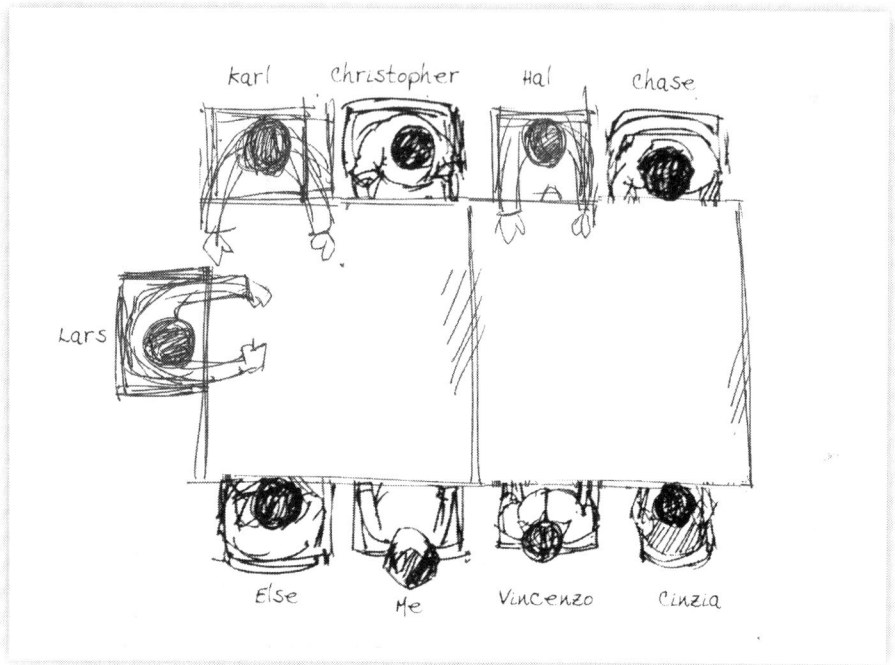

PAELLA DINNER

Christopher sat next to the Danish man, named Karl, and took an instant liking to him. Of course, the Danish man was completely drunk! I was seated across the table from Christopher, next to the woman, named Else, who took an instant liking to me. She chatted and asked me questions, all the while touching my arm, my shoulder, my hair, my waist. I didn't know what to make of it, hated it, but endured it wordlessly. I certainly wasn't going to make a scene or take the risk of insulting the woman. The Danes were completely bombed—their light complexions were mottled with red patches, their blue eyes were glassy and unnaturally bright, and of course Christopher was well on his way almost immediately. He asked what I wanted to drink, and I answered, "Sangria!" which brought cheers of approval from everyone.

The Danish woman warned me the sangria would be strong.

"Oh? But why would it be strong? It's just red wine."

She laughed at me, her voice a woodwind serenade. "I'm sure there are other ingredients," she announced and checked with the waiter, who confirmed there were three liqueurs in the sangria besides the wine itself, including rum, Pernod, and Cognac.

It was especially good. Best I've ever had. I became light-headed very fast and had to switch to *coca lite*, diet coke—I have to have some wits about me or someone will have to carry me home—not a pretty thought. The group continued ordering pitchers of sangria and rounds of beers throughout the night. It is the most amazing consumption of alcohol I have ever seen. I nursed a couple of sangrias and used my *coca lite* to keep me conscious.

The paella was fabulous. I loved it but knew I wouldn't be able to finish. My stomach was queasy and flip-flopping all through the evening, as it has been doing all week. I'm just not able to eat normally since I've arrived here. Sitting across from Christopher has me tied in knots. I am watching him and talking to him and listening to him talk to the others. I am completely captivated with him. My palms are sweaty, and I am breathless. My cheeks are rosy with heat, and my eyes are shining. I don't have to look in a mirror to tell; I can feel these things. This is the strangest phenomenon. I don't know what is happening to me. I almost feel as if I'm in a frenzy of some sort. All of my vitals are racing inside. It feels to me as if there is no one else in the room but Christopher and me. I am completely focused on him.

When he finished eating his meal, I asked him, "Would you like my mussels, Christopher?" His face lit up, "Really? Yes?" Then he frowned and said, "No, they are yours; you must eat them."

"But I don't like them," I assured him.

"Are you sure?" He had a guilty look on his face but took the proffered food with relish. Within a few more minutes, I had given him all of the food on my plate. I had eaten perhaps a third of the helping.

I noticed Chase glancing down the table disapprovingly at Christopher sharing my food. I felt a brief moment of self-reproach but then decided I didn't care. If we wanted to share, there was nothing wrong with that. I couldn't imagine what ridiculous rule of British decorum Chase believed Christopher to be breaching, but it was something, judging from the intense expression of censure on his face.

Christopher wolfed down his food so fast I couldn't believe it. I am discovering Christopher is a very hungry man. The act of offering Christopher food feels more like an act of love than of physical sustenance. I think he receives it that way. He is very grateful for every morsel. "Thank you, Darcy.

Very generous of you," he said in his rushed English accent, even as he is scooping huge portions into his mouth. He has absolutely the worst table manners I have ever witnessed in my life. It is a puzzlement because I know he has been brought up in upper-class English society. Like Chase, he is a member of a famous family.

He has tried to tell me several times about his father, who apparently is a man of position. But I won't listen. The very first day I arrived, he brought up the subject. He was obviously self-conscious and a bit unsure whether he wanted to tell me about his father but somehow compelled to do so (I read all this in him within seconds). As quickly as I understood his vacillation, I stopped him and said, "Don't tell me. I don't want to know about your father. I'm only interested in you, Christopher. We're going to be friends. I don't care who your father is." He was visibly shocked. And he did retreat from telling me. But two other times this week he has brought him up and tried to tell me. I've stopped him both times. I can tell his father is an issue with him. If he's an issue, I don't want this person interjecting his personality anywhere near our friendship. I have a feeling this man has done painful things to Christopher. I don't want his identity mucking up my pure feelings and loyalty to Christopher. And I don't want to hear any self-pitying confessions from him about what a bad son he's been.

Anyway, I know Christopher is very aware of proper behavior and manners; he just doesn't use them. I think he must be doing it for attention, but he shows absolutely no outward concern or awareness that anyone may be watching. I soon discovered that he may not have asked me for my extra food, but he would have no qualms about asking a total stranger at another table for theirs.

He got up after finishing and began socializing with total strangers at other tables! I was so shocked. It took the strangers by surprise, and it was so rude to us. I was appalled by this behavior. Chase rolled his eyes and looked the other way. But Hal got up and joined him! I would have thought it was a cultural difference had Chase not found his behavior equally offensive.

When they returned, Christopher began talking about his gardens— I don't know how we got onto that subject. Chase, Cindy, and Vincenzo were engrossed in their own conversation about world politics, which I drifted in and out of—the EU and how it will destroy the autonomy of all the European nations. It seems Vincenzo is very conservative, a staunch defender of Italia the homeland and its preservation. But Christopher is talking about gardening, and we have a lovely conversation about flowers and shrubs. He wants to know all about my gardens. I'm thinking there is no end to the interesting nooks and crannies of his interests.

Then Christopher confides to us that he had lost his mother when he was eleven years old. My heart absolutely bleeds for him. It's as if it happened yesterday the way he was talking about it. And his experiences aren't that different from Jaime's, which we compare. Then Hal confided that he lost his father when he was twelve. Christopher made a comment that Hal is a mommy's boy, "Aren't you, Hal?" at which I took instant umbrage.

Hal shrugged indifferently, drunkenly, and said, "Yes, I am," very matter-of-factly. I was thinking, *those would be fighting words back home.* But Hal received them passively. I was insulted for him.

Christopher turned to me and asked, "And Jaime is a mommy's boy too, isn't he?"

"No, he is NOT!" I replied emphatically. Christopher didn't believe me. "I wish he were more of a mommy's boy. He's way too independent as far as I'm concerned."

Christopher wanted to hear more about Jaime and his independence. So I told him about some more of our conflicts. "You really mother him too much," Christopher sat forward and said heatedly. "You have to stop that, you know. He's eighteen years old. He's a man now." He was getting all worked up about it, and I was laughing at him. A man? No, he's still a boy.

"I think you're a beautiful mother, Darcy," Hal stuck up for me with a slur.

"Thank you, Hal. And you are a beautiful son."

"Why, thank you, Darcy."

"Why do they always have to leave?" Christopher asked, suddenly interrupting Hal's and my mutual admiration society.

"Who?"

"The people we love. They always die and leave us alone. And I don't know why."

"Yes," piped in Hal, "they always leave. It's so sad." His voice was reverberating with held-in emotion.

"I know. It's not fair," I added, now feeling as if I were going to cry. If one of us started, the others were going to follow, I just knew it. It was going to be a cry-fest.

At that point, I was interrupted by Vincenzo, who asked me a political question about the UN. Hal and Christopher carried on their conversation as if I had never been a part of it. As I listened, I heard they were becoming quite maudlin.

I realized that a big part of Christopher's problems must lie in the death of his mother. Suddenly he seemed like a poor waif to me. Abandoned as a boy, probably with no one to take care of him properly—I was imagining sterile nannies and an absent father. It tugged at my heartstrings as I watched him out of the corner of my eye.

Just then, a large group of people arrived for dinner—it was 2:00 a.m., and Chase leaned over the table in my direction and pointed out to me how great this country is. "Nowhere else in the world do people begin dinner so late. I love this country!" he cried out exuberantly. He balled a fist and struck the area over his heart two times with a reverent expression. Each time a new group of people arrived, he had to interrupt the conversation and announce, "It's the middle of the night!" and repeat this salute. He was so animated about this twenty-four-hour action thing!

But this group that had just arrived was seated behind Christopher and Hal. One of the women in the party was a tall, blonde Israeli woman—she was one of the most beautiful women I've ever seen. Apparently Christopher felt that way too—as soon as he saw her, he was out of his seat like a shot.

She brushed him off like an irritating fly. He persisted. He was instantly smitten by her. He hung out at her table—then Hal followed, too. I was very annoyed at both of them. But I had seen similar erratic behavior in Christopher earlier this week. The drunker he becomes, the fewer boundaries he possesses. Everyone is a potential best friend.

Then, out of nowhere, he hit the Israeli in the face. Pop. Right in the nose! Not hard, but the action was sudden and unpredictable and absolutely frightening. She batted him away once again as if he were a fly. Her actions were confident and precise, like a military person. I was more upset than she. She really was one of the most magnificent women I have ever seen, with her blonde hair down to her waist and that strong nose, so proud, so beautiful a creature.

"Did you see that?" I said to the rest of the group. "He hit that woman. Christopher hit that blonde woman over there!"

"He did WHAT?" Chase turned to look, but Christopher was talking casually to the other people in the Israeli's party. In fact, he was pulling up a chair.

"I saw it, too. He hit her twice," declared Cindy.

I'm amazed to hear there was a second time but relieved that someone else saw it. Chase doesn't half believe it, I can tell.

Later, I overheard Christopher telling her that as beautiful as she was, a woman's beauty could never equal the beauty of a man—how to win a woman's affections! The upper torso of a man, according to Christopher, is *the* most beautiful creation on earth. Later, Christopher told me Chase was gorgeous—he had a beautiful, tight ass that Christopher would love to get his hands on. Actually he waxed on eloquently about Chase's ass, which we studied and admired together. I felt like Alice in Wonderland—was I really admiring a man's body parts with another man? I'm coming to accept the notion that Christopher is probably bisexual. He seems to have strong attractions to people of both sexes. This information, to my amazement, does not faze my attraction to Christopher in the least. I couldn't disagree Chase's ass was a thing of beauty, however. I think it will be the better part of valor to keep this tidbit about Christopher's attraction to Chase's ass to myself. I'd love to be there the day Christopher would make a move on Chase!

I'd have to say I was fairly *disgusted* with Christopher tonight. When he finished with the Israeli (or she with him), he returned to the table and asked me to dance! The idea was appalling, alarming. I told him to be quiet and then lectured him on how to act in a restaurant. And I reproached him for hitting the Israeli.

"Didn't do," he denied vehemently.

"I saw you do it. You hit her right in the nose." I was outraged. I demanded an explanation.

Christopher looked over at the Israeli. "She looks fine, doesn't she?" he announced with satisfaction. "Anyway, there's nothing wrong with hitting a woman as long as you don't hurt her." His eyes connected with mine like a gauntlet thrown.

"What are you talking about, 'It's okay to hit women'? Are you crazy? What is the matter with you?" I demand indignantly. "Why do you say things like that? You know damned well you don't go around hitting women."

"As long as it doesn't hurt, there's nothing wrong with it. It's done all the time." Christopher is slurring now and gurgling his words. He is just trying to get my goat. He knows he is succeeding.

"That's a disgusting thing to say," I tell him. "I can't talk to you when you say things like that." I turn toward the others to join in their now-heated discussion about the euro—Vincenzo is ranting about how the EU was trying to take away the identity of his homeland, *Italia*.

I hear Christopher lament to Hal, "She was the most beautiful woman I've ever seen and I blew my chances with her. I just have the worst luck with women," he whined. I pretended not to hear because he was making me so nuts, if I'd had to respond to that bit of lunacy I would have had to strangle him with my bare hands. I'm seething inside. The sangria isn't helping.

I'm wondering to myself, what do you think she was most unimpressed with, your drunken, uncouth behavior or your telling her you preferred men's bodies to hers—that was fetching. Or could it have been the way you smacked her in the nose? I cannot believe that Christopher is talking to what he thinks is the most beautiful creature on the face of the planet and telling her that her body is not as beautiful as his own. What *is* that exactly?

And what is my problem exactly? I must have lost my marbles completely to be attracted to him! I'm beginning to worry if I should be out here in the real world. Apparently I have no discrimination.

By the time we leave the restaurant, Christopher is completely out of control. Once out on the street, he bounds off and joins other groups of strangers with cries of glee. He is jumping and flailing in the air—I was upset with his behavior even though I knew I had no right to be. Actually, inside, I am devastated. I am crushed by his behavior. Even more, I am crushed by my own caring.

Out on the carnival street, Christopher socializes with strangers and then returns to me, hugging me and pulling at me to dance.

"Dance with me, Darcy! I want to dance," he pleads with me. Christopher loves dancing.

"No." I stand rigidly using my stiff body to fend him off. "Don't."

He wraps his arms around me and puts his forehead against mine, "Please …" Any other time, that was an action that would have sent my head reeling. But I was very turned off. His breath is thick with alcohol and cigarettes. My evening is being destroyed. And I feel he is out of control. He is scaring me. "Please, Darcy, we'll find a place to go dancing."

"I don't think so, Christopher. Not tonight."

But Christopher was not easily daunted. He pulled me even closer, and I started pushing him away. "I love you, Darcy. Dance with me!"

"Take it easy, old boy," Chase said calmly, putting his hand on Christopher's shoulder.

Christopher released me immediately and pouted. "But I want to go dancing."

Chase wedged himself between us at this point. "Not tonight," he said matter-of-factly, with final authority. Accepting that authority without a whimper of argument, Christopher bounded away, down the street to another anonymous crowd. "Hi! Wanna go dancing?" I heard him greet the strangers.

Inside I am devastated as I watch him disappear into a crowd of strangers. The cool night air feels good against my heated face. Outside, in the street, it is like Mardi Gras. The street is jammed with reveling partiers laughing and socializing in the middle of the alleyway. It is bedlam.

Chase was animated himself. He was signing Spanish *pesetas* for Vincenzo to take home to Italy as a souvenir. Soon the *pesetas* will be no more; Spain will switch over to the euro. Chase enlisted me to join in and sign, too. All the while, he was making fun of Cindy, his new favorite pastime since the other night when he discovered her ignorance of the world. "Cindy, who is Juan Carlos? Who is Franco?" He kept grabbing my arm and bringing me into the conversation. "Cindy, who brought democracy to Spain?" He didn't let me drift toward Christopher, though I edged in his direction repeatedly. Chase edged over step for step each time, grabbing me back silently, embracing me back into the fold. I had the distinct impression he understood how I was feeling. And that embarrassed me to no end. Suddenly I am feeling pretty damned foolish.

I need to get out of here, I thought to myself. I can't stand this anymore. It's like that for me, Paco—I have my limits emotionally, and when I reach them I know it's time to retreat.

"Will you help me find a cab, Chase?" I asked him, suddenly.

Without a question, he nodded his assent, and with no further ado Chase strode off into the crowds, without even so much as a glance back to see if I was behind. I had to hustle to keep up through the throngs of raucous, drunken people. At one point, I grabbed the back of his shirt so we wouldn't be separated in a particularly dense crowd. We did lose the others, but it didn't seem to bother Chase. He was on a mission and was not to be distracted, whether we all made it or not.

"What about the others?" I called out to him.

"They'll follow," he replied confidently.

"But what about Christopher? We left Christopher!"

Chase made an obscene sound in his throat. "HE left us. He went off with total strangers," he verily growled in disgust. "Let him go. He's not worth it." He wasn't brooking any further whining nonsense from me, and I decided to shut up.

Finally we came out of the labyrinth onto a wider street (still only wide enough for one car to pass at a time, but a two-way street). Cars were honking at crowds of people who had wandered into the street and blocked their passage. I asked him to take pictures of the amazing scene, which he obliged with forbearance. I had the distinct impression he was upset with me. But, of course, he was a gentleman and never offered a word of rebuke. Then he hailed a taxi and tucked me safely inside with a friendly wave goodbye.

We'd left Christopher with strangers in an unknown *calle*. I felt bereft. As if I had left something of value behind. What if something happened to him? What if someone mugged him? I felt desolate. There was nothing I could do. I was not his protector. I comforted myself with the fact that this was not new behavior for Christopher, just my first time to witness it.

The ride home was so beautiful: the streets full of life, colors, and sparkling lights; it distracted me from my melancholy. Soon I was engrossed in scene after scene of glowing Spanish architectural glory. The cab driver wended his way through the Plaza del Sol and headed northwest, around the roundabout to the Calle de Alcala, through the breathtaking Plaza de Cibeles and around the magnificently lit fountain of Cibeles, the sculpture of Cybele, or Ceres, the Phrygian goddess of fertility, the Earth Mother. She was standing in a lion-drawn chariot surrounded by a fountain spewing great plumes of iridescent, glowing water, which made my mouth drop open with awe. "Go around!" I cried suddenly to the cab driver. "!*Por favor, otra vez!*" And I motioned him to drive around the roundabout over and over so I could study the incredible and staggering beauty. With great amusement, the driver circled the incredible fountain for me repeatedly as I laughed with delight. Finally I said, "*Bastante.*" And around the roundabout we skimmed for the last time, barely touching the earth, flying north in our own chariot, into the Paseo de Recolletos, which took us to the Plaza de Colon, where the Italian white marble monument to Christopher Columbus (*Cristóbal Colón* in Castilian Spanish) towered adjacent to the roundabout. The enormous roundabout encircled yet another even more breathtaking fountain with one, two, three, oh my god, there must be fifteen or more fountains shooting up into the air! "Again?" asked the driver, and I answered with a huge smile of glee.

When I emerged from the cab at Calle de Bravo Murillo, I was smiling from ear to ear, my heart was singing with joy, I felt light and giddy—wow, wow, wow! This is the most beautiful city I have ever seen! What a spectacular ending to my first week in Spain. All this because I said "yes" to a crazy idea just a few short weeks ago.

Paco, how did I get so lucky?

Chapter 4

Sunday
November 29, 1998
Afternoon

Today I am alone. In my room. And grateful for the respite. I need the down time to gather my wits and try and reconnect to myself.

I am smarting from the memories about last night and from the fact that today is my first son's birthday. I feel so different here in Spain; it feels weird to think about him. As if it's not my life, but someone else's back in the States. Yet, it is my life and it is, indeed, my lost son's twenty-fifth birthday today. A special birthday for him. He is probably feeling really old today. A quarter of a century. I remember how traumatic that was for me. Seems like such a long time ago.

It's funny thinking about Ryan—I thought that if I went to a new country I would be a different person. Well not really a different person, but that I would be able to get out of my roles from back home, be able to explore different parts of myself I haven't been in touch with for years. But I find I am more "me" than ever. Last night, after knowing me only seven days, Christopher called me "the great mother force." I am simply amazed that my essence was that easily extrapolated by a stranger. I find it both reassuring and terrifying at the same time. If that is all I am or ever will be, then my life must be over because I'm not a mother anymore. My son has grown and flown away. And yet, there is a strong mothering need in me; I recognize that.

It is, however, easy for me to walk away from the SOS signals Christopher is sending out. In the same night he asked me to come back and live with him, he also asked me to be his mother, and he held me like a lover. He speaks to me with his eyes like a lover, and when we are together there is a compelling pull of attraction. He is a drunk. And on this, my first son's birthday, I can't help but be reminded of his father, Steve, who was a druggie. I was so attracted to him. And then (when it was too late for me) he turned out to be such a rotter. I was so young and naïve to have met such a sick manipulator. But then it's the weak and naïve whom the sick manipulators prey upon. I was ripe for the kill.

With Christopher, you can add in cruelty and violence. I watched him strike that Israeli girl in the face, a woman he had known less than an hour. I cannot believe he could look me in the face in all seriousness and say it's fine to hit a woman as long as she doesn't get hurt. I wonder what his definition of hurt is. I don't care to find out.

I knew before I went to bed the first night that whatever Christopher was like, his environment was not one in which I could live. Of course I was jet lagged and dazed and didn't have a handle on exactly what was going on. But I could smell substance use in his lapses, I could see the mountains of empty liquor bottles, made note of his parading around in front of me in his underwear and the frissons of fear I felt for my safety when I turned out the light that first night.

And so, today—already day number eight in Madrid—I know that I am a different person than I was twenty-nine years ago when I became Steve's umpteenth victim. I realize that the Darcy of today smelled the danger and got the hell out as fast as she could. Today I am strong. Today I am aware. Today I am proud of myself.

But the attraction to this man is still there.

What is that?

Pure physicality?

Pure horniness? But I'm not attracted to any of the other men like I am to Christopher. I find this fact frightening. Perplexing. If it were just horniness, then I would be attracted to any man who passed by, wouldn't I? I don't have enough experience in these things to know. But maybe I haven't changed. Maybe I'm not really stronger, wiser, and smarter. Maybe I'm a woman who becomes attracted to the wrong men. How would I know? I've been married to the same wonderful man for twenty-one years—maybe I lucked out and lived happily ever after in ignorance of my stroke of luck in meeting you to begin with. And now I have to wonder, where does that leave me today? I have no experience with my own sexuality other than within the confines of my marriage. I am terrified to think I have to go back and start over, horrified to think of what I might find during the exploration—what if I find out I'm permanently flawed in my choices of men? What if I find out I'm a sicko, too?

God, it's cruel getting older. I am feeling the same sexual drives as ever—no, more! But I don't "look" the part.

Here came this absolutely magnificent, elegant woman, really one of the most outstandingly beautiful women I have ever seen in person, and Christopher was to his feet as soon as his eyes beheld her—and later he had the nerve to whine that she was the most gorgeous woman he had ever beheld in his life, and he blew it. And what is my problem exactly? Why is there even a question in my middle-aged, experienced mind about this boy?

I must have lost my marbles completely to be attracted to him. Further evidence of my complete lack of common sense. It's only been eight days, and this man named Christopher has touched me and held me. I have not been touched or held by a man in five long years.

Today I am alone again. In my room. And grateful for the respite. As of today, I no longer trust myself. I don't even know who I am any more. Paco, I'm scared.

◦⟲

Evening

Paco,

I was feeling so blue this morning that I couldn't concentrate on my homework. So I decided to take two hours off and go see El Prado museum. All by myself. To my great satisfaction, I figured out the subway system just fine. But when I arrived, there was a two-block-long line to get in. I didn't have time to wait in a line like that, so I decided to go to the Retiro Park instead, which was just a half-mile West of El Prado.

The walk felt wonderful. And the park is beautiful. It's huge and stately—the architecture of the white stone entryway arch is magnificent. The trees are just dropping their leaves—it's fall here in Madrid. There were thousands of people in the park—families and children everywhere. I relaxed and strolled for two hours and just people-watched. In the park center, near a beautiful circular fountain, I heard the same Ecuadorian music group that I'd heard playing last night, only this time with Retiro Lake as a backdrop. It was exactly what I needed—the outdoors, walking, and beautiful, haunting music.

When I returned to my room, I had a little more concentration in me and I tackled my homework. So now, I have to finish my language comparison paper. It looks like it's going to be about fifteen pages long, handwritten. I'll probably be working on it well past midnight.

I feel a little lonely today being by myself. I think I'm getting used to being with people day and night, something new for me, the single virgin widow all alone in her empty nest. It's nice to have this room to retreat to, but I'll be glad to see all my new friends tomorrow.

Still in all, I can't stop wondering if Christopher made it home safely last night. The great mother force. Unbelievable.

Monday
November 30, 1998

Sean,

This morning I'm embarrassed. Again. I think I made quite a fool of myself on Saturday night. And, indeed, Chase is telling Ethan and Dylan about how drunk I got at the restaurant. But it turned out that Chase, Cindy, Vincenzo and Hal went on to several other bars before they were finished for the night. Their stamina is amazing. I'd been more than ready to call it an evening at 3:00 a.m. So young they are!

I took a lot of razzing and abuse for my drinking behavior and sexual talk on Saturday night. But it was okay. And in fact, from this moment on, sex is a vibrant, humming entity among all of us. It's no longer taboo to laugh and joke around like it usually is in mixed company—it's the most fun topic of all, and it is limitless fun, even in class. There is no end to the opportunities to use it and laugh and laugh and laugh. I've never laughed so hard, so frequently, and with such abandon in my whole life as I'm doing with these men. And a good percentage of the laughter is about sex. It's a pretty sexy group—of course, it *is* a group of single men in their 20s and 30s we're talking about here. But I was right in there, shocking the most stoned-faced of them all. Make no mistake, I am loving this.

No one knows what became of Christopher last night. When class began this morning, Christopher wasn't there. Liam looked at the empty desk. "Anybody know about Christopher? Where is he, then?" he asked with an Irish lilt, as if he expected us all to know.

"He lives by himself," Hal explained. "So, none of us knows."

Liam started class without him. The class seemed empty without him there. I was becoming more worried. What if something had happened to him? No one would know. We had left him drunk in the street and unable to take care of himself. Liam started his lesson, and I drifted into academic-time begrudgingly. Two hours later, Liam made another remark about Christopher, declaring, "Someone should ring him up."

"He doesn't have a phone," I offered, gloomily.

A half-hour later, Christopher opened the door and waltzed in. "Sorry," he said to Liam with a casual giggle. "I wasn't really late," he added. "I got up on time but forgot my books." It was a lame excuse, and it angered Liam. His face turned beet red.

"Take a seat, Mr. St. George. We'll have no more interruptions, then."

"Sorry." Christopher rushed to the empty seat beside mine with a boyish grin. He smiled at me endearingly. I scowled at him. He turned and smiled at Cindy. She lowered her gaze to her book. I was relieved he was all right but was very irritated at his puerile behavior.

I know, I know, what do I expect from a boy?

☙

Wednesday
December 2, 1998

This afternoon, Inés told me she's leaving on holiday for a week. I am *thrilled* to think I will have the place to myself. Thursday night will be my first night alone—I told Christopher I was going to be alone hoping he would bite. His response? "Party house!"

Oh my god, so young. I am completely out of my mind—what the hell is happening to me? At home I am known as a mature and logical adult.

Here's the thing about Christopher—I'm deciding I can't stand the sexual tension between us and that I have to do something about it. My reasoning (such that it is) is that if he rejects me, it will be over and I can get on with enjoying Madrid, as I had originally intended to do—how have I gotten so sidetracked? There's a part of me that would rather be humiliated than go on in this absolute frenzy. The thing about Christopher is it isn't just such a strong, persistent physical response. We get along like a house afire; we are two peas in a pod, intellectually and energetically. He reminds me of you way too often and on too many intellectual levels. It's irresistible to me. I know this. I'm painfully aware of this. ...

Tonight I gave my third lesson, and out of four elements—reading, grammar, oral, and writing—I only got to one, the reading. I did an effective job on the one, but after the preceding bad lesson, I was upset—completely crushed that I had done such a bad job teaching tonight. My team tried to encourage me and calm me down, but nothing they said made me feel any better. I was feeling as if nothing I did in this program was working. I would never cut it. I was convinced they were going to throw me out. I was a raving lunatic about it immediately following class.

And you know, tonight was the first time Christopher happened to come to my team's classroom after class. Having spied my distress immediately upon entering the room, he came to me directly.

"Everything, okay Darcy?"

"No, everything's awful," I replied. "I did horribly on my lesson. I think I should just leave."

"Rubbish!" he exclaimed, immediately hot with outrage. "Bullocks to that! Bullocks! You're a brilliant teacher. It couldn't have been that bad. What happened?" he asked. So I told him, and I told him how upset I was with my own performance (I didn't have to because I was so distressed over it everyone could see, and everyone had gathered around trying to console me).

Cindy and Chase invited me to come to Sol with them for dinner, but I didn't want to go that far. I said no, much to their consternation. They tried to convince me, but I wasn't having any of it—really, I felt so distraught I just wanted to go up to my room and cry and start packing. I'm not used to failing so miserably; perhaps this kind of teaching is just not for me. It's highly regimented and tightly structured to include so many elements.

Dylan approached me with Christopher in tow and asked if I'd like to come down the street to McDonald's with them for a bite to eat before going back to my room. At first, I said no to them, too. I was suspicious of Dylan asking me because I didn't trust him. But then he said some very kind words of reassurance to me about his lesson and how awful it was and how absolutely bad he was as a teacher and how good everyone knew me to be. He confided how embarrassing it was for him to stand before a class and how out of his comfort zone it was for him to relate to the students. It was heartfelt and really a nice offering of sympathy. He even told me I shouldn't consider quitting. Dylan, who just ten days ago told me to quit before trying! Dylan. Now why would Dylan want to be so kind to me?

Christopher's sincere alarm and concern felt very nice, and I did want to be with him, so I accepted their invitation—Cindy became immediately upset with me for going off with those two and got Chase to come and try to persuade me into coming with them. But I really didn't want to go to Sol. I was truly smarting, and I was worn out and not feeling very well. And of course, Christopher …

So, off I went with Christopher and Dylan, the two of them joking and telling amusing stories to cheer me up as we walked around the brightly lit rush-hour-congested curve of the Plaza de Castillo. Once inside, Christopher asked me what I wanted to eat and Dylan found a seat in the nonsmoking section in spite of the fact that the two of them smoke like weeds. I was touched he would do that for me without my even asking. It really was quite nice of him, uncharacteristically thoughtful of him, for Dylan really doesn't socialize all that much with the group and has completely ignored me since the incident in the apartment the first night. Usually after school he goes off by himself to his apartment and his friends—he's lived in Madrid for a while and has a whole circle of friends of his own outside of school.

The two of them were very kind to me during dinner, solicitous and gentle, reassuring and doing everything they could to settle me down. Still, I told Christopher I was considering going home.

Christopher's face was crestfallen. "No!" he cried with sudden emotion. "You can't do that. I need you here. What will I do with you gone?" He reached out and held my hand, and his eyes, oh his eyes, absolutely pleaded with me. …

The three of us had a lovely dinner—they kept me laughing throughout. Dylan was surprisingly solicitous and kind. He asked me all kinds of personal questions—all my classmates always ask me questions about my life whenever they can. The burning question is "How old are you?" Which uncharacteristically, I refuse to answer. But they are all so young and yet they include me as a part of their group, and I instinctively feel if they knew the actual number it would change the way they relate to me. I don't want to lose their camaraderie. I don't want to feel any older than I already do, and I know that my oldness would be magnified in their eyes should they know the number. And so I steadfastly refuse. Dylan asked if, by the end of the course, I would tell what year I had given up smoking. (He had already extracted the fact that I had quit when I was 25.) "Oh, all right," I said. "But only on the last day."

After dinner was finished, Dylan suddenly decided to leave. Much to my surprise, Christopher said goodbye to him and remained with me. I was glad

Dylan was leaving for two reasons: first, I didn't trust him—why was he being so nice? And second, of course I wanted some time alone with Christopher.

As soon as Dylan was out the revolving door, Christopher and I started talking like two crazy people with only a few hours left to live! I asked him about his studies at the University of Edinburgh where he was a philosophy major. He loved talking about philosophy—and I loved listening. His ideas weren't so far from your ideas—I remember thinking, I'll ask him about the tree in the forest with no one to hear—our favorite disagreement Paco, remember?

He answered exactly like you. As he wrestled the question out loud, I could feel myself falling and falling and falling for him. He is *extremely* bright, he is full of energy, he wants to do good things for the world—he told me about teaching in Africa during his gap year, the year between high school and college when many Brits take off and do service somewhere abroad. He is so anti-materialism, pro-"green," as he calls it. Oh, he is such a lovely guy. And he was sober that whole evening with me.

Then he brought up the subject of sex. He told me about his girlfriend and how he didn't love her, marriage love, but that she was his best friend. Mostly we discussed when two people should have sex for the first time. It was not a clinical discussion. The sparks were flying. We talked about men and women's relations—how we relate, what the problems are, roles, etc. It was a lovely, lovely night. We parted at the Plaza de Castillo Metro station stairs.

One good thing for both Christopher and me tonight is that neither of us has a long program to teach tomorrow. Tomorrow it will be Chase and Ethan in my group and Hal and Cindy in the other teaching group. I need the break. Inside, I am reeling over doing so poorly on my short lesson tonight.

As soon as I returned to the room here, I plopped down on this rickety old bed and cried and cried over school. Christopher and Dylan may have cheered me up and distracted me for a bit, but the fact is I failed to deliver my lesson correctly twice now. I feel like shit. I didn't really think this whole trip through beforehand—I had no idea what teaching English as a second language was all about. I may have to face the fact that this kind of teaching may not be for me. Crying makes me feel a little better, sad but spent. I'm just going to call it a night and go to bed.

Once asleep, I know will dream of Christopher.

∽

Friday
December 4, 1998

Tonight after class, we all went to the Chinese restaurant for an early dinner—Cindy, me, Chase, Hal, Dylan, Emma, and Christopher. Ethan and Michael are often missing from social events like this evening—Ethan because he has his wife to get back to, Michael for unknown reasons, always a mystery, she is. The table was round with a lazy Susan in the middle.

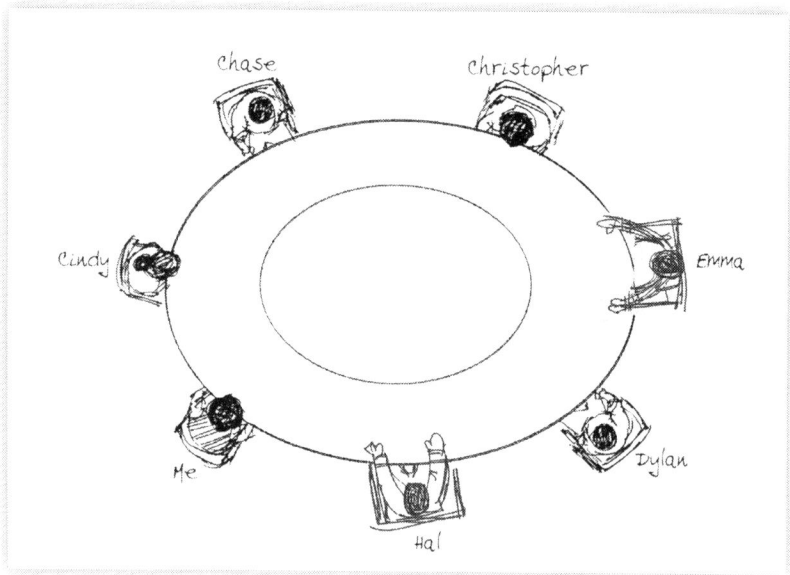

DINNER SEATING AT THE CHINESE

By now, we are all becoming very comfy together. Christopher ate everyone's food off the lazy Susan perched in the center of the table. I noticed he was asking Emma for her leftovers, but she was ignoring him and flirting with Dylan. Nevertheless, Christopher was stuffed by the end of the meal—even he realized what a P-I-G he'd been and kept uncouthly commenting on his state of overindulgence.

I sat between Cindy and Hal. Hal ordered veggies that had to be sent back because they had been batter-dipped with egg—Hal was really upset. And he was very upset with me for ordering shrimp. I could feel him withdrawing from me with repulsion over my fish eating. I felt self-conscious and uncomfortable; maybe it was my own conscience nibbling away at me. Hal never said a word, much too gentlemanly and kind. I was having enough trouble finding nutritious things to eat; I didn't need to feel guilt on top of it. Hal is my idol—I wish I could be as pure as him. I think we don't like to make friends with our idols. No fun at all.

At the Chinese, Chase was fun and well mannered in the restaurant, continental in style. He was sitting next to Christopher, the pig, whose behavior was intentionally outrageous, unconventional, purposely offensive, and me, absolutely loving his obnoxious displays. Me, giggling inside over the entire contrasting spectacle—Christopher, the pig, next to Chase the gentleman on one side and sexy Emma on the other. At one point at the end of the meal he took his index finger and middle finger and wiped his plate clean, licking his fingers of every drop of oyster sauce—exactly the way you used to do at our table, Paco—but hungrily, determinedly, purposely pretending not to notice everyone's absolute shock until his plate was clean.

Chase was horrified at Christopher's behavior right next to him, though he never overreacted, simply rolled his deep blue Scottish eyes and shrugged at me with that characteristic British understated disapproval and pointed his thumb over at Christopher with a clownish look of exasperation and a twinkle.

I thought it was disgusting and endearing—me, never one to censure bad behavior early enough.

I only had eyes for Christopher. By now, I was in what I was coming to recognize as a complete sexual frenzy over him—his arms, his hands, his smile, his laugh, and his bottomless green-hazel eyes simply made my legs weak and my pulse race uncontrollably. I could not keep my eyes off him nor my hands. It was all I could do to control myself with any semblance of dignity because I did fear the effect my attraction to Christopher would have on the group—I know that it would be bad news—*never* acceptable to the group, and that I would lose my status in the group if they ever found out—a status I truly do not want to lose. I am quite sure, without a doubt, if anything ever happened between Christopher and me, everyone would hear about it—Christopher would not be discreet. This I know for certain. And so, I find myself in this increasingly impossible state of tension, wanting him and knowing I have to be careful. Knowing really I can't have him. Well, in my rational mind. In the old Darcy mind.

Of course, Christopher does everything to provoke me tonight; don't forget, he was the one who started this whole thing by propositioning me. He touches me as often as he can, and I have begun to touch him with regularity. And he seeks me out. But still, there is an innocence about him, a self-involvement that warns me he may not be experiencing the same thing as me—though I am out of my mind, I still have some touch with reality, even at my most emotional moments.

And so when we left the Chinese, Christopher declaring his satiation and tiredness, I invited everyone to my apartment, which was close by, in hopes of keeping Christopher and getting rid of everyone else. Actually I had asked Christopher if I could do laundry at his house and he had agreed, so we all went to my apartment to pick up my laundry. I'm completely insane! I know. I know. And still I can't stop myself from this madness. Emma declines the invitation, saying she has to meet up with some friends near Opera. But everyone else decides to come up to my place!

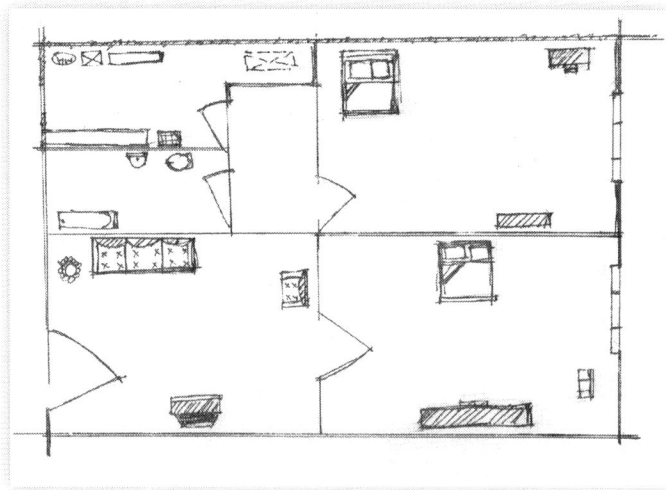

THE APARTMENT

The apartment is very small but seems even smaller with all my new friends crammed into the living room. They turn on Inés' TV, which makes me nervous, for that is something I had not yet ventured to do. They watched sports, and Christopher fell asleep on the floor. I brought out pillows for everyone and blankets. I was sitting on a side chair, Chase on the sofa next to me, and Cindy next to Hal, who was on the other side of Chase. Christopher was sprawled on the floor adjacent to the television.

I'll never forget Chase's behavior at the apartment—he walked in, all six-foot-plus of him, tall and imposing in presence—went through every room with Christopher—everyone else following close behind—and upon completing the inspection to his satisfaction, silently picked out the main features of the apartment. He took me aside and said quietly, "Could I stay here with you for a few days? Since the landlady is away. Would you mind?"

I was so taken aback I couldn't believe my ears. My first reaction was instant recoiling at the notion of having a relatively strange man live in the same house with me all alone. After all, what do we, any of us, know about each other? But Cindy had just told me earlier how absolutely trustworthy Chase was and what a perfect gentleman he was—she'd confided that the night after moving in with her to a smaller hostel away from Sol, Chase had slept with her in the same single bed and hadn't *touched* her the entire night. Not once had any part of his body touched hers. ... I'm wondering how that would even be physically possible. ...

Now, I did not *believe* this little story. I absolutely thought she was *lying*—either it never happened or it happened and they did make love.

There was no way I was going to believe that any man could sleep with Cindy without touching her because all the men were so gaga over her. They were all hot for her. And she and Chase had become an item; they both lived in Sol, and then suddenly Chase had moved in with her. Out of nowhere. I remember back when Chase helped Cindy move to Sol, I had wondered if he had an agenda with Cindy, that he had eyes for her.

When Chase asked my advice about helping Cindy move her things to Sol, and I told him yes, he should do that, and he quite openly liked hearing that—that convinced me he had the hots for her. I mean, it would be an incomprehensible concept that he wanted to help out of plain old goodness—a person who sees need and wants to help? Oh dear, how cynical I sound. ...

Besides, after Chase helped Cindy move to Sol, they had become quite an item. They were inseparable, always together. They arrived together in the morning, they ate together, and he was very affectionate toward her—I truly think and have accepted the fact that they have become lovers, though

I would never ask. (And of course the assumption made me pull away from Chase again, or at least ignore him for a longer time because surely any man interested in being with Cindy was not a man I would be interested in; nor would he be interested in me.)

So when Cindy made this pronouncement a week later, I simply did not believe her. And tonight when Chase asked to live with me, I said, "Well yeah, sure," slowly, "but I thought you were staying with Cindy?"

"I was, but she moved to a smaller place and it's a little too crowded for both of us, and I think, well, I think it's time for me to move somewhere else." His eyes and expression made it very clear it was Cindy he was leaving, not the room. That was the salient point to me—in that case, he was welcome to stay with me—especially since I knew he had slept side-by-side with Cindy and *apparently* not touched her.

I'm so aware of men now, but still, I need my space, my security, and my own space that I control and feel comfortable in. I still feel scared, especially now with all these new experiences, feelings, longings. I need to get used to this new me without pressure.

But what a revelation. Suddenly I was looking at Chase with different eyes. Suddenly I looked at Chase—for a moment at least—and wondered, who is this man? Is he for real? I was only slightly nervous about him sleeping in my apartment. Really the question wasn't whether he was safe. The question instantly became, could I stand having such an attractive man in my abode? What new emotions would this create? There was only a bit of a question about his honor, his trustworthiness. I have to say, reckless and daring as it felt, the risk I was taking was exciting to me, not scary—so I knew he was trustworthy, because scary is a turnoff to me. And I was definitely not turned off.

When Christopher fell asleep on the living room floor, I felt abandoned. We weren't going to be doing laundry at his house tonight, that was for sure.

Meanwhile, Chase was acting outrageously. He'd picked up on my fear of "the landlady" and how I didn't want anything disturbed. I asked them nicely not to touch her knick-knacks and not to go into her bedroom and not to make much noise because of course all the neighbors would know and would gossip and I didn't want trouble with these people—one woman had already yelled at me in Spanish and tried to prevent me from entering the building. She was about 4 feet 4 inches tall, so I kept walking past her, saying, *"No comprendo, no comprendo español!"* Turned out later she was the *owner* of the building! Ay,yi,yi!

Well, Chase found this information irresistible—simply irresistible, and no sooner were we all seated than he got up and started snooping around the living room. I was *instantly* nervous—after all, these were young guys, irresponsible, unpredictable—people who needed to be held in check lest they get out of control—oh yes, I was well aware of the age difference even on the most fundamental, primal levels.

"Chase!" I yelled in a stage whisper. The walls are like paper; I desperately didn't want the neighbors hearing us. "Don't touch her things!" "Don't move that!" "Don't pick that up!" "Put that BACK—please, Chase, don't do that!"

I couldn't look half the time. And the more I suffered, the more it egged him on—he opened *every* damn cabinet, moved *every* single item in her living room, played with things, threw them to the others, pretended to drop them—I had to literally go to him, touch him by the arm, and *plead* with him to stop.

Which he finally did. After he got bored of it. Even as I was watching him in near-hysterical anxiety, I knew he was fully in control of his actions—he wasn't going to drop anything or go nuts, he was simply trying to drive *me* insane (which wasn't hard to do since I was already pretty far gone). It was all about tormenting me. I found out tonight that Chase is an incorrigible, incurable tease.

He even opened Inés' bedroom door and had a look inside, against my express request that he not. I was *beside* myself, even though I knew what he was doing—the tension inside me was so high. But soon Chase tired of his antics and returned to his seat next to me.

Later, once we settled into the boredom of watching soccer in Spanish, I asked everyone what their passion was—what they wanted most to do with their lives. Chase answered the simplest, most beautiful answer possible—he wants to work with children. He worked with children in California during his gap year, and it filled him with joy and fulfillment, and he's known ever since that this is what he wants to do with his life.

For the second time that night, I looked at Chase with new eyes. What an incredibly nice person. Apparently he had more depth than I had at first credited him with. Pretty shallow of me.

The group watched sports in Spanish, and Chase was completely animated and loud, chattering sports stats and memorabilia to anyone who would listen. When TV got boring and Christopher woke up, Christopher went out to the store and bought some *cava* for us all because I had said I wanted to taste some Spanish champagne, one of my favorite drinks. So we all drank *cava*, and then everyone decided to go, claiming tiredness. I said to Christopher, "I guess we're not doing my laundry tonight; can we do it tomorrow?"

"Sure," he replied, noncommittally.

I was less than thrilled with his lack of enthusiasm. What did I expect? I knew how outrageous any expectation would be. Yet, I can't deny how I felt. And I felt disappointed. It is just there.

∾

They are so young.

I am not.

As much as I'm trying, I cannot get away from that fact.

I'm not as young as I feel inside. Apparently. I've never noticed this before. It's an extremely rude reality to wake up to. It's such a cruel reality to me. As long as I was married to you, I was protected from this reality. You and I were growing older together. Now I'm alone. Waking up old amongst the young people. Kind of painful.

Inside, in my deepest heart and soul, I am young and vibrant like them.

And my newly awakening sexuality is young and hot and pulsating and needy. The sensuality I feel is the same as when I was twenty-two. It's the *same*. But I am not.

The contrast between my inner and outer realities is profoundly jarring and very disturbing to me. We do relate on a highly sensual and sexual level, but it has limitations—limits that add to my frustration and infuriate me—I hate the limitations! I hate the fact that had I been twenty years younger the history of our group would have been profoundly, utterly different.

Someone would have committed adultery of the heart.

I know that as surely as the sun will arise on the Madrid Plateau in the morning.

Of course that barrier also is the exact quality that *created* the very freedom to relate so freely in a sexual way—everyone participated, married or not, committed or not. Had there been no natural barrier between us, this may not have been possible. So the barrier removed barriers between us. Life is such a conundrum.

But still, it is excruciating for *me*. Not so much for them I don't think.

Chapter 5

Saturday
December 5, 1998

I value my status in the group. That fact is brought home to me when I fantasize sleeping with Christopher and fret about all the possible outcomes, all of which involve the group finding out and me losing their respect. To tell the truth, I couldn't bear that possibility. It scares the shit out of me because I know my sex drive is becoming stronger than my sense of rational self-preservation—if I have to choose, carnal knowledge is definitely going to win out. I fantasize being forced out of the group. I have even fantasized staying with Christopher until he's finished the CELTA, though I never would. I am disgraced. The fantasy goes on and on.

The conflict is unbearable. And it grows by the minute in proportion to my attraction to Christopher. I can't concentrate in school. All I can do is focus on Christopher. His fingers, I could imagine them touching me, his lips, I can imagine them kissing me. ... It goes on forever ... like a schoolgirl. And try as I might, I can't stop it. It's a nightmare. Yesterday I missed easy sentence parts questions from Liam because my mind was on body parts. It is *humiliating*.

Okay, so I'm making an absolute fool of myself over Christopher—let's get it out in the open and be done with the episode. I'd like to gloss over it and pretend it isn't happening, but it is and I'm not going to run away from it or try and make it prettier than it is. It's as ugly and stupid and foolish as it gets for a middle-aged woman. ...

I've pretty much decided to get Christopher alone and tell him how I feel. He has agreed to let me do laundry at Ancora, and he's been saying he wants to cook for me all week, so we combined the two tonight. This morning was a Saturday, and we all had observations at school; we had to observe the teachers in their classes and analyze their work. Chase was supposed to stay overnight at my apartment last night, but he never showed up, which pissed me off because I sat up waiting for him. I was scared to death I wouldn't hear the doorbell and he would be left stranded out in the *calle* in the middle of the night with nowhere to go. He knew he had screwed me, so this morning when I met up with him and Cindy, he brought me a peace offering—Swiss candy. I didn't care about his candy—I was ticked off at him. I expect more from him; I expect him to be responsible. I need him to be responsible.

After observations were over, we all met up at Pans, a little coffee and sandwich shop streetside beneath the school, a place where we always meet before and after school. At Pans, we sipped our *café con leche* and gossiped about the teachers we had observed. Christopher and Cindy felt the morning had been a complete waste of their precious weekend time. I always appreciate observing other teachers and find I learn new teaching techniques regardless of how good or bad the teacher is. So I thought it was a great opportunity. Very generous of the teachers to invite us in.

Soon Christopher was restless and wanted to go. He's a restless guy.

We left Cindy and Chase, waving to them through the plate glass window as we bounded around the plaza corner toward my apartment. We made our way through the gold-leaf decorated wrought iron door into the quiet, cooler darkness of the huge tiled lobby. Christopher had me laughing before we were out of view of Chase and Cindy, and we never stopped laughing from that moment on.

On the way down to the subway, laundry parcels in hand, we laughed and chatted and skipped through the Plaza de Castillo like two children on holiday. I was just happy to have him to myself—he acts differently when we are alone—there is a kindred closeness we share openly when we are alone. We spoke of philosophy—it was fun to hear his outrageous view-points as well as his serious ones. He's very concerned for humanity and has a consciousness about serving—he spent his gap year in Africa and tells me stories of African violence, hunger, and Middle Eastern sexual practices. Very exotic to my American ears.

We descended the wide steps into the Bravo Murillo subway station, skipping down the steps as if we hadn't a care in the world.

"I'm going to show you an underground market that you won't believe. It's brilliant," Christopher exclaimed while skipping ahead to an escalator that would take us down to the second and then the third levels beneath the street. There are four levels of subways in Madrid, one on top of another. And on some levels there are shopping malls that line the tunnels where one can buy just about everything from food to shirts and colorful Spanish scarves to cameras and sunglasses, even a photocopying facility. Anything commuters may need on their way to and from work can be found in these subways. It is the most amazing sight for a Chicago girl who has to wend her way through urine-stenched, filthy tunnels in the Chicago subways.

When we were in the subway, Cindy and Chase ran to catch up to us. Cindy took me aside and said they had watched us from the window of Pans.

"You are such a cute couple," she told me.

I responded with a grin. "We have a lot of fun together." Then we went our separate ways, Christopher and I down yet another steep escalator to the line below, Cindy and Chase off through a side tunnel in the maze to a line that would take them on back to Sol. Christopher and I took the Metro south to Ancora, where he excitedly guided me to this phenom of an underground market.

Oh my gawd, it was as awesome as Christopher had described it. Aisles and aisles of vendors, like Chicago's Fulton Street Market, but all underground, invisible to the passers-by on the Calle Ancora above. Christopher loves the market. We raced from one fishmonger to the next, at each one Christopher pointing out beautiful fresh and exotic fish. At one, we found some beautifully pink trout that barely cost USD $4.00 a pound. We decided on a menu, and then we split up to save time, each of us going to different vendors for different elements of the dinner. I bought some French Roquefort and fresh French bread as a surprise appetizer for Christopher. Christopher bought salad fixings, and then we ascended to the street where we found a liquor store and bought some *vino tinto*—Christopher approached a stranger and asked for advice on which wine would be good for our dinner. He is forever startling me with his familiar ways with strangers. Everyone is his friend.

At the apartment, Christopher made the dinner—he cooked up trout with garlic potatoes and made a salad with olive oil. When we first entered the kitchen, I discovered the walls were now papered with colorful charts of our lessons. He had color-coded grammar points and parts of speech! I was amazed to see that he'd told me the truth about his study habits—he's always complaining that he studies more than anyone in the course, yet no one respects him—never mind it is his own outrageous behavior that robs him his rightful respect in the group.

I was completely wowed and exclaimed with delight, "You fox! You are studying your head off over here while everyone else is partying!" It was pretty impressive, and it confirmed my initial impression of him, that he is brilliant and, at heart, a serious student underneath the drunken chaos he creates around himself.

We had one glass of wine with dinner. Then we started our homework, for this was to be a laundry and study day—we both have our big 75-minute lessons to give this Monday, and Christopher is crazed about getting it right—really he is quite obsessed with it and agitated. He ranted and raved about how bad a teacher he is and how he can't think of a good enough lesson. He begged me to help him brainstorm, which I did, but nothing we came up with was good enough for him. Further evidence to me of his brilliance—not just anything will do, it has to be exceptional; it has to be unique and outstanding. He will settle for nothing less.

He smoked like a fiend and paced the little workroom back and forth, racing over to the open French window to exhale his cigarette smoke, as if that's going to help—the smoke got blown right back into our tight quarters by the breeze wafting in through the window. He is the funniest guy. So endearing in his impossible ways.

I did some homework, but of course being alone with Christopher, I couldn't concentrate a bit. I wanted to talk. But Christopher actually did quite a bit of homework while I puttered about. After an hour or so, he started pouring the wine and I started getting very giggly.

Christopher began telling me about his girlfriend and how they got together. According to him, she was a worse alcoholic than him—oh yes, he often seems aware of his drinking problems. He told me how they had initially had sex by "accident." I love it. Couldn't wait to hear his rendition of accidental sex!

Things were heating up between us; there was a lot of innuendo and body language and deep eye contact, as there always is between Christopher and me. Suddenly he said we should call it a day for the homework and go to Sol to join up with the others, who are planning a night out. He left the flat to call them up as well as his girlfriend. It was good that he left.

I am feeling *very* mellow—I have no idea how much wine I have consumed—Christopher has been filling my glass the whole time we talked—I tell Christopher to turn off the lights when he leaves and I bask in the light of the heater and the radio music. The music was divine—I hadn't listened to the radio in eons, and it sounded wonderful to my mellow ear.

When he returned, he announced we were going to meet Chase, Cindy, and Hal in Sol in one hour—he wasn't able to reach his girlfriend.

I told him I wanted to talk to him about something. Reluctantly he sat down on a chair opposite me—I was sprawled on the sofa with my drink.

I replayed the conversation that we had had earlier in the week about the tree in the forest and how he said there is no such thing as a void and a reaction, that reactions are to another entity—we aren't constructing reality by ourselves, it's interactive—and I told him that I was feeling a lot of energy between us and I wanted to know if I was making it up or if he was feeling it, too.

He got very cerebral on me and started talking bullshit, and I saw he was freaking out. So I backed down and made the subject very bland and true—there was a lot of energy between us.

He turned to me and asked, "You aren't talking about sex are you?" And I said, "No, not necessarily," which seemed to calm him a little.

Then he told me I was upsetting him—he didn't know how to respond to my question and he was afraid—I told him I was sorry, not to worry, it was nothing, etc. And I told him the truth: "Christopher, you're always saying I don't trust you, and I want you to know it's not true. From the first moment I met you, I trusted you implicitly—remember? I told you that you were a nice guy. I don't trust many people, especially men, and I want you to know I completely trust you—it's very special."

Christopher started making sounds in the back of his throat. Alarming sounds of distress. I was frantic—I'd upset him tremendously without even touching him! Now what was I going to do? Finally he said, "I am completely undone by this. I mean, what am I to make of it?" He was uncomfortable, and the fact that I trusted him after all we'd been through this past week had him completely unglued. Ay,yi,yi!

I apologized profusely for causing unnecessary trouble and suggested we leave. I was mortified. And I was thinking to myself, woa—that was a close call—I've just averted a disaster.

So we left and raced through the streets of south Madrid like lunatics, and Christopher was holding my hand and pulling me along after him—he almost got us killed running in front of oncoming cars!

I called out to him breathlessly, "You know that thing about trust back there?"

"Uh huh," he called back.

"Well, I take it back."

Christopher laughed, and then I laughed as we raced to the subway station. We replaced the discomfort with lightheartedness and jokes. I thought I had escaped certain disaster by the hairs on my forty-something-year-old chinny-chin-chin.

We met up with Chase and Cindy by the Caballero statue in Sol. Chase announced he had something he must show me and led us all on this grand march down one of the eight narrow streets that led off north from the plaza. On the way, they were all teasing me about my state of insobriety. They told me Christopher had called them and asked for help. "She's lying on my sofa with a glass of wine and told me to turn off the lights!"

I explained with tipsy giggles, "I was *very* mellow." Then I asked Christopher how much I'd had to drink, and he said, "Oh, at least half a bottle," to which I was shocked—everyone knows I don't drink that much. So I blamed Christopher for my behavior, and the attention turned to him. I got away with the deflection and breathed an internal sigh of relief.

Finally, we arrived at Chase's destination. We walked in this crowded, dark, and smoky bar. It was decorated in blacks and reds, and Chase was watching me intently with a foolish grin on his face. "Darcy!" He called my name and pointed to the walls, "Look!" The walls were decorated in penis and vagina art—it was a sex bar! Penises and vaginas everywhere! Then he grabbed my hand and led me out to the street, where he was gaily laughing at my horror.

Christopher was acting drunker and drunker, and we decided we would go to a Mexican restaurant, which Chase said was close by—more than a mile later, we were still tromping through the streets of Madrid, god knows where and how far from Sol it was—I was worried about finding my way home, but relaxed when I remembered the weekend before and realized Chase would make sure I got a cab when it was time.

We came to an intersection that was a roundabout. Everyone walked into the intersection—I'm the one who abhors their casual behavior in the *calles*, but I went along and was not paying attention.

Suddenly a bus began to careen around the roundabout in our direction. Out of nowhere. Everything happened so fast, I didn't know what hit me—Christopher, who was on the other side of the group from me, clowning around, suddenly wrapped his arms around me and pushed me out of the way of the oncoming bus.

I sputtered, "What's wrong? What's going on?"

Next thing I knew we were back up on the curb, Christopher's strong arms wrapped securely around me, and the bus streaked past us.

"Oh my god!" I cried out, realizing, well after the fact, that it would have hit us. As quickly as he appeared by my side and wrapped his arms around me, Christopher bounded off across the street, joining Hal and Chase up ahead.

In complete awe, Cindy grabbed me by the arm and shouted, "Darcy! Christopher just saved your life!"

The group carried on as if nothing had happened. But Cindy gripped my arm as we tromped along behind, and said with *great* passion, "Christopher cares for you, Darcy; he just took care of you and saved your life!"

"I thought he was just stumbling around."

"No!" she insisted, "I saw the whole thing, and he was watching out for you—he saw the bus coming, and he was watching out for you. Christopher cares for you!"

She was, like, *nuts* over this—to her this was the definition of love, and she had never seen Christopher exhibit any selfless behavior up to this point. Cindy was now reverent about Christopher and me.

I remember thinking to myself, *it's the trust thing—it forces him to act better—he has to live up to that higher standard because he does care about me and I have put my trust in him.* I felt very warm inside, but I knew in my heart Christopher was a child. A lost child. Much later that night, at a tapas bar, Christopher cornered me against a wall and leaned into me, pressing, touching me, sensual and hot, his breath warm on my skin, totally carnal in his awareness, and he said in his thick, deeply rolling, nervous English voice, "You scared me back there, old girl—all that talk about energy. I don't know. I don't know."

"I'm deeply sorry, Christopher; I didn't mean to scare you, really. Just don't think about it—it's nothing, really. Let's forget it, ok?"

Christopher was quite sheepish. He started muttering gibberish, English gibberish, and I was now worried that everything would not be okay, that he would not let it go. So what will I do?

Later, when Christopher took me to find a cab (we had made a pact that we would leave wherever we were by 1:00 a.m. because we both had lots of prep work for our first long lesson on Monday. We agreed that we absolutely must have a sober and rested day tomorrow). At the cab door, Christopher pulled me into his arms and we hugged—an intimate hug, a full-body contact hug, not brotherly or innocent in the least. He was acting quite drunk, but I said to him, "You aren't as drunk as you're pretending, are you?"

A clear-eyed, sober gaze returned my inquiry. "No," he confirmed in all seriousness.

He uses his drunkenness. He uses it to behave exactly as he pleases. It pleases him to touch me. I don't care what he says. It pisses me off that he is feigning innocence as a trump card of refusal to my innuendo. Immature. Dishonest. Disappointing. What on earth do I expect from a child?

I got in the cab and hoped he got home safely. There was no way for me to know if he did, for I don't have a phone. I'm always worried about him.

But before that parting, we had gone to a local bar for a couple of hours and watched sports and eaten tapas while waiting to get into this fabulous Mexican restaurant down the street—Chase was vibrant and enthusiastic about soccer and left Cindy to seek me out and talk about sports. We had a fun time chatting and laughing, and him making fun of my lack of sports knowledge—but he told me a lot about soccer and the players—he's a total fanatic. He gets so excited about the subject. It's sweet actually. It's his passion, his bliss.

Once at the Mexican restaurant, we settled in to some *serious* drinking. Because the drinking before was just casual pints of beer and lager, mind you. The margaritas were now *flowing*, and they were the *strong* kind, the authentic kind, not the candy-namby-pamby kind we have back home. I drank one and started on *agua mineral*—already, I was feeling no pain. I warned Christopher about the drinks. We must have had seven or eight rounds of margaritas alone! Hal had a constant order in. And Cindy was drinking on every single round.

Christopher got up, left our table, and began approaching other people in surrounding booths. He was asking them for food. He even asked one woman if she was going to finish her Bloody Mary! I could not believe my ears—Christopher's behavior was beyond outrageous—I have never seen such bad behavior. I told Chase to look, and Chase became angry, then disgusted. We began yelling at Christopher to return to our table. I was worried he was going to get us thrown out of the restaurant—you can't just go begging to other tables in a restaurant without causing a major disturbance. He finally returned and complained that a table of French people were rude to him. Making disparaging remarks about frogs! Then he called the waiter over and asked the waiter to bring him some "cheap beer." Hal, who had had every single one of the eight rounds of margaritas, was laughing his head off over the cheap beer.

Cindy got completely *bombed*—she was completely out of control—and soon it was time for me and Christopher to leave. Christopher was docile and willing to leave, which amazed me. Even in his drunken state, he was serious about his studies. To me, that was further proof of its realness.

Before leaving, I turned to Chase and said, "I'm worried about Cindy; she is too drunk."

Chase said, "Don't worry. I'll make sure she's ok. I'll take her home before I come to your place." But I was nervous about leaving her in this state. Not that I was worried about her being with Chase, just that she was way too inebriated. I made Chase promise repeatedly, and he did so with complete solemnity. After taking her home, Chase was supposed to make the move over to my place.

I kissed Hal goodbye. Then I went over to hug Chase, and he held me and kissed me, first on one cheek, then on the other. I loved the way his lips felt on my cheeks—and I was pleasantly surprised at his demonstration of affection, though I was sure it was just a matter of ritual and decorum for him. Nothing special—very continental and, in that sense, a pleasant novelty for an innocent Yankee girl to experience.

"Watch Cindy," I admonished him.

"I will. It'll be fine," he reassured, as Christopher pulled me away through the crowded restaurant to the lively night scene outside.

Chapter 6

Sunday
December 6, 1998

I am looking forward to Chase living with me for a couple of reasons. First, who wouldn't want a gorgeous man to live with her? Second, I don't know what will happen, and wondering about it is exciting. Third, I think it will be nice having a man in the next room at night. Comforting. A comfort I haven't felt in the five years since you left, Paco. I think it will be reassuring and help me sleep better at night knowing he is there. I could picture getting used to that.

Anyway, he moved in tonight—he was supposed to come last night after bringing Cindy home, but he never showed up. Cindy has managed to sabotage his moving out every other night 'til now.

The first thing I asked was what had happened last night after Christopher and I left.

He'd lied. He promised to take care of Cindy and that everything would be fine. Well, it hadn't been fine—when Christopher and I left, apparently the manager of the restaurant invited Chase, Hal, and Cindy to play a free shots game. The wheel kept pointing to Cindy (so it must have been fixed), and she kept drinking the shots of tequila. Chase said he had to carry her home, where she vomited all over the room. Then she fell into the toilet and hit her head on the porcelain—apparently she has a big goose egg on her forehead.

I got so mad at Chase. He had promised to take care of her, and he hadn't! I can't believe he'd let her drink any more at all after we'd left—she was completely drunk even then. To make matters worse, he defends himself to me, saying he drank a lot of her shots to keep her from drinking too much. Then later tonight, he maintained that he couldn't tell her what to drink—she was an adult, and she *wanted* the shots!

What a load of crap. I wasn't buying any of that at all. I steadfastly held him accountable, which riled him.

I feel so betrayed because I'm relying on Chase for safety myself. There is something about him that is different—he isn't like other men—he is responsible and strong and can drink like a fish without getting drunk. I want to believe he will protect us and be there for us—so it's a disappointment that he wasn't there for Cindy. I guess I took it personally. I need to know he is safe. I need to feel he would protect me if I were drinking. I need to know he will do what he promises to do.

So, it was awkward at first. After we argued over Cindy. Then the reality of how awkward the situation was hit home—how does one behave with a stranger living in such close quarters? So we went our separate ways this evening and studied, me in my bedroom, Chase in the living room. At one point, he went out to make phone calls and took the keys. Later, after he came back and resumed his studying, I went down to the Calle Bravo Murillo to make some calls of my own. I called my sister-in-law, Anne, to let her know how I was. She told me some bad news. Uncle Joe passed away last week.

Paco, your uncle Joe died, and I wasn't there. I missed the funeral. He wasn't ill, though he was elderly. I hadn't even imagined something might happen to him. I feel pretty shaken up. On the phone with Annie, I sobbed and sobbed right out on the street in front of Spanish strangers. I couldn't stop. I was desolate, disconsolate—now all there is left of that generation in your family is your mom, and she is so frail. I feel so alone.

When I arrived back in the apartment, I felt even more awkward—I didn't want to tell Chase because it felt too personal to share with him, and I don't want to impose my sadness on him. If I cry in front of him, there might be no stopping me again—I know I would be half grieving for you, Paco, and that is way too intimate and private to share with this new friend. I thought I could just avert my gaze and walk through the living room without him noticing—he was doing homework, after all. ...I entered the living room and looked at the floor while walking through—I said hello—it sounded normal to me. ...

He knew immediately. "What's wrong?" he said, instantly sitting up in his seat.

"Nothing," I fibbed, but he began to lean forward, so I added quickly, "I got some bad news on the phone. I just want to go to my room." My lip was quivering.

Chase was up like a shot. He followed me right into the bedroom (I notice my bedroom door is not a boundary that he recognizes with any trepidation—if he wants to enter, he does so. He does not ask permission). He asked, "What is it?" So I told him and I burst into tears.

It was awkward, just as I had feared—he touched my arm—I wanted to be held but didn't feel comfortable enough to go there—he would have held me—he waited for my move. I stood my ground and talked and cried. I told him I just needed a few minutes alone, please. He wanted to help but didn't know how—and to be fair, I didn't want him to have to deal with my grief, especially since my grief had been such a recent topic in the bars. I needed privacy.

Chase is such a helping person. He always offers to help people in distress—he is not afraid. He's very sensitive, very attuned to others, and he does not flinch. I often find myself thinking he is a force of goodness. In that way we share a kinship—it is one of the attractions between us—one of the things we recognize in each other.

I retired for a little bit. Then I went to the bathroom to wash my hot, swollen, tear-stained face, and when I returned, I left my door open to signal I was done. Minutes later, he came into my room and asked if I was hungry, offered to take us out. I said I'd rather stay in and offered to make sandwiches—he was grateful for anything I had to offer. So I prepared the sandwiches, and he set up the plates and prepared our drinks.

After dinner, he came into my room—I was sitting at the desk next to the shuttered window, which was adjacent to the bed. Chase came right in and sat down on the bed. So forward. So *without* an agenda! So refreshing. It was the most remarkable thing. He spent at least an hour regaling me with police stories from Scotland—he was so wonderful to me, humoring me, making me laugh, keeping my mind off Uncle Joe and the funeral I had missed.

He told me he'd been married in Scotland, so I asked him what happened. He told me about his wife, his son Nicholas, and his girlfriend. The story was vague—I didn't get a feel for timeframes or his real feelings. He did talk about divorce and how he felt as if his life was on hold until it was over. Thus, he thought this would be a good time to travel with his girlfriend, Lauren. He did allude to the fact that his wife would not agree to his side of the story (as he was telling it to me) and that given the chance, she would think she was entitled to more of his assets.

I was beginning to think of Chase as "the perfect man." I had told Cindy I could see no flaws in him, none that were serious anyway. I did hear a warning bell when he made this admission, though.

But mostly I think of Chase as wonderful.

❧

Earlier, after arguing about Cindy, he had gone to take a shower. Then he went to the living room to study and watch TV. I went to the kitchen to check on my laundry, which hung outside the kitchen window on a pulley clothesline crisscrossed over the inner cement courtyard below. The hallway stunk of vomit—we had just eaten, and for a moment I wondered if Chase was bulimic—his body is a perfect male specimen, and I know the physical is very important to him—in that way, we are like Mutt and Jeff. I opened the tall, levered kitchen window and saw his hiking boots and socks were perched outside on the ledge to dry. I realized it wasn't bulimia—it was from the drinking the night before. Chase must have had a terrible hangover himself—he never said a word to me. So I never said anything to him. I still don't know if he had vomited or if that was the remnants of Cindy vomiting all over everything, including Chase, or if, indeed, he had intercepted half of those shots as he had so steadfastly insisted and become ill himself.

∽

I am a jumble of emotions and raw primitive urges—I have my 75-minute class tomorrow. Chase went out. So I retired for the night. I left my door ajar.

When he returned a half-hour later, I called out to make sure it was him. After saying good night, he drew the curtain across the living room doorway and turned on the TV. There was no sound. He didn't turn the volume on! I was wowed by this thoughtfulness about even the tiniest detail—Chase is a detail man—in that sense he is a fully developed man, not immature like Christopher, though many men never mature in this considerate way—I think Chase is the most considerate and genuinely caring man I have ever, ever met.

Quite a sexy quality.

I got up (the bed springs squeak every time I breathe. So Chase knows my every move in here), and I went to my door—Chase was inches away from my door. I could see the back of his blond head as he silently watched TV, the eerie dancing shadows playing on the living room walls like a 360-degree film surrounding him. I smiled. I knew without a doubt the shadows represented some sort of world sports review.

I closed my door and for a split second considered whether I should throw the flimsy bolt. I knew in my heart there was no reason to bolt my door—Chase is the consummate gentleman—even had I been the siren who lit his fires—for me, it was the act of ultimate faith in him not to throw the bolt. It was also still risky and breathtakingly exciting (within the boundaries of certain knowledge of safety)—unrealized potentials loomed in my imagination. I touched the bolt as I wavered between the pros and cons.

I chose to trust him.

I chose to feel the tightening of my chest as my breathing caught in my throat. I was choosing to live. This is what Spain is all about for me—the choice to live in the moment.

Oh my god, this is so *exhilarating*!

Quietly, I tip-toed back to my bed, knowing Chase had heard every-thing that had just happened, knowing Chase *knew I hadn't thrown the bolt,* knowing Chase had registered there *was* a bolt to be thrown because Chase was thorough—he noticed *everything*, believe me. I notice him noticing all the time.

It took me awhile to fall asleep with Chase awake just feet away in the next room with the unbolted door between us. Only when he turned off the TV and retired, himself, did I fall into slumber.

I didn't hear the door open. The first I knew of his presence was his touch as he lowered himself to my bed. He said my name on a low, breathy, Scottish whisper and came to me in the night. He laid himself on top of me—the full, glorious weight of his all-male body pressed into my body on the thin mattress until I couldn't breathe.

My eyes flew open! Chase!

I sat up in the darkness, my body still feeling the impression of his warm breath on my cheek. He'd been lying on me just moments before. Where was he?

I looked around the empty darkness of my tiny little bedroom. I was alone.

Oh my god! It had been a dream! But it was *so* real, I had to look to make sure. I jumped out of the bed and went to the door, pulled it open, and looked into the pitch dark living room. Chase was sprawled on the sofa—I didn't know if he was awake or not. He didn't move. I went back to my room and spent a restless night trying to get back to sleep.

I cannot *ever* remember a dream so vivid, so palpable that I could not tell the difference between the essence of the dream and reality. It's the kind of dream I wish I could have about you, Paco. The kind of dream where we are reunited. Where you are truly there.

∽

This is the birth of my attraction to Chase. Up until this moment, I've been looking at him cerebrally, trying to find faults with him, distancing myself from him. But at this moment, I feel an urgent need to touch him. On every level.

I know he is taken. He is not only spoken for, he is speaking for another woman. Even if I were the siren who lit his fire (and I am *not*, no illusions here), to transgress this commitment would ruin our budding relationship. It would bring guilt and regret and all the other negative emotions into our reality. As it stands, we have a purity between us that defines who we are to one another. If anything, I am attracted to him physically *because* of who he *is* (as opposed to Christopher, to whom I am completely physically attracted—Christopher makes me moist by looking into my eyes, simply by being in the same room. And by the way, I am profoundly grateful *not* to be assigned to the same teaching group as he—I *never* would have been able to overcome the physical distraction. With Chase, it is a more balanced attraction involving every part of who he is)—Chase's physical beauty is something I fight against because I know it gets in the way of us connecting in a real way—I don't trust it, and I don't relate to it, and it doesn't turn me on. If I had a matching physical beauty, we could have connected in an erotic *explosion*, of this I am quite sure. Because we are connecting on every other level. As it is, I feel a lot of physical self-consciousness and awkwardness around Chase—I am acutely aware of his physical superiority—and I *hate* it.

∽

Monday
December 7, 1998

I've been "aglow" from the second week on. I am positively radiant—everyone notices it every day.

"Darcy, you are glowing! What is it?"

"I am happy," I say, and think, between Christopher and Chase, if I get any more sexually turned on I'm going to self-incinerate.

My relationship with Christopher has gradually shifted to a more motherly role—I am turned off by the alcohol, but I never stop feeling that incredible physical awareness of him. I have no physical attraction to Hal or to Ethan, and of course none to Michael, whom I consider a woman, or Dylan, whom I am repelled by and afraid of.

But every day I awaken happy, knowing I will see Chase and Christopher once again. Knowing I will spend all of my day and night with these two exciting men—and that it was preordained by fate and circumstance—and we have a solid relationship, all three of us, that I have quickly come to rely on and look forward to experiencing each and every day now. I don't have much of these two men, but I do have the next two weeks with them within the confines of this relationship we have developed together, both as a group and individually.

"Darcy, you look positively radiant. What's happened?"

"I don't know," I say casually and shrug—but I am *acutely* aware of the sexual frenzy that has taken me by *storm*. Painfully aware of the two men who stoke the now ever-present blush in my cheeks. My cheeks feel as if they are on *fire*, all day and every day—it's the most amazing phenomenon, to be sexually turned on all the time—I have never in my life experienced this physical sensation. Of course, I have never been so physically needy and so unfulfilled.

I feel the freest with Chase because I am relatively sure of his safety. I can flirt with him and bait him, talk sexy with innuendo, tell off-color jokes, look at and appreciate his body openly and *touch* him any time I want to and he will allow it, encourage it, bait me back, egg me on, touch me back even, without worry that either one of us will go too far or lose our sense of who we are in our relationship. It is *so* warm, so comfortable, yet so on the edge and tantalizing, I never really know where it will go. But I do know where it will not go.

⟳

Today, I gave my first 75-minute class. I was *frantic*. When Chase did his first long class last Thursday, he was a basket case. I spent all my time on Thursday helping him "because we were a team." Chase's words. I had my doubts as to whether my support would be reciprocated.

I don't know, dependability and reliability are difficult commodities to find in a man, I think, except for you of course, Paco—you were there for me every single minute of every day for 21 years. I highly doubt I will ever experience that kind of absolute faith in another man in my lifetime. But it's more than finding qualities in a man, isn't it? What we had was a union, union of spirit, lives, our minds, and hearts. Out of that kind of oneness comes faith. Faith that you would be there. Because you always were. I didn't really understand that until you were gone. It is your absence that highlights your thereness. Your thereness was the invisible foundation upon which my whole life was built. I had no idea what would happen once the foundation crumbled away from me.

⟳

There weren't any foundations built in class today, that's for sure.

Chase never even asked me if I needed help today, and he knew how nervous I was. He went out with the group for Chinese—a long 1-1/2 hour lunch—and left me to fend for myself. I felt so angry with him, so betrayed, so abandoned. It really hurt. What hurt the most was how familiar I am with this state of abandonment and aloneness. I know what to do with it too intimately. Dig in and move on.

So I ended up sputtering and fuming through my preparations in a small, windowless prep room by myself. Terrified. I was hyperventilating—I had to do a situational presentation, which I wasn't able to write, wasn't able to wrap my mind around, until the last ten minutes before class. It came to me out of nowhere on the precipice of despair, from where I have no idea. Inspiration ignites in the darkest of moments.

Usually, one team member is assigned to observe their team during each class. Today, Teams A and B were scheduled to switch student observers. Chase was assigned to observe the other class during my lesson. Just as well—I didn't need to be distracted by his self-involved face.

Hal came from the other class to observe me. Afterwards, he told me my lesson was one of the bright spots of the course for him. He confided he was feeling really low until he saw me teach—it was such a thing of beauty, it raised his spirits way up, and now he thought that maybe he would be all right (his words). The Welsh are dramatic, what can I say? It heartened me to hear such praise, even if I didn't believe it. I had made a lot of errors I wasn't happy with, but it was the first lesson I wasn't devastated over. Hal made me feel even better about it.

And Hal told *everyone* how brilliant I was. Much to my self-conscious delight. I was glad Chase was hearing that. When he asked how it went, I shrugged casually and said that it had a few problems but went well. On this side of disappointment, I was glad I could stand tall before him and know I had done it on my own. When the going gets tough, I tend to get tougher.

Tonight, when we got back to the apartment, I was still upset with Chase. After dinner, he came into my room and sat on my bed, telling cop stories about Scotland again. I thought about Eddie but didn't share with him that my brother was a cop—I just wasn't feeling very close to him tonight.

He told me about his last day on the force—the day after his going-away party (just three weeks ago, wow, he was a cop only three weeks ago). At the party, his buddies were lacing his beers with some kind of vile Scottish liquor to get him really drunk (they would have to go to such extremes to see Chase drunk, I am quite sure). Chase knew they had laced his drinks but drank the beers anyway. He says he got really drunk—threw up everywhere and passed out—he doesn't remember getting home that night.

I asked him if he knew—why did he drink the beers? Why would he do that to himself?

The answer? Because it would be completely unacceptable to refuse a drink from his buddies. Not possible. Even if it was poison! He would rather die.

Incomprehensible!!!!!

Though talking with him was good enough, tonight I begged off early—I am not comfortable with Chase right now—I think I have mis-judged him. Given him too much credit in the haze of my attraction to him, an attraction that is new to me. This physicality is freaking me out. I just don't feel comfortable in my own skin any more. I don't understand the things I'm feeling, Paco. I don't remember feeling these things with you—I must have—we were crazy about each other. From the first moment we met, I do remember we couldn't keep our hands off each other. But it was so long ago ... and so much has happened in the interim. I don't know what's normal and what isn't. It's the weirdest experience. I just feel so sad.

I went to bed at a reasonable hour. But I couldn't sleep. I tossed and turned on the thin, squeaky mattress. Chase watched silent TV for a long time tonight. I know it was too early for him and his lifestyle.

I'm SO old.

Chapter 7

This morning I got up at 7:00 and studied. It's the Feast of the Immaculate Conception, a national holiday in Spain. We have the day off. But we have two papers and a lesson plan due tomorrow. I'm not sure I can get everything done in one day. Chase got up around 10:30, and we had some breakfast together. It was awkward again—I was in my jammies still—so I showered with Inés' hand-held showerhead in the tiny makeshift bathtub shower-curtained area. Then I got to work on my tape lesson—a lesson on listening. In order to do it, I had to use Inés' tape machine in her bedroom.

When Chase saw me head into Inés' bedroom, he jumped up and followed behind to help me operate the stereo equipment. He started looking through Inés' CD collection and found an Enya CD, which he played for me—he couldn't believe I had never heard of Enya before. Her music is beautiful.

Chase just sat on Inés' bed and his face lit up while the music played— I really love the way he loves music—I haven't paid too much attention to music for a very long time in my life. It used to be one of the most important things to me, but somehow, Paco, you and I got sidetracked with Jaime and our youthful passions were put aside. Chase is so sentimental about it. I can remember feeling that way about Elton John, the Eagles, Led Zeppelin, ELO, Crosby, Stills, Nash, and Young, and of course the Beatles, Cream, Hendrix—once upon a time. It touches me, this. I have to get one of Enya's CDs when I get home.

There are some other singers Chase has used in his lesson planning I must find when I get home, too. Some guy named Lou Reed, very deep, sexy voice. The guys love him. Hal used a song of his, "Walk on the Wild Side," in his lesson. It was cool. And last week Chase used a Scottish singer in his lesson. The song was about a man who loved his lover so much he would walk one thousand miles to see her; he would take a bullet for her. Chase played the song over and over, and the class absolutely loved it. The Brits all knew this song by heart; the Spaniards eagerly learned the words and fit them into their grammatical placeholders. It was very happy, lots of laughter and singing along by everyone. Chase is making music come alive for me again.

After finishing with my school tape, I looked through Inés' music collection and found a Beach Boys CD called *Pet Sounds*. I put it on. The distant echoing intro notes rang out from Inés' bedroom into the living room beyond where Chase sat cross-legged on the sofa studying. Brian Wilson sang, "Wouldn't it be nice if we were older?" and a jolt of joy surged inside me. From the living room, I heard Chase sing, "And wouldn't it be nice to live together," and I joined, "iiin the kind of world where we belong," on my side. *We could say goodnight and staaaay together. ...*" We laughed and sang beautiful harmonies together like that, one Beach Boys song after the next from our respective rooms. Completely spontaneous, so much fun!

When the album was over, Chase came to the bedroom doorway and asked if he could work at my desk while I was in Inés' room. It made me uncomfortable to have him in my messy quarters, but of course, I said yes. A few minutes later, from the bedroom, he cried out, "Darcy, come here and see!" I ran in thinking, *What the hell could be the matter?* Lo and behold, Chase had opened my shuttered window—the window turned out to be French doors leading out to a full balcony!! I'd had a balcony all this time and hadn't known!

Chase of course made so much fun of me—"HELLOOOO, Darcy! It's a balcony! You're living in the dark all this time—oh yeah; it was REAL hard opening the shutters—pull the cord like this." He pulled the chord with two limp fingers! "Yes. Very hard. HELLOOOO!!!" And of course I was embarrassed and laughing at myself as well as at Chase's antics and abuse. The ice, once again, was broken between us.

We laughed and joked and sang, and he danced—he *loves* music—can't resist swiveling his hips and gyrating in the sexiest way. We studied in different rooms but kept coming into one another's room to talk or laugh or sing, or me just to keep seeing my fucking balcony. We ate lunch out on my beautiful, wonderful, gorgeous balcony overlooking the tree-lined alcove street below. I took out my camera and snapped pictures of Chase lounging on my balcony. Such a delightfully sweet discovery.

But it's bittersweet. We went down to Prêt A Manger in the plaza and got sandwiches to go. Sandwiches for a picnic on my new balcony. As we luxuriated in the open air above the bustling business district below, Chase started with a nervous cough, "Em, Darcy, em, well, there's something I need to tell you. I'm leaving tonight."

I looked up with shock. "Leaving? Tonight?" No. It's not possible. Not now! Not when we're getting along so well. My heart completely sank. Completely disappointed.

I said to him several times, "Please Chase, you can't leave now—we're having too much fun!" and "Chase, don't leave—it just won't be the same here without you."

He explained that he had found another place to stay and was leaving tonight.

He said it was because Inés was coming back soon, and it wouldn't look right if he were still there.

I don't believe him. Either I did something wrong, or it was something else. Cindy feels that his girlfriend back in Greece is calling all the shots. Maybe she had decreed the move.

So, that's the way it was—just as it became so fun and happy between us, Chase left tonight.

I'm here alone.

It's very lonely here now. It's so quiet in this apartment. No laughing. No more songs. Just silence all around me. There's a void that once was Chase. I don't like voids, Paco; they make me so sad. ...

But Chase and I have forged something solid between us today—a bond of friendship that I suspect will sparkle in both of our eyes for the rest of the course.

Earlier this afternoon, he sat upon my bed talking about his sex life and Sophie and Lauren—

"I'm not attracted to just everyone, you know," he told me.

"Oh?"

"It takes a dynamite woman to light my fires."

"Does it?"

"I don't go for just any girl. It's always been that way for me. That's how I knew I should be with Lauren. I mean, she convinced me I should be with her, not my wife, and that's something."

Yes, I think, that's something all right—it's adultery. And sweet Lauren is a home wrecker. There is no way around that—someday she will pay a price for that. I would rather not be in her shoes the day Chase looks at her with ice in his eyes and says he doesn't love her—that will be a living hell on earth for her—I think that will happen someday. Chase still has love in his eyes for his wife, a special softness. I can see it. It is *very* disturbing. I can't stop worrying about Nicholas. Nicholas is not yet one year old.

Chase is mightily impressed with Lauren's ability to convince him. I think he was bewitched in a weak moment. I pity him for his weakness—he is making irrevocable mistakes. This is the big time—welcome to adulthood, boys.

Even the leaders are vulnerable.

I think in the long run I am lucky to know Chase the way I do. I have the luxury of forgiving him because we have no ties, we have no commitments, we have no child between us, and so his betrayals are still forgivable. I know in my heart there is a woman out there in Scotland somewhere with an infant all by herself abandoned for whatever reason by this very same, wonderful Chase. There is a woman out there who would not forgive him so easily. And that thought permeates my heart and makes me very sad, too. … So much sadness to feel in this life, Paco. So much sadness.

〜

Wednesday
December 9th

Today something pretty profound happened. We were called in to do tutorials with Liam—meetings in which he is to tell us our standing in the class. Up until this moment, the course has been hard and there has been pressure, but we have become pretty carefree and confident in our ways and our status within the group.

Chase went first—his absence sobered Ethan, Michael, and me as we waited in our practice room for him to return. Michael leaned over to me and whispered that she was afraid. She hadn't been doing so well, and she knew it. I told her not to worry about it. "Liam's not going to tell you anything you don't already know, right?"

Nodding with a nervous smile, she gratefully answered, "Thank you, Darcy," and resumed her lesson planning work. I always support Michael in spite of the confusion she has caused interpersonally within the group. She looks like a woman, she speaks like a woman, she relates to me like a woman, but still there is dissent within the group about whether or not she is a man. Maybe it's naïve of me, but if someone tells me she is a woman, and she talks like a woman and looks like a woman, I pretty much believe she is.

The subject comes up frequently. Christopher gets quite hot about it. "THAT is a man!" he exclaims with great outraged passion, whenever the subject comes up. Chase says, "Darcy! Look at her—she has no chest. She has no breasts!!!" How would I know if she has breasts or not? Lots of women are smaller. We all know she is peculiar, but most of us continue to refer to her as "her." I have become friends with her and sometimes we go out at lunchtime for walks and talk. She's very sweet to me. I like her, and I find her interesting. Well, she's very mysterious. She doesn't socialize with the rest of the group after class, always has something else she needs to do. She lives with friends somewhere in Madrid. Kind of like Ethan and Emma; she has a life outside of this class. Sometimes I envy that.

Chase returned from his tutorial closed-lipped but not unhappy. He just nodded an okay when I asked him how it went.

I was next. In preparation for the meeting, we'd had to fill out a pre-tutorial form telling what we thought of our performance in the class, including rating our progress. I rated myself "excellent" for progress and explained my rating as based on how far I had come from the beginning of the class.

In the conference, Liam was very gentle. He told me all my strengths as he saw them and my weaknesses, all of which he had written in a report to the university back in England.

Then he kindly referred to my self-assessment and said he understood why I had put down that rating and acknowledged his agreement of my improvement, but said I had misinterpreted the "progress" part and that our assessments were far apart. The possible ratings were unacceptable, acceptable, excellent, and superior. He had rated me "acceptable." Period.

My cheeks became flushed. I told him I understood—I had misread the form and I didn't disagree with his assessment. I lied. Of course.

The rest of the session was tortuously long, and I have only a vague memory of it. I returned to the planning room in a daze.

I was *mortified*. I didn't disagree with his assessment, but I had *not* misread the form. It asked about progress. I felt as if I had been set up, ambushed. My cheeks were *hot* and red, red, red. I returned to the room and slid into my seat, my eyes downcast—not the first time Chase had seen this kind of entrance from me.

Chase, of course, was on me as soon as I came through the door.

"Darcy?" I didn't look up. "Everything okay?"

"Yes, fine," I replied, eyes on my work blindly.

"Darcy? Okay?" he demanded now.

"It was fine," I said through clenched teeth.

Michael put her hand on my arm, "How was it?" she asked tremulously. It was her turn next.

"It was fine," I said to her without looking at Chase. "I'm fine."

She knew I was lying. Michael left shaken. Well, what was I to say? She knew I wasn't happy—that was plain for all to see—but I didn't want to go into it with her right before she had her own conference. And I didn't particularly want to go into it in front of Chase and Ethan—Ethan who sat silently by and watched, carefully scrutinizing every single action and breath I took.

Chase persisted once Michael left. "Darcy, what happened?"

So I told him—"It was brutal. Liam was very critical. I didn't get the rating I thought I should have gotten."

Chase became impatient. "So what?" he cried out in his deep, Scottish guttural voice. "It's not about ratings, is it then? At the end of the day, it's about getting a certificate. Are you in the program or not?"

"Of course I'm in the program. And it *is* about ratings. That's why they rate us."

"No!" Chase became extremely upset. "It's not about ratings. It's about getting the certificate and becoming a good teacher; at the end of the day, nobody cares about the grade you get."

"Chase, it's important to me. I'm not used to not getting the grade I set out to get. And I have the distinct impression it's now set in stone."

Chase argued on. I stopped him short by asking him if he got a superior—he balked, wouldn't respond. He got a superior! Suddenly it hit me right between the eyes—Chase was number one in the entire class!

I was so *pissed off*. Here he was, chastising me for caring—without acknowledging his own position. That's outrageous. He was criticizing me when he was sitting on top. I told him, "Don't criticize me for wanting a grade when you know you've gotten a grade, the top grade. That's so hypocritical!"

But he persisted, wouldn't let it go, telling me this grade thing was all wrong. Grades are meaningless. Meaningless to whom? Only someone who is on top! What a bunch of bullshit.

Michael returned and said it was fine. I thought it was over and went back to work grumbling and muttering under my breath, knowing a glowering Chase was looking on.

Then Cindy came into our planning room complaining her head off about her tutorial with Liam, and of course, *brainlessly*, Chase argued with her, too. She ended by saying, "I deserve the top grade because I'm Cindy. I don't need to earn it!" Which of course made Chase *nuts*, and he blew her off, slamming his books shut and asking Ethan if he wanted to go to lunch. We all left together, though our spirits were definitely divided and troubled.

When we returned from lunch, Liam approached me as soon as we entered the lobby and asked to talk with me. He took me into a private room and said Michael had told him I was unhappy about my grade.

I was thunderstruck. I denied it.

Liam went on to tell me it's a cultural thing—Americans have an "attitude problem." He spent fifteen minutes explaining my attitude problem and how to fix it.

I told him I had no problem with his rating, but I sure had a problem with Michael telling him my business. So, then I got a lecture on how I should thank Michael because *she* was helping *me* in the course. Then he said he wanted to talk to Cindy, too, and set her straight.

I returned to the planning room *steaming*, simply steaming.

Chase demanded to know what happened—of course now everyone was aware I had been taken into a private room by Liam.

I told him, "Michael told Liam that I was unhappy, and now he thinks I have an attitude problem!"

Chase said, "You gotta watch that Michael—watch what you say to HIM."

"I'm not saying anything to her ever again," was all I said in return. I could see that I needed to keep my mouth shut in front of the British people.

Suddenly I realize the deck is stacked against the Americans. I can see that it's them against us in a British system, and we cannot win under any circumstances. It's very clear to me. The only way to survive the course is to put my nose to the grindstone and mind my own business. Chase is right about one thing: The goal is to pass and get the certificate. I really had lost sight of that part.

But when Cindy heard what had happened with Michael, she went *ballistic*. She wanted to punch Michael out. "How dare she tell on us to Liam!" But I told Cindy, no, she couldn't say a word to Michael because I had a 75-minute class to do tonight and I had to work with her; she's my partner tonight, she's on *my* team, and I can't pass without working well with her. Cindy simply had to keep her mouth shut for now. Reluctantly, Cindy agreed but under extreme, extreme protest.

I returned to the planning room. Chase was working on his class, and I told him what happened with Cindy. He said, "Jesus, this is becoming a bloody soap opera," with utter disgust.

I realized several things at that point:

1. I needed to focus on my teaching right now and I was so angry with Chase I didn't want to be anywhere near him. I packed up my teaching supplies and moved to a private room to prepare.
2. Chase would have *no* patience, as in *zero*, with a pack of women fighting over a "he said, she said."

3. Chase was right about continuing to fight—it was not in anyone's best interest, especially not mine. I needed to refocus my energies on *me* and *my* teaching. Somehow I had allowed myself to become too distracted by these men and too disconnected from my own goals.

I vowed to keep my distance from all of them when it came time for me to give a lesson. I'm not going to depend on anyone but myself from now on. I've had to depend on myself ever since you left, Paco, and I know deep down I can do that. This is the one truth I have come to know in my life.

I told Liam in that second meeting that the grade or any grade didn't matter to me, and I meant it. Once I saw the system was fixed, I was freed to focus on what was left, what was really important to me, what brought me to Spain in the first place. I was going to concentrate on improving my skills and becoming the best teacher I could be for my students back home. I'm a newly certified secondary teacher back home, and the lessons Liam is teaching us are brilliant. He is the best teacher, hands down, I have ever had.

But I am more convinced than ever the grades are already determined and set in stone. The next two weeks (barring any screw-ups) will be perfunctory. I believe Liam has already sent in the grades, that he's already made up his mind who is getting what grades. Inside, that *enrages* me, indeed. But, hey, I'm an American girl in hostile redcoat territory. I think that's the reality of this course. Suddenly Chase's lampooning of us Americans doesn't seem so funny any more. Suddenly I'm experiencing the British anger at America in action. This is the system I find myself in. I didn't create it, but I sure as hell recognize it for what it is. The deck is stacked against me because of my nationality. I'm smart enough to know that. And I am *very* capable of taking this knowledge and faking my way through the rest of this charade. But I feel disillusioned now. Liam may be a grammar guru, but his brilliance has become a bit tarnished for me.

Thursday
December 10th

I did okay on my lesson today; it was a fucking miracle I didn't bomb after yesterday's chaos and emotional trauma. Afterwards, I needed everyone to help me with my tape for the next lesson. Ethan had promised to help me after class, but he left—he forgot. So I asked everyone to help, including Chase.

Michael gave a horrendous lesson—in fact she froze and then ran out of the room in the middle of it, leaving me to finish her part of the lesson with no prep! Which I got in trouble with Liam for doing—some nonsense about me not fulfilling my role as the class reporter (my assigned role while Michael was teaching) because I was doing her teaching—what about the students???? She ran out, and the students were just sitting there not knowing what to do. Was it more important to rigidly stick to my randomly assigned role than to pick up the lesson and teach the students??? Who's got a values problem?

So Michael wasn't in the mood to help me—so much for team spirit. Absolutely no one on my team was there to help me. Since my own team was evaporating before my very eyes, I asked everyone from the other team to help me. Team A all said yes. (I must have a tape by tomorrow, and this is my last chance to get it. If I get graded down for having the wrong teachers on my tape, who the *hell* cares at this point—it's all set in stone. I am feeling *bitter*.)

Hal went first. Then Dylan did his, then Christopher, then Chase finally deigned to help after seeing everyone else generously helping me (wouldn't look good to the group would it?), then Cindy, and then Michael finally agreed and went last.

The subject was, "If I won the lottery, I would ..." Cindy said she'd buy property all around the world. Chase said he'd buy race cars and go on the racing circuit. Christopher said he'd spend it as quickly as he could on a lark. And Michael said she'd use it to overthrow her government, which was evil and needed to be destroyed. Actually, except for Michael who was disturbingly intense, we had a lot of fun—it was truly a class effort. I'm so grateful they all came together tonight to help me.

After making the tape with both groups, we all went down to Te &
Me for a drink. But Cindy couldn't stand being in the same room with
Michael—she was still angry over the Liam episode—she is a simmering
pot about to explode; it was kind of scary. She left the bar within minutes,
saying, "Either she leaves or I do. It's a creepy feeling being in the same
room. I have nothing to say to IT ever again!" she exclaimed.

Chase just shook his head in disgust over her carrying on. And I could
see in his eyes repulsion that she would let her feelings about Michael get
in the way of socializing with the group. The group is more important than
anything to Chase. Usually Chase exudes self-confidence and calm focus.
He does not get rattled, except when dueling with me, or when he's angry
at one of the others for their transgressions against the group. Chase can forgive just about any outrageous behavior, but not actions against the group.
Nothing riles Chase more than when he feels someone isn't acting in the
best interests of the group. Chase is a team player. I've never really been on
a team before. But I'm learning all about it now from Chase.

Now I realize Chase has excelled beyond me and everyone else in the
class, and that he has chastised *me* for caring—without acknowledging his
own position—I am so *pissed off*. It's taken me a while to realize Chase and
I are deeply competitive. But Chase hid his competitive soul from everyone—it's easier to hide your competitiveness when you are number one—
you can feign casualness about your position, and that's what Chase does.

A lot of disappointments are happening for me now. I'm so disillusioned.

Chapter 8

Friday
December 11, 1998

This morning Ethan added his taped answer to the question, "If I won the lottery," answering that he is a religious man, had been brought up with very strong faith, and if he won the lottery he would use the money to travel to Africa or South America and become a missionary so he could spread the word of God to the pagan people. He spoke into the machine with a soft, convincing voice, a serious expression, and just the right amount of British formality to completely convince me of his sincerity—he never wavered, never blinked, and when he was finished, he stood tall and quietly confident, his manner naturally a little stiff and rigid. It all makes sense to me now—his quietness, his reticence in our rowdy group, his formal manner. He's extremely religious! Wow.

I feel a bit let down to think of Ethan as a religious man—I still don't know Ethan that well (I haven't spent much social time with him until this point). I thought I could like him and be natural around him, but with this revelation I feel I have to be more respectful around him and not be so sexual in my talk. Note to self: Start treating Ethan with more deference and respect (god only knows why, but it feels important—my Catholic childhood training comes out). It's kind of disappointing to think his reserve will never melt; I will never be able to transcend it because it is a part of the spiritual, more serious person he is.

Ironically, Chase became the captain of our team today. It happened so naturally, so seamlessly, I never even thought of him as our captain until just now. Now that I think about it, he always gives all the credit to everyone else. But this afternoon when our team was really put to the test, it was Chase who stood to the challenge. Gareth appeared at our planning room door and suddenly announced that our next team task was to create an entire week's lesson plan for next week, due by Monday. Chaos broke out among us—an entire week's plan! Over the weekend? Impossible! What were we to do?

Chase walked with confident resolve over to the whiteboard, picked up a marker, and said, "Okay, let's get this on the board."

An hour later we had a fully detailed, organized plan of action outlined on the board, fully color-coded by lesson elements. It was one of the most impressive demonstrations of leadership, organization, and sheer intelligence in action I have *ever* witnessed. I was *wowed*. From this moment on, I will walk into the raging sea if Chase tells me to. I mean, I have leadership qualities, but Chase *is* a leader—there is a difference. He is a born and bred leader. He doesn't have to think about it. It's instinctive—it is a thing of stunning beauty (far more than his physical beauty). And then he retreats modestly as if what he's done is nothing, and he encourages his teammates to excel—wow—what an experience for me to witness—what a shining example of excellence.

We had planned to go to a Chinese for dinner tonight. It's Friday evening, and everyone else had already been at Te & Me for a couple of hours, so, no one was feeling any pain—both of our teams had just gotten the group timetabling assignment from Liam today and spent the whole afternoon planning. I am still disappointed in Chase as a personal friend; he has let me down big time, but I am now impressed with him as a leader.

I was late joining everyone because I had to meet with Marta, one of my students, after school and do a personal history of her, which turned out to be a lot of fun. Marta is a med student who must pass the CELTA exam to continue with her medical studies. Many of her text books are written in English! I can't imagine that she must learn from books not in her own native language. In the interview, she tells me about her brothers and sisters and how they celebrate holidays. She's funny and very sweet. It's obvious to me she really wants to communicate what her country and her culture are like. She is very proud that her country is now a democracy. I think the Spanish people have been through a lot to get their democracy. They appreciate it so much more than we Americans who take it for granted.

When I got to the bar, Chase and Ethan were hard at work together planning their classes for the next week's worth of timetabling. I felt bad to see them hunched over their papers because during the planning session this afternoon they had given me a set of music assignments I'd liked and felt excited about doing and then at the last minute they'd yanked all my assignments and given them to Michael (over my vociferous complaints—well, no, really I objected but let it go, though I was reeling over it inside—the "team spirit" took over me ... arrgghh), and then they gave me drivel—the new assignment didn't make sense to me, and I didn't like it—I was supposed to do some kind of vocabulary analysis of different geographies and cultures, whatever that means. Chase *assured* me we'd work it out together. This was a team effort, and we were the *best* team, and we were all going to help one another. Yeah right, I've heard that before and been burned. I'm leery now.

Excuse me if I'm cynical, but I've been screwed on this team stuff before.

So when I arrive at the bar, I see they're busily working by themselves and they ignore me. My heart sinks and I'm angry. I sit down next to Hal at the far side of the table. I make a comment to Hal—kind of a disparaging one.

"Hal, this is supposed to be a working occasion for my team, so if they ever decide to work with me, would you mind changing places?"

It was a *team* effort, but their half of the team hadn't saved any table space for my half!

Chase, without looking up says, "Darcy, come join us; we're planning." I start grinding my teeth.

So Hal and I exchanged seats, and Ethan and Chase briefly told me about *their* lessons. Ethan wanted to interface his lesson with mine because he and I were sharing a topic, culture. Otherwise, it was all about them.

I have a *bad* feeling. I complain, "I was supposed to do music in diverse cultures. You took away my subject and gave it to Michael, and now I don't know what I'm doing at all."

Chase says, "I know you didn't like that, but it had to be done—for the team. It improved the slot. Are you okay with it?"

"No!" I exclaim. "I don't know what I'm doing."

"What do you mean? Look, you're doing a vocabulary lesson on global cultures," he elaborates. It makes zero sense to me. What is the focal point? What lesson will I be doing? What vocabulary will I be teaching the students? Where is the vocabulary list? What is the purpose? How will my lesson tie into their elements? It all has to flow, all has to become one integral teaching unit for the students.

"Yeah but I don't understand it—what will I *do*?" To say a topic is not to know exactly what I will be teaching, how I will be tying the themes to actual teaching and grammar points. How will it tie in to what they are doing? I don't even know what they're doing—they're planning without me!

"Don't *worry* about it; we're going to figure that out at a meeting tomorrow night," he says.

Then he proceeds to set up a meeting for Saturday night at 6:00 p.m. at some bar near Ethan's house.

I have a bad feeling about the whole thing. I know when I've been brushed off. And Ethan and Chase have been furiously working—they are completely planned out. They know their subjects, their materials, the reading, the grammar points, everything. I don't even understand what it is I'm supposed to do—or even where I should look for inspiration. I know nothing. Their pieces dovetail together—Chase is making up a game about burglars, and Ethan is doing a quiz on the grammar concepts used in the game. I'm supposed to do some vocabulary lesson on multicultural history and geography. They are working together as a team; I have no one to work with on my planning. Michael hasn't joined the planning either. My piece is solo. And it doesn't fit in with theirs at all.

Paco, I'm all alone. Again.

I tell myself not to panic.

Meanwhile, Cindy is drifting in and out of our vision. Her team is in a state of total dysfunction, and she is wistfully watching ours working together off-hours (little does she know my predicament). She comes over and whispers to me that she feels bad to be in such a bad group. Suddenly, she announces to the group that she has a headache—she's going home. She wants to spend the weekend traveling in Spain—Toledo and Segovia.

This is funny: She had invited me to go and I said no, I didn't think so because there was too much homework to do over the weekend—that was *before* the timetabling and three papers that have just been assigned.

But Cindy had already bought a ticket to Segovia. When Chase was staying with me, *he* had invited me to go to Segovia separately.

"Oh come on, we'll have such a good time and it's so beautiful." I had said I didn't think so—where would we stay? I'm too old to be bumming around with a bunch of twenty-year-olds.

No, it's just a day trip—I'm trying to envision keeping up with the "long-leggeds," and I say "I don't think so" to Chase, too.

Now by today it's absolutely out of the question—we're swamped with homework.

So Cindy asks if I'm going, and I say no way. ...

So now she's hemmin' and hawin,' and she goes over to Chase (who is ticked she's not going out with us tonight—never mind we're already out, we haven't *gone* out yet!), and she says, "So Chase, are you coming to Segovia or not?"

He hesitates so long, I'm really not sure how he will answer, and I'm thinking, so much for our meeting tomorrow night. Then he says a flat-out and emphatic "No!" No explanation, just the purposely belligerent answer in his deepest vibrato Scottish lilt.

Cindy shrugs, says she's leaving, and whispers in my ear, "I just can't stand the company in this place. I have to leave." Looking all the while at Michael, who's socializing at the bar with Christopher—Christopher who is *fascinated* with her questionable gender. Ay, yi, yi! My gaze lingers on Christopher for one agonizing, longing minute, then returns to Cindy, who's spewing fury at all of us. I was like, give it up—what is the matter with you?

She leaves. Chase sets up the next night's meeting, okays it with all of us, and everyone agrees it's a good thing and we will all be there—Ethan draws maps for Michael and me. All the while, Christopher is whining about what a sorry team he is on, that they haven't even planned their week yet and no one's meeting over the weekend. It's settled then, we are meeting tomorrow and we're done for the night (my misgivings notwithstanding). Now we were going to have dinner at the Chinese and relax.

Actually, I've had no alcohol through this point, only *agua mineral*. So, we pay and leave. Dylan declines to come (this week, Dylan has been coming for after-school beers but not anything else). Michael, when we get to the corner, suddenly says in her sweet, thin voice, "Oh, but I've already had Chinese this week. I can't eat it again. It will make me sick." How could anyone get sick from having Chinese more than once in a week? You see? Now that is mysterious. We agreed to meet the next night, and she, too, walked off in the opposite direction down the crowded Calle Bravo Murillo. We thought it was peculiar and sudden, but a lot of how Michael behaves is peculiar.

So we leave, Ethan, me, Chase, Hal, and Christopher.

We verily skipped on down to the Chinese only to find it is closed—it's still *siesta* time (5:30 or 6:00), and so we began wandering around looking for a place to eat—a lot of suggestions were bandied about, including going to Sol—I didn't relish the idea of Sol but was amenable to anything the group wanted to do—finally we found this little Italian Alps-style bar and restaurant down the street from the Chinese. It was closed, but when asked, the manager agreed to serve us drinks and *tapas* until the restaurant opened at 8:00 (!!!!) We were thrilled—starving, tummies empty, but thrilled.

I ordered an *agua sin gas*, but Chase won't hear of it—he got me a *vino tinto* despite my protestations about an empty stomach and getting drunk. We lined up at the bar initially, but then we scattered around a bit, me sitting at a table directly next to the bar, Chase sitting next to my table on some stairs leading to a dining room on the upper floor, Hal and Christopher standing at the bar next to my table, and Ethan leaning his back against the bar and facing the rest of us.

At first, we congregated with the boys where the beer is flowing fast and furious. The barmaid was serving us *tapas,* too. Hal had two beers and then switched to *coca* and water! Everyone was completely taken aback—Hal is our very *biggest* drinker—he explained he now knows, since his tutorial with Liam, he has to sober up if he's going to pass the course. He has decided passing is his top priority. Soon he moved over to a table and switched to a pot of tea.

This really shook up Chase—he whispered to me aside, "Hal is drinking TEA in a pub!!!!" He spat out the word *tea* as if it was a vile, unimaginable heresy. "What has the world come to anyway?" But you could see the admiration shining in his eyes. Hal is facing his responsibilities to himself and to his group. Nothing can earn Chase's respect more than this. But still he goads Hal and makes fun of him. Hal scrunches up his shoulders and leans closer into the table while talking with Christopher.

Meanwhile, mind you, Christopher is in the fast lane for drunkenness—he is now *celebrating* their group's disarray—Chase has to look the other way when Christopher speaks on the subject.

He doesn't say a word, but I know he is outraged by Christopher making light of his group's disintegration. To Chase it's the worst display of incompetence and disloyalty, and for Christopher to be drinking to it and lauding it is nothing short of disgraceful to Chase. It is only going to end badly next week. And it's going to bring all of us down in the end. It's not just disloyalty to his own class, but also disloyalty to the group as a whole. We are the fall class. It makes us all look bad. To Chase this is an intolerable state of affairs.

Very quickly, Christopher was outrageous—knocking things over, slurring his words, hassling the barmaid, etc. The regular.

But the group interaction was friendly—I was a little reserved—I was still smarting over the week's events, over Chase's disappointments, and over my current status non grata in next week's lesson planning. But I decided to take Chase's challenge and drink the *vino tinto* and loosen up—there was time enough to worry about school later—it was Friday night, for Pete's sake. There was plenty of time on Saturday to confront Chase and get things straightened out.

So, much to Chase's delight, I have a couple of *vinos* and we laugh and have fun—but as always, someone soon asks me about Jaime again—I believe it was Chase—how old was I when I had him? That was after someone had asked again about you—how long were we married? Were we happy? Did we ever argue? They are endlessly curious about our marriage.

Chase wanted to know all about you—and I had no problem obliging. When he asked about how you died—he wanted to know the whole story, I said to all of them again (who were all hanging on my every word), "I don't mind telling you, but it's a downer subject and I don't want to ruin the group's mood. ..."

No, no, no, don't worry about that—they want to hear the story. The whole story.

So, Paco, I told them how you were a runner and how you came home tired that night and how you always ran when you were tired—it helped pick you up, reenergized you, and how we were going to a dinner party that night that you really looked forward to, authentic Mexican food prepared by an authentic Texan—and how I had suggested you go for the run. I told how I had just started school to become a teacher and how I was on the bed with all my new books scattered around me and what your last words were to me.

"Oh there she is; she's got her new books." you'd crooned so affectionately, so happy to see me studying again after all those years. And then you'd bounded down the stairs.

"Bye, bye, have a good run!" I'd called after you as you disappeared down the stairwell. I'll never forget those words; they will ring in my heart forever. I never said I love you. I never said so many things, Paco; oh, how I wish I could have those two seconds of time to do over. ...

And then I told them how you left to go running and never came home again. There was complete silence in the bar. All eyes were trained on me.

I told them in more detail what a shock it was to me—how it debilitated me for years and how I've come to wonder if perhaps it wasn't news to you—perhaps you knew you were ill, but you didn't tell me—I told them how you would have protected me from this knowledge and how angry I was at you for that if you had done it, and how only recently was I feeling a bit forgiving if that had been the case—well, I'm trying anyway. Not quite there yet. ...

Chase interrupted to defend you, saying that of course you would protect me from that information—"What else could he do? And he was protecting himself as well." Never really thought of it that way before, Paco—that makes me wince inside to think. That gives me pause. Funny, that Chase could have given me an insight into you. Such a human insight too, so real.

I think Hal and Christopher drifted off at this point, leaving just Ethan, Chase, and me talking together.

That was when Chase asked me about Ryan. How old was I? What happened? Where was Ryan now? I told them I was eighteen when it happened—Chase asked the burning question, "How old are you, Darcy, or is that a rude question?"

"It's a totally rude question," I said flatly. "And I prefer not to answer."

Chase guffawed and was embarrassed, but I don't care—I just didn't want to *say* that actual number.

It would leave no hope. So rude for *me*. Too rude for me to bear. And so embarrassing to even feel. I just can't face it or look at it right now. I don't know who I am anymore, but I do know that I don't feel the age that number represents.

I told him how I was forced into giving my baby up for adoption and how traumatic it was—they were shocked and dismayed for me. I was uncomfortable discussing this subject with them in such detail. Their questions were getting more and more personal and I was nearly squirming in my seat with rising self-consciousness. But I didn't know how to stop it.

Ethan excused himself to go to the bathroom. Chase leaned forward immediately and whispered, "I killed a lad when I was a teenager. At least I thought I did."

My turn to be shocked. "W*hat?*"

He nodded. "I was responsible for a death. It was horrible. A boy I went to boarding school with committed suicide. I knew it was my fault."

"But he committed suicide. That's not killing him!" I frowned. "How could that have been your fault?"

"I'd made fun of him the day before at school. In the locker room. Ohhh, I was merciless with him," he whispered in his Scottish brogue. "You see, he was in the shower and....well, he had an...well, his John Thomas was saluting," he rushed through the words very quickly. "You know, his..."

The sudden look of understanding on my face told him I did, indeed, understand.

"I made some very crude remarks about it. About him. About his, em, stature. Ohhhh, it was brutal. Boys can be a bit cruel you know. But that's what we did. I didn't think anything of it. And then the very next morning we heard he'd committed suicide. They said he had been depressed. I must have pushed him right over the edge."

"Nooo, but you can't assume that!" I reached out and touched his arm as he spoke.

He went on to describe what a horror it had been for him. No one else had seen it. No one else had heard. And he didn't say a word to anyone. He didn't dare tell a soul.

Oh my god, he kept it a secret. That must have been so horrible for him.

He sat up a little straighter. "I never talk about this. None of my friends know."

To this day, he's still accepting responsibility for the death of this boy! "But Chase, this boy had problems much bigger than you making fun of him."

"I tell myself that now. Yes. But then. As a young lad..."

I looked into his eyes and saw raw guilt and regret. I asked, "What happened after that? How were you?" Because I imagine this must have had a profound effect on Chase back then. "Were you affected afterwards?"

Emphatically he said, "Gutted. It changed my life really. Completely changed me."

To my utter frustration, I didn't get to ask how, because at that moment Ethan returned and the subject immediately changed.

Chase wanted to share that secret for some reason, and it instantly brought us closer together. I think he shared his secret as a way to make me feel better about my secret, about my baby. Because he saw me squirming in my chair. He knew of my discomfort. I think Chase was reaching out to *me* to make me feel better. To show me I wasn't the only one with something unpleasant in her past.

The new intimacy this realization created was immediately palpable and present between us when we looked at one another—a new warmth emanated between us. Then, in front of Ethan, Chase began talking about his wife Sophie and Nicholas and how much he missed them and how he always felt Sophie was his soul mate and how he wasn't *sure* divorce was the right thing.

He had told me earlier about Lauren and how extraordinary she was. But it was tonight that he revealed more about the timeline of events. It was only now that I realized with utter horror—holy shit! This has all just happened—he left his wife while she was pregnant or shortly after the birth of their son Nicholas—*he must have cheated on his wife while she was pregnant*!!!!

Oh my god, this is a capital offense!

But I *brushed* it all aside.

I focused on Chase, the man in pain, because he was *surely* in a lot of pain. He missed his son—he even missed his wife. He said, "I'm not sure this is the right thing. I could still go back and live with her. I could do—I wouldn't be happy, but I could *do* it."

I was thinking, if he wasn't sure, then he should go back and fix this mess. It's not too late, and Nicholas needs a father! I can't help it—I've loved my soul mate and lost him through no choice of my own. You are gone, Paco. Forever. To me, everything is fixable. Everything short of death.

Ethan tells us he is a newlywed—his wife, Mary, and he were married in April. We do a lot of kidding about why he always checks with Mary before doing anything with us and why he's so quick to go home—lots of laughing about sex, and it is sooo much fun. It is special to joke about sex with two men who are married and can share that married knowledge and joke about it from the other side of the street. I am thoroughly enjoying myself with these two. I think to myself, this is one of the best times I've ever had in my whole life. My cheeks are simply aglow.

Chase and I tell each other we like the freedom of being out of marriage—lots of jokes about the ball and chain and how free we are now—nice to make your own decisions and not be tied to someone else. Chase asks me, "Do you want to get married again, Darcy?"

I reply instantly with no hesitation, "No."

"Why not?"

"Because I've already been married to the perfect man and I doubt I will find another." But I think to myself, I've already been married to the perfect man and it didn't work out, did it? You are gone. As perfect as an imperfect human can be, Paco, as perfect as you could be. Still, you weren't perfect, I wasn't perfect—it wasn't perfect, and though it sounds simplistic and stupid, it didn't last forever. The happily-ever-after myth isn't even true for true soul mates. I can't imagine trying it ever, ever again.

The three of us talk about marriage—a lot about sex in marriage, the ins, the outs. Christopher makes an over-the-shoulder comment about how we're having a "therapy session," and I feel bad for a moment that since they've never been married, they feel excluded.

But then it went away.

We were having so much fun, and I didn't really care about Christopher. Well, I cared, but he was drunk as a skunk already and wouldn't be any good in a conversation anyway. Nothing I could do or say would prevent him from slamming the drinks down or slow his determination to get drunk. Christopher was on his own path. Quite resolutely.

Ethan went to the bathroom again, and Chase leaned over and said, "I feel as if we've gotten closer tonight. We've shared some personal things." His eyes were warm, and his face was uncharacteristically serious. He meant it. And that fact touched me deeply. I understood Chase did not confide in a lot of people. It felt very warm and special.

We continued talking as if there were no tomorrow. We covered so many subjects—Chase asked me once more if I ever wanted to get married again and I repeated my "no."

"But why not, Darcy?" He seemed distressed by my adamancy.

"Because I've already been married to the best. Anything else would be a step down. Besides, I can't picture myself married again. And I'm fine the way it is now. I've gone through hell to get where I am, and I'm not unhappy to be by myself, just unhappy to be separated from my Sean. I don't need to be married to be whole. I wish Sean were back, but that's not going to happen, so I'm happy with who I am single."

"That is beautiful, Darcy." Chase is always reverent when I speak of you this way. I could tell I touched him deeply when I reached into my heart and spoke honestly of my love.

Then I told him about taking Jaime to Ireland—he was *amazed*. He was reverent about my mothering, too. He recognized the specialness of my motherhood and revered it. But of course he was *merciless* in his razzing of my over-protectiveness of Jaime. And he told me great tales of his childhood and going to boarding school and sneaking out over the weekends and going *across the English Channel* and riding trains over the French countryside in contests with his classmates to see who could get the farthest over the weekend. Amazing stories—he was only fourteen and fifteen!!! And traveling abroad on his own—simply incomprehensible to this Yankee mother's mind. I was thinking the entire U.K. is derelict in the raising of their children! Have they no nurturing sense? Have they no sense of protecting their young? Sending them off to boarding schools to fend for themselves—I was horrified by his upbringing or lack thereof. And Chase was horrified by my over protectiveness and my ruination of my son's new manhood. And we are completely reveling in our differences, completely enamored of the other for the differences. It's the most peculiar thing. I honor him for his differences from me. Wouldn't have him any other way, really. Isn't that unconditional acceptance? Isn't that completely rare? I am feeling reverence over what is happening here.

Suddenly, I don't know why, but I feel this new connection to him, and I long to communicate more of myself to him. I know he will understand my heart, my soul, in most matters. I know Chase could understand me in a special way that would be comforting.

Hal announces he is leaving. He has just finished his second pot of tea at the bar.

Chase is horrified. "Aw, Hal, no! We haven't eaten yet. It's early." But Hal insists he has to go home and get a good night's sleep so he can study tomorrow. Chase persisted, but to no avail. Hal leaves.

Christopher stumbles over to the pay phone at the end of the bar and makes a collect call to England.

For some reason, this riles Chase. Violently.

"A CHARGE-CALL!" Chase exclaimed with disgust, as if it stripped Christopher of all human dignity. He was unreasonably outraged by it.

Chase urged Ethan to call Mary and get her to meet us for dinner somewhere—it was nearly 8:00 p.m. I was very tipsy. I'd had three glasses of wine, the most I've done yet. I could easily go home now and call it an evening.

Christopher refuses to get off the phone for Ethan to make his call. A half-hour later, Chase announces we would just leave and call Mary from Ethan's neighborhood.

We got up to leave. Christopher *ignored* us. I motioned to him to get off the phone, and he ignored me. Finally, I went over and told him, "We're going to dinner." He ignored me.

Chase said, "We're leaving, Christopher."

Christopher looked at me beseechingly, saying with his eyes, "Don't go, don't go," but he didn't say a word to me.

When we got out on the street I said, "I feel bad; we've abandoned Christopher."

Chase took exception to that—he scoffed and ranted about Christopher ignoring us and ended with, "He's on a bloody charge-call for god's sake!" As if that fact alone justified any action on our part. It was so strange.

I followed Ethan and Chase, as usual. It was impossible for me to keep up with the long-leggeds, and they just left me behind always. I half ran up the rear.

We hiked to the subway, where we took a different line than usual, one that took us to Alonzo Martinez. Chase sat while Ethan and I stood by the train door together. Of course, Chase offered me the seat first, but I wanted to stand. Ethan stood taller than Chase, at least six-foot-one or -two it seemed to me, but then I'm only five-two and everyone seems tall to me. But when I looked into his eyes, it felt as if he shrank away from me, as if I were invading his privacy by looking directly into his eyes—Ethan is inscrutable to me—he is one of those rare human beings I have no clue as to what they are thinking.

I knew he didn't approve of my attraction to Christopher or my association with him.

But tonight, he simply watched me and Chase—and I didn't feel any disapproval, but I was keeping my hands off of Chase for fear of Ethan's censure—after all, Chase is spoken for—by *two* women. If Ethan disapproved of my flirting with Christopher, surely he would object to my flirting with Chase. But I sensed no reproach—he just watched down at me from up high.

Positively unnerving.

We went to a *tapas* bar. It was kind of cool—it had a big, black velvet drapery over the entrance, and when you emerged through the entryway you were greeted with vivid red walls punctuated with fifteen-foot-high pocket-shuttered windows.

Waiters in red vests and white pressed shirts came to the table to take our order. The plan was to have a couple of beers, then call Mary, then Ethan would go and "square things with Mare," an expression that would reduce Chase to paroxysms of laughter each time Ethan pointedly repeated it to us. Then he would get her and bring her back. We would have drinks, and *then* we would go to this Italian restaurant in the neighborhood, where we would have a round of before-dinner drinks! I think there was some kind of cultural rhythm to the sequence that was understood by the Brits. Not by me, though. It seemed a roundabout way to meet Mary for dinner. Why didn't we just all meet her at the Italian?

Oh well, they were definitive—I was just along for the ride.

We had several rounds of drinks with Ethan. I'm drinking *agua*, much to Chase's dismay. I'm still completely goofy on the three glasses of *vino* from the Italian Alps pub.

⌒◌

When Ethan left, to square things with Mare, Chase started talking about what a great group we have and how everything is going to be great— suddenly he apologizes for taking my subject away and softly assures me he'll help me with it. Yeah right, heard that before.

Unlike Group A, which he tears after. Chase proceeded to get very riled about Group A and C-I-I-N-N-D-Y; her name he rolled off his outraged Scottish tongue with a brogue. He says the *I* way in the back of his throat with disgust.

He is *so* mad at her for not going out with us tonight. He's even madder at her for going away over the weekend. He rants and raves about her lack of team spirit. "And C-I-I-N-N-D-Y ..." he exclaims over and over. "I can't BELIEVE C-I-I-N-N-D-Y would do this!" I am becoming *convinced* his over reaction is because he is hot for her—he cares for her, or why else would he be so riled?

He just couldn't believe her behavior. He's upset about her reaction to the grade and her reaction at Michael and her reaction to her group—he gives her credit for having to bear a terrible team, even carry it on her shoulders, but to give up on them the way she has, is simply unforgivable to him. He expects a higher standard of behavior from her, and he is *sorely* disappointed in her.

He talked a lot about team spirit and how great the three of us are: Ethan, me, and him. And we're going to help Michael get by. But then, once again, he harped on Cindy. He always comes back to her. He just couldn't believe she was leaving town for the weekend.

In her defense, I pointed out the hard time she's had to withstand with her team—well, it was Dylan and Christopher, wasn't it? Hal was great. And Emma did her best to pull her own weight though her heart wasn't really in it. But between Dylan and Christopher, Cindy couldn't get a thing done. Even with the cooperation of Hal, who tried his best to help smooth things out on their team. But every time she tried to lead them, one of the two would disagree and come up with ridiculous counter-suggestions that would cause terrible rows within the group, and then they got nothing done by the end of a session together—by today they were no longer speaking. It was like the Tower of Babel on Team A.

I told Chase, "You know, we're all supposed to be one big team, everyone in the course, and what have we done to help Cindy? What recourse did we give her?"

That gave Chase pause. He felt bad, for maybe a minute. I suggested we call her cell phone and offer to help her—invite her to our meeting tomorrow night. He hesitated, for about a second, and then rejected the idea completely.

He was high on our success and disgusted by their failure. Their passing the course from his point of view would be bad for us, too—it would devalue our certificates. "It's a bloody joke!" Chase said with loathing. It mightily offended his sense of fairness and justice that they could be so disorganized, so lazy and uncaring, and in all probability would be passed. And the fact that, in spite of our hard work, we could be pulled down by the likes of them made him insane, completely insane.

❧

Finally, Ethan arrived with Mary. She had short, graceful brunette curls asymmetrically framing a cherubic, alabaster, round face and a high, musical voice, very charming and pleasant.

We had one round of drinks and talked about normal, adult subjects. Then we left and pressed through rush hour crowds on the wide boulevard. Ethan walked side by side with Mary, Chase with me.

The Italian restaurant was magnificent. It had frescoes painted on the walls in light terra cotta colors, greens and clay, gold, and pinks, and curious sculptures hanging from unusual perches above—a combination of Italian nouveau and renaissance. Warm and charming ambiance.

We were seated at a table in the rear, a nice candlelit table tucked away in a corner. I wasn't sure how the seating would go, so I chose a seat on the inside. Ethan took a seat opposite me, and Mary followed and sat next to her new hubby. Chase took the seat next to me.

Suddenly the feeling became very grown up—as if we were a foursome— as if we were on a date, very mature, very sophisticated in this renaissance Italian atmosphere. And indeed it *was*.

The Brits ordered a round of gin and tonics—I wanted water, but Chase insisted I have a *vino tinto*—he ordered a whole bottle.

This is after drinking since 3:00 p.m.—enormous quantities of alcohol. Ethan kept staring down at me. ...

We talked about the menu. Chase leaned into me and talked about the entrees with great animation. I could feel his solidness along my entire torso, my arms, and my hips, and my hair brushed against his at the temples.

"I'm going to try these bad boys," he said, referring to a camerón y aguacate salad—shrimp and avocado—that had caught my eye, too. He ordered *pasta carbonara* and I *pasta pescado*, pasta with fish. We were playful together but properly subdued for the setting.

But once the first course arrived, it was so wonderful, Chase and I just began to relax and have fun together—there was lots of teasing and touching going on.

Chase pressed his leg, the full length of his long thigh, against the full length of mine. Chills went up and down my spine at the contact. I pressed back.

Now, that couldn't be an accident, could it? We were touching in this manner for most of the dinner—it was unbearably erotic behavior under the table, but above the table it was even more provocative and tantalizing. I would touch his arm, he would touch mine. I would look up into his eyes, laughing, laughing, always laughing, and the laughter was an intoxicating opiate to me, making me laugh even more.

I touched his leg with my hand. He arched his brow suggestively at me.

Our shoulders were now touching as we spoke to Ethan and Mare. We leaned into one another, our full weights—completely and unabashedly reveling in the closeness of touching. When we spoke to each other, we pulled apart and devoured each other with our eyes.

We were like two lovers during dinner. And it came so naturally. I couldn't believe how good it felt. I couldn't believe it was me, flirting with a fully grown man who was fully flirting back. I haven't done this since I was twenty years old and met you, Paco. ... I am flirting!

It was who we were:

Chase and Darcy.

Chase and Darcy, having dinner with friends.

We are adorable together. I know it. I can see it on Ethan's and Mary's faces.

I was so happy tonight. I was exuberant—I was aglow like a torch. This was one of the best nights I have had on the trip. Chase and I were so close. And Chase was so solicitous. He made sure I had everything I needed ... well. ... We shared, we imbibed—I felt free and so happy inside.

You know what? Know what it was? Chase made me feel desirable tonight. When his eyes met mine, it was with pleasure shining in them. I was pleasing him. I haven't felt that in a very long time, Paco. Not for a very long time.

Then he did something I hadn't seen him do in our three weeks together—he pushed his drink aside and ordered *agua*. Chase drinking *agua* at dinner. I observed in silence.

I ordered an Irish coffee. And boy, did that have a punch.

But Chase stayed with the *agua*. It was simple. He'd had his limit. He knew it and didn't go beyond it. It was an impressive show of self-discipline. His behavior was not at all drunk—I never would have known he'd reached the border.

At the end of the evening, after Ethan and Mary went on their separate way, Chase put me in a cab and walked on his own up to Sol, where he was now staying with friends again.

As always, the cab took a major thoroughfare up to Plaza de Castillo, the second-largest plaza in the city of Madrid. It was at least a ten-minute drive, and the city was radiant with magical, multicolored lights. As always in the cabs at night, I became inebriated with the city's magnificent beauty. It was a breathtaking sight, the white Byzantine building facades, the lights, and the beautiful roundabouts, each with a flowing sculptured fountain in the center. Fucking gorgeous. It simply took my breath away, each sight more beautiful than the preceding one. I didn't ever want to go home.

I was completely and totally in love. With a mesmerizing and seductive city. And a mesmerizing and seductive man. His looks didn't hurt, but it was him I was falling for—his essence, the *man* who looked down into my eyes with such laughter and warmth and life and sheer, unadulterated caring.

And as the cab driver maneuvered his vehicle through the magical streets of Madrid, I knew I was totally and irreparably falling for him.

A man I could never have.

I am feeling the first frissons of doom.

But you know it doesn't matter. I am determined to feel what I feel and not think about December 19th when I will return home. This, to me, is heaven. And I've come a long way from the bowels of hell to experience it. Whatever it is, I am going to live it to the max. I'm not going to censure it or try to control it.

When I arrived at the Plaza de Castillo, I went directly to the phone banks along the street and called my brother, Eddie, back home in Chicago. I was intoxicated with wine, Irish whiskey, and love. I told him how happy I was in Spain. I told him I never wanted to come home. I told him I wanted to sell my house and come back to Spain.

He told me when I returned home, we'd have to talk. I knew I had made him nuts. But I was so happy! In my heart I know Eddie, though insane over this pronouncement, is happy to hear me so happy. I know he's been worried about me.

Isn't life unbearably beautiful? How can we humans survive such searing beauty?

When I am with Chase, I feel sheer joy. I am happy, contented, and fulfilled. To me, it's a miracle to *feel* so intensely for someone I'm not having sex with.

Well we are having *something*. And it is very physical. But it isn't like anything I've ever experienced before. There are limitations and intoxicating new freedoms for me. All I know is that I am falling for Chase in a very big way, a very intimate way. Even in spite of his faults.

Paco, we are all so much more than our faults, aren't we?

Chapter 9

Saturday
December 12, 1998
9 am

I have to do chores today and get my homework done for the team meeting this evening. I am unfocused today—hard to concentrate on mundane things.

I have a Scottish man to dream upon.

But every time I begin to dream about him, reality creeps in to remind me not to go too overboard. This morning I'm thinking about that last day Chase was here in the apartment with me. When he was talking about Lauren and the sirens.

I think there is a message to me in Chase's words—a message of caution—he is only turned on by the sirens, the Cindy's of the world. And I am certainly not a siren. I hear the warning loud and clear and take heed.

But the warning didn't hold water last night when Chase decided to play footsie with me under the table, did it?

༄

11am

Paco,

I forgot to tell you, Christopher came up to me in a bar earlier this week and said, "You really gave me a fright the other night, old girl."

"What?" I asked bewildered. For a minute, I thought he was referring to the bus incident.

But then his face softened and his voice went deep and swirling in the back of his throat, the way the Brits do when they're getting emotional. He was looking so young (which he is) and scared. "I mean really, you really wound me up. I didn't know what to do—actually you almost gave me heart failure." He was revving up, and now I knew, he was referring to last Saturday night. "I mean, for a while there I thought I was having a Mrs. Robinson. I didn't know *what* to do!"

"Mrs. Robinson!" I declared shocked, outraged. "No, it wasn't like that. Don't worry about it, Christopher." But of course he *was* worried and didn't know what to do with it.

By now he had already not come to school on time this week, and I was annoyed with him. Him and his errant, selfish ways. Irresponsible and totally uncaring about the rest of us. I was feeling abandoned and turned off by his alcoholic self-centeredness.

"Lookit, Christopher, there is a lot of energy between us, don't you see it? We talk and laugh, and I feel a special bond with you."

Christopher was hopping from one foot to another (emotionally as well as physically) like boys do when they're uncomfortable. I'd created a monster, and it wouldn't go away!

"Christopher, please, forget it," I told him. "I'm sorry I scared you. I didn't mean to."

"No?" He was gurgling again. He sputtered and then went off for another beer.

Mrs. Robinson, indeed. I decided at that moment, I would express my *real* feelings to him before we parted, but when it was safe for both of us. I don't know why I feel so compelled to be *real* with a boy like Christopher, but it feels like a matter of honor to me. I'm not going to bear false witness to myself, or what I felt. There is honor in retreating when you're wrong. And I retreated instantly in that moment.

As far as I can see, there is no honor whatsoever in parading around in front of a strange woman in your underwear and propositioning her and then feigning innocence.

He is too young. That's the explanation, pure and simple.

However, I still care for Christopher, a lot. Even though I'm withdrawing from him, I intend to watch out for him and help him when I can. We are still having some very special moments together. And you know, what I said to him was the truth—there is a lot of energy between us. I don't think that is going to change because of his age or his lack of maturity or the wrong timing in our lives. There is an attraction between us that is compelling and dynamic. But there is a more mature energy and attraction bombarding me from a different direction now. And my attention is definitely distracted.

If Chase were afraid of me, he would walk in front of the fear and face it down—he would never run and pretend innocence.

But make no mistake—I am *not* going to be turned down by Chase. This relationship is *completely* in his hands. Completely run by him. To be turned down by Chase would be *unthinkable* to me. I would rather *die*.

I will just enjoy him in each and every moment. All judgments and all fantasies shall be played out in the safety and privacy of my own room. Within the confines of my own mind.

I am so aware of how lucky I am to even *be* in this situation with five young men surrounding me and basically adoring me and taking such good care of me—I am loving every single precious minute of this. And my cheeks can attest to how turned on I am. For me, it doesn't have to end in lovemaking for the experience to be a total success. This is the most positive sexual energy I have ever felt since—well, Paco, since a very, very long time ... since you. Bittersweet is this. So bittersweet.

❧

2 pm

Okay, I've gotten my chores done. I've also gotten my first assignment half done. Now I'm starting my lesson planning—I still don't know what to do. So I've been stewing about it for an hour. I cannot wrap my mind around this cultural vocabulary lesson, and it's making me nuts. It's time to get ready to leave now. I don't want to be late to meet Chase and Ethan. They've promised me we will "sort it out" tonight. We'll see.

❦

Late Tonight

I'm so proud of myself. I traveled on the foreign Metro all by myself and found the destination. I'm making my way around a foreign city with few *problemas.*

Everyone was late for our session. I took pictures of the Alonso Martínez roundabout and fountain—there's always a fountain in every roundabout. and then I went to get some food—I'm starving and spy another Burger King across from the plaza Santa Barbara—haven't eaten since last night—jeez, these people eat so late and at such weird times. When I got back, still no one was there. I was surprised by Ethan's tardiness; he always seemed like the stable one, and it was his neighborhood after all. But that's the way it is, isn't it? The person whose neighborhood one meets up in is often the last one to arrive.

Finally it was Ethan who showed up. We went into this odd wedge-shaped tin-walled bar that straddled the center of a main boulevard, right at the mouth of the Alonso Martínez Metro station. It looked like a bar in a sardine can.

I told Ethan about the trouble I've been having with the smoke. We checked out the bar, and no one was smoking—there were only two other people in there. In Spain, it's not even considered evening yet at 8:00 p.m.!

So we got drinks, me a *coca lite*, him a pint of some *birra*. Ethan led the way to a round wrought iron bistro table where we pulled out our work and began coordinating. I was annoyed with Chase for being late. You know, this is the down side of youth. They are so *unreliable*. It's really a mystery of life that nature puts children inside of men's bodies.

Ethan and I were just about finished coordinating our two elements for Monday's lesson when in came Chase. I didn't look him in the eye—I didn't want to see coldness or indifference where last blazed warmth. He got a drink. I discreetly pushed his chair further from mine while he was up at the bar. I glanced at Ethan afterwards to see if he had noticed. He simply met my gaze with an expressionless, relentless stare. I never know what he's thinking. Ever. It's unnerving.

Chase is not interested in talking shop. Suddenly, it dawns on me that he probably hasn't done any work that day. Indeed, he starts off talking about some soccer game he'd watched this afternoon. My annoyance with him grows into indignation—we had all made a pact to work tonight, and he isn't prepared. What is his problem?

Michael didn't show—we waited 45 minutes for her. Chase was angry and insisted we leave and go to another bar. I hesitated—if we worked at this bar, maybe she would come. Ethan and Chase had no hesitance about leaving. Michael was history to them.

The idea of studying is history, too. We're going bar hopping! And we're calling Mary from pay phones—none of them worked, so we searched out a working one. Ethan went off on his own to find one, and Chase and I were left dawdling and taunting one another—revving up to friendship while rimming the looming pit of unresolved and growing conflicts. The friendship dance—the intimacy dance.

We're standing out on a corner in the Alonso Martínez roundabout amidst the blaring horns and colorful neon Spanish lights. We're talking about fountains and roundabouts, and Chase starts talking about one of his favorite subjects—Greek roundabouts—they are *illogical*, can you imagine? (What is it with men and logic? They are obsessed with it. And it's completely irrelevant to anything. Why can't they figure that out? Really, it's most illogical.) The Greeks have the rules backwards, so they're always in gridlock! The Greeks turn left onto a roundabout, and it completely causes gridlock. Chase *loves* to describe Greek roundabouts in gridlock, and it is very funny when he does—according to him, the whole country is in a permanent state of gridlock! His deep voice drops low into his larynx and resonates with Scottish outrage. We were laughing and bouncing up the hilly street, and he stopped dead in front of a Spanish *apothecaria*.

"And Darcy, what is a four-way stop?" I did a double-take—what does he mean, what is a four-way stop? Everyone knows what a four-way stop is. On he continued, "HeLLOOOO! Everyone stops and stares at each other. WHAT is that?"

Oh, apparently not everyone does understand the four-way stop! It had never occurred to me that there could be uniqueness to it. I laughed with glee at the prospect. "That, my dear Chase, is the American way!" I proudly exclaimed.

"It's absolute LUNacy," he declared. "Who else but an American would dream up such a thing?"

That's right, I realize, it could be purely American. "It's a thing of beauty—it's democratic—we have to be civilized and give each other the right of way. It's equality in action. See?"

"Its CARnage, that's what it is—utter CARnage. It's totally illogical!"

We're revving up now, and I'm pushing into him as we walk, swiveling my hips into his, leaning my arm into his, and he's pushing back. Illogical indeed. What a pile of crap.

We're back on track—it's going to be another fun night!

Ethan gets a hold of Mare—she's making dinner—so she'll put dinner on and then join us for drinks, then Mare and Ethan will go home for dinner—strangest system I've ever seen. So casual, so adaptable for the drinks thing. I'm growing to like it, *mucho*.

We returned through the expanding Saturday evening crowds to the red-walled bar and ordered rounds. I was drinking *agua sin gas*—once again to Chase's disgust. But for some reason, I wanted to be sober tonight. I am concerned about throwing myself on Chase—I'm still smarting from my ridiculous behavior with Christopher, and I don't want to make a complete fool of myself with Chase. It would be far too mortifying. I feel much more protective of my relationship with Chase. I want more from him than I could have even thought of with Christopher. In the end, I want Chase to respect me.

Mary was taking a long time. Ethan and Chase talked sports—real fast and in their thickest accents. Between the accents, the speed, and the exotic sports slang, I couldn't understand a damn thing they were saying. It was as if they were speaking a foreign language—they might as well have been for all I could make out. I watched and listened quietly. I didn't mind—I am endlessly fascinated with the way they speak and the slang they use. There is music in it. It's quite beautiful to my ear.

"Right, Darcy?" Chase asked suddenly.

"I haven't the faintest idea what you are talking about!" I exclaimed, much to Ethan's complete delight—he grinned ear to ear. And Chase's instant smile told me he knew that very well—he was making fun of me again, one of his favorite pastimes.

Then he told me some perfectly stupid sports fact about some unknown athlete that every Brit knows, but I don't. Of course, that was his point. Americans know nothing. Americans are isolated from the rest of the world. Americans are number one, and they don't care about anyone else—his all time favorite bug-a-boo.

Yeah, yeah, so what else is new?

I can't argue with the truth.

Then Chase regaled us with Scottish cop tales from the small town near Edinburgh where he worked. I've already heard most of them except the leashed-dog-stuck-in-the-moving-car story: Apparently an older woman shut her car door but inadvertently closed it on the leash of her Westie, who had jumped out the door at the last minute as she turned away to go around the car. The woman drove off with the Westie running alongside the car. Even with the police tailing behind her, lights ablaze and sirens blaring, she drove on and on, unaware she had a problem. Miraculously, the poor terrier survived the ordeal. Chase was completely unglued by this woman driving the streets so oblivious to her surroundings. "It's CARnage out there, COMPLETE CARNAGE!"

Ethan is laughing his head off. I love it when Ethan smiles and laughs. He has this deliciously dry English sense of humor. Most of the time he has this inscrutable, deadpan expression, but when something tickles him, his face turns red and the corners of his straight, thin lips turn up ever so wickedly. It's delightful. But he holds his cigarette up between his index finger and his thumb like a stereotypical German soldier. It's eerie—that gives me the heebeegeebies.

Finally I asked for some wine—Chase jumped up to order for me. I insisted on paying for rounds. They have paid for everything for the past two solid weeks, always refusing to allow me to pay. They turned my money away once again. It's the most remarkable thing I have ever seen—I'm both impressed and uncomfortable about it at the same time.

Shortly after my drink came, Mary arrived and had a drink with us. Once again the conversation became more adult, more civilized and serious. We all straighten up for Mare—she is a great civilizing force among us, even me. Soon we moved on to another bar and have wonderful *tapas*. Chase was in the mood for pizza, but we ordered *tapas* instead after he asked me if I like pizza and the look on my face told him no, I didn't.

"You don't eat pizza, then?" he asked with surprise and consternation, as if it weren't possible for an American, much less any person in the universe, to dislike pizza. Really, he was incredulous. After that, he would not hear of having pizza—yikes—I have to be so careful around him because he is such a gentleman and he cares about what I like and don't like—he pays close attention to such details and remembers them. I'm not used to this kind of politeness, this kind of attentiveness.

Chase and I are the only ones eating because Ethan and Mary are going home for dinner. Chase and I like exactly the same foods on the menu; he ordered some kind of *aioli*, garlic potato salad, a shrimp and avocado concoction, and calamari, which I have never had and he insists he will teach me to like. I am in a constant state of confusion during this evening; there seems to be an independent rhythm to the course of events which is unknown to me—is there any order to a British evening out? Does someone know what's going on?

By the time Mary and Ethan left, it was 11:00 at night. I suggested pizza.

"No, I'm good," insisted Chase, referring to the *tapas*. "Let's walk to Sol—it's not far. I'll take you to the Plaza Mayor. Would you like to go there?"

My heart lightened. I would love to see the Plaza Mayor. It's one of the places I had wanted to see, but haven't had the time. I'd heard Cindy and

Hal talking about it and had wanted very much to go there. "Okay," I said cheerfully.

But walk to Sol. Oh, boy. Knowing Chase, I should have known his idea of a short walk could be a long, long walk indeed. And alongside a long-legged. I was thrilled.

But I was doing well tonight. I must be getting used to trailing after Chase at top speed through crowded—no, jammed—midnight crowds. On our way back along the Calle de Fernando VI, Chase stopped in front of an unusual smooth sand-colored stucco building surrounded by ornate wrought iron fences. He told me it was the Society of Authors and Editors building, the authors union. If it had been daylight, I would have loved to go in there. But it was too late now. So on we proceeded until we came back to the Calle de Hortaleza.

We had to walk into the bumper-to-bumper car-lined street to avoid the throngs on the narrow sidewalk. Walking between cars stuck in single-lane traffic jams. I reached out and grabbed the back of Chase's shirt so I wouldn't lose him in the masses—if he were to get away from me, I'm too short to see or be seen in the middle of a sea of Saturday night revelers. He just traipsed on and seemed not to notice. Or mind. His back felt strong to my clinging fingers. Solid.

The concept of solid dissolved for me the day you died, Paco. It feels reassuring and welcome. I thought that was something I would never get to feel again. Actually I thought it was a mirage, a cruel illusion that melted before me forever. Feeling it again is disconcerting but welcome all the same.

༄

At one point in the red bar with Mary and Ethan, Chase had told Mare that I'm a sex-crazed woman. I had been *horrified*. And determined to let him know my objections. Once we got past the crowds of the Alonso Martínez neighborhood, the streets became almost uncomfortably empty and quiet—in fact, the store fronts had become more dilapidated and seedy—I wondered how safe it was, for about a nanosecond until I remembered it was six-foot-plus copper Chase I was tripping beside.

I gasped for breath beside him and said, "So, I'm a sex-crazed woman, huh?"

"Yeah, sex-crazed," he answered casually.

"Thanks a lot. Now Mary thinks I'm a nutball!"

"It was just a joke. She knows that." Chase is speaking to me offhandedly, not taking the subject seriously at all as he single-mindedly pressed forward.

"No, she doesn't, and now she'll always think of me that way."

"She won't do!" He was now becoming impatient as he realized this was more serious than he had first thought and that it could turn into a thing he would have to justify. "It was just for fun, Darcy."

"Look, I'm an American girl, you know, from the Puritan colony? We don't think those kinds of things are funny."

"That's the point," he said over his shoulder as he raced down the street, weaving and bobbing between parked and moving cars, me keeping up as best I could. "We aren't in the States, and Mare is a British girl. She won't think anything of the remark."

I caught up with a winded price, and shoulder to shoulder I said, "I don't act this way at home, you know. My family wouldn't recognize me."

Chase smiled down at me, the smile invading and crinkling his warm blue eyes. "That's good, then."

Good? What? Not something to be ashamed of? I considered the possibility. The thought was appealing. Why of course it is! That's what's made this experience such a good one for me: it's liberated me from my normal life, shaken me up and made me see life, my very own self, in a different light. I smiled my agreement back, a big, happy, liberated smile. It's not about getting out of my normal roles; it's about expanding who I really am.

"I'm having the best time!" I suddenly shouted into the Madrid night air. "I *am* sex-crazed!!!!"

Chase looked at me with a delighted grin. We both laughed together like two giddy kids on a holiday.

Just then, a large and boisterous group of partiers reached us on the sidewalk, and Chase veered out into the street into another group. I grabbed another handful of his clothes to stay connected … solid.

When we emerged from the crowd like emerging from a dense fog, I could see we were nearing the pulsating, glowing Sol, which was now visible, like a vision of the Emerald City, maybe a half-mile ahead. Just then, we walked in front of a sex toy store, and Chase pointed it out to me.

"Look lively, Darcy, soon we'll have to fend off the ladies of the night!"

"Where!" I cried incredulously, "Where are they?" I thought he was teasing me again.

But Chase started pointing them out to me, and they were, indeed, on every street corner. Lazing against every light post. In every manner of dress and undress. I would have never, ever noticed them as hookers, just as people standing there. Chase pointed to one and said, "See that one? That's a man."

I was shocked. Completely shocked. She looked just like a woman to me. I didn't believe him. In fact, I thought he was lying to me and making fun of my ignorance and naïveté. Then Chase insisted they were all men! He is so bad. But could they be?

I think we had Michael on the brain.

Chase made a pit stop at a packed McDonald's in Sol. I was hot and sweaty after our trek. The thought of waiting for Chase amid the nostril-to-nostril crowds inside was not appealing to me. So I stayed outside. I was surrounded by groups of foreign men—well actually, technically, I was the foreigner. A white van of Ecuadorian street musicians was half-parked on the sidewalk immediately outside of the McDonald's in front of me—we had seen two different groups of the musicians playing in offshoot streets on this side of the huge square. Men came and went from the van. A man in the front passenger seat handed each one something I couldn't see—I imagined it was a drug transaction—then I got scared and searched the throngs for police. If there were trouble, I didn't want to be in the middle of it.

Where was Chase anyhow? He was taking inordinately long. And I didn't like the way these groups of men were staring at me.

I became annoyed at Chase for leaving me outside in the middle of the night. He had absolutely no worries about my safety. He *assumed* I would be safe, and I found that annoying even if it were true Madrid was safe.

How safe could a drug van be?

On the other hand, I reminded myself, Chase was a trained cop. He could probably smell real danger a mile away.

Then I reconsidered and thought, nawww, I had better street instincts than most. I'd be better off trusting myself.

Which was exactly what Chase was doing, wasn't it? Trusting my abilities to take care of myself?

You know? It's hard to stay annoyed with Chase for long.

Finally, Chase emerged, and, with a barely perceptible nod in my direction, strode single-mindedly once again up the street (uphill, of course). I ran uphill to catch up as he wove through a web of side streets and red cobblestone alleyways; finally, one led through a massive Roman arched entryway, where we emerged into an enormous open-aired courtyard, the Plaza Mayor, a huge rectangular square surrounded by red-brick edifices. Chase leaned in and pointed out the nine entryways; each, he explained, was a portal to a street beyond, and each designed differently, uniquely, by different architects hundreds of years ago. It struck me again how well he knew the city, much better than anyone else in the class, but he had said this was his second visit. Still, it made me wonder ... what if Chase were a spy? What a great cover being an ESL teacher would be. He could move from country to country with anonymity ... oh, this imagination of mine. It never quits.

"Darcy, come here and see!" Chase ordered me. He walked confidently to the center of the square without looking back to see if I would follow. He looked up at the edifice of the long rectangular building in front of us. It was brightly lit with blindingly powerful spotlights.

Chase lowered his head close to mine and reached up and pointed. "Look!" He had that playful tone to his voice that I adored, but I didn't know what he wanted me to see. I squinted and stared up.

"It's paintings. Look at the paintings, Dahrcy," he said impatiently.

I focused on the massive windowed wall before me, and in between each window, the wall spaces had paintings on them—sweeping modern lines, in colorful blues and reds, Spanish style, reminding me of Miró. "Wow," I breathed softly as I studied them.

"No," he contradicted persistently. "Look carefully," he directed me intently. He awaited my reaction.

"They're beautiful," I breathed, as conscious of our heads close together as I was of the paintings beyond.

"They're nuuudes," he said.

I looked more carefully, and oh my god. Every painting was a nude—there may have been one hundred of them and every single one was nude!

"OH MY GAWD!" Chase put his hands on his face and mocked me.

"Oh, my god," I breathed in awe. It was so cool. So beautiful.

"Come on," he said abruptly. I didn't want to leave. I wanted to study each and every one. He walked off deeper into the plaza where there were rows and rows of booths, street vendors set up in the square to sell Christmas wares—it was well past midnight. The booths had legitimate products and bawdy things like a pair of Groucho mustache glasses with a huge penis for the nose!!!! Outrageous things. Chase said I should buy one for Jaime—yeah right. There were trick condoms, even. Trick condoms!

I told Chase about my friend Sarah insisting I bring condoms to Spain. Just in case. How she insisted I must bring condoms with me wherever I go from now on and how I had gone to the pharmacy for the very first time and been confronted with choosing which kind to buy. I've never made love to a man wearing a condom. I had chosen a variety-pack, since I hadn't a clue what I might need someday. Someday. If I were ever ready for that again.

"Do you have a condom, then?" Chase asked, completely taken aback by the idea.

I smiled and lifted my purse. "I do." It was very fulfilling to have the tables turned and see Chase's nonplussed Scottish eyebrows leap onto his forehead. Funny, really, he had been trying to shock me. Very sweet.

All in all, though, I have to say I felt uncomfortable with Chase in the square tonight—why were we there? Why did he bring me there? What was I supposed to do? This was our very first time to be alone together outside of the group. How should I act with him? I felt self-conscious and out of place. He was shopping for his girlfriend but didn't actually buy anything.

"Dahhrcee, what do you think, should I get this Christmas stocking for Lauren? What about this one?" He would ask about each item and go from booth to booth at breakneck speed. He told me about the little gifts he'd been buying to fill Lauren's Christmas stocking and I felt bad—I thought it was a deliberate superimposing of Lauren on our evening, and it worked.

Actually, it was like a bucket of cold water to me; from that moment I sobered and became circumspect. It reminded me of all the wonderful moments we had at Christmas, Paco. all the warmth and love I used to put into shopping for you.

I wanted to go home.

I was done. That's how I do these night outings. I stay 'til I'm uncomfortable or just simply "done," have had my fill, gone to my own limits and can't go any further. I was out of my element. I mean who am I? I'm a widow who's been in a 21-year committed relationship with my soul mate who's raised their son all by herself. I'm a fuck of a lot older than these boy-man-children, and yet I'm attracted to their maleness. How the hell am I supposed to act? I'm not a vamp. I'm not on the prowl. Hell, I wouldn't even know how to act if I were. I'm simply a woman alone feeling new things. Intense physical things I haven't felt since I was their very same age way back when. Well, maybe not even then—good girls weren't allowed to feel these things back then. Maybe that's why I've never felt this way before.

Chase spotted Santa hats and got very excited, like a little kid—"We'll buy Santa hats for everyone on the last day of class." He became very animated about the idea—he even tied the idea to team spirit, the same way they wear ties in England to identify themselves as having achieved certain honors or as members of certain societies. Well, Chase decided we would wear Santa hats the same way. He promised he was coming back before the week was out and buying enough hats for all of us to wear on the last day of school. I didn't believe him. I thought this was just more immature bravado that would never come to pass.

Then he spotted caricature artists set up at the far end of the now-slick cobblestone surface of the square. And he wanted me to sit for one—oh no. No way, José. That was *not* going to happen—even so, Chase wouldn't leave. He insisted we stay and watch.

He *loved* it. We would ooh and ahh as each new stroke was added to the drawing in progress. He was like a kid who's had his imagination set afire—wild horses couldn't have dragged him from that spot.

A man smoking a cigarette came up beside us. Soon the acrid smell of smoke was choking me, so I moved away. The square was becoming more and more crowded in spite of the late hour. It was a carnival atmosphere—there was a fire-eater at the other end. I watched the scene in amazement.

Nevertheless, I still wanted to go home. Sadness engulfed me. I felt odd and out of place. If we were lovers, then we would have acted in a certain way together, and I may have felt like acting in that way and sharing the moment with Chase, but I kept thinking of his Lauren waiting for him in Greece.

I'm sorry, but I really didn't want to be on the wrong side of his commitment to someone else—and the reality was Chase was committed to two other women—his heart was a little crowded. And you know, I have waited a long time. I'm a widow. But it's kind of like being a virgin. I'm a virgin widow! I've been without my mate for five long years. And it occurs to me that there would be some value to waiting for the *right* man—that my "first time" could be something really special. Just a thought, fleeting as it might be. A thought that wasn't on my mind when I was in my twenties, that's for sure. Then I couldn't wait to give it away! If fantasies came true and Chase came to my bed in the middle of the night, did I really think I would send him away because he wasn't the "right" man?

I may be old, but I'm not demented! Fantasies are fantasies—they don't come true. And I was tiring of this one tonight. It was making me sad. It was making me feel very old.

Actually, Paco, I kept thinking of you. I was missing you and wishing you could be here with me and share this vibrant and exciting city, thinking of how we would have laughed and explored together. Traveling the world together. Life's journey. Oh god, we had so much fun together. I will never be able to experience that kind of sharing again. Sharing with you.

Will I ever feel normal again? Will I ever feel at ease again?

We stayed long enough for Chase to watch two or three entire drawings. Then we left. Chase asked if I wanted to go for a drink—he led me to a Spanish tile bar—it was very crowded and smoky. He looked in the bar, then he looked at me, and said, "Come on, we'll find something else." That went down well. Very warm feeling. Very cared for.

He found an Irish pub called, of all things, O'Neil's. In the middle of medieval Madrid! It was half full. Chase led the way up to the bar—I have never stood at a bar before. When I was Chase's age, it wasn't considered proper for a girl to do that. It feels very strange but kind of fun. Liberating. What's the big deal?

Chase wanted me to order a Guinness—yeah right. Of course I had to listen to how it was classified as a food group in England (shades of you, Paco). I ordered an Irish coffee.

The pub began to fill quickly. It was really hot and stuffy. I knew my hair had fallen and my cheeks were burning, burning hot. It was difficult to talk. We are standing very close together—closer than my comfort zone would have liked. I am feeling so raw tonight. I would have loved to touch him. Resisting, resisting. I try to think of something else.

Chase tapped my arm, leaned in to me, and pointed to the side. A couple right next to us was devouring each other in a passionate kiss.

My knees went weak. He was making love to her right in front of us! I am *way* too horny to witness a scene like this. And I am way too sensitized to Chase to share this scene with him. It feels very awkward.

I took a huge gulp of my Irish coffee. It was very strong and sent my head reeling.

They mesmerize me. My eyes keep wandering back to them. I want to feel that way again someday. I take more huge gulps and feel the heat.

There isn't much one can talk about in a situation like this.

I prayed for Chase to finish his Guinness so we could go. I knew he was aware of this uncomfortable lull between us. I wondered if he could guess what I was feeling.

Chase reached over to the bar and handed me a Guinness coaster decorated with words in Spanish. "A souvenir," he said softly in my ear. I looked up into his deep blue eyes. The sexual awareness pulsated between us. A souvenir of a sexy moment in Madrid.

Finally we left.

The cool night air was such a welcome relief! Chase bounded across the ancient cobblestone street. I bounded right after him—only my legs had somehow become jelly.

"Uh oh," I said and swayed. I looked around for a wall or something to steady myself.

"Dahrcy! Everything okay?"

I made my way toward him. Actually, I teetered toward him, my head staying rigid in a fixed, determined direction but my legs wobbling in all different directions.

Chase held out his hand, "Come on," he encouraged, his voice lilting on the "on." He did not, however, come back for me.

I looked at his hand, a hand I had studied for at least a week now. I wondered if it would be proper to take that hand—"Darcy, take my hand!" he ordered.

I put my hand in his, and he closed it easily around mine; warm and friendly it felt.

I thought I was in heaven. We walked through the narrow, ancient side streets, hand in hand, Chase leading me through the throngs I surely would have gotten lost in on my own. I giggled and ran to keep up. Irish coffee silliness washed over my senses.

We stopped at a postcard vendor just at the opening of the Far East end of Sol, beneath the Tio Pepe sign, to look at postcards. Chase held my hand all the while, showing me cards and speaking to me in his low, sensuous Scottish voice. He held my hand while showing me cards with his other hand; our shoulders and arms were one, and we leaned into one another, huddled together to inspect the cards.

"We can do better," he said finally. And so on we went emerging fully into the Plaza del Sol.

It was a magnificent sight! The people, thousands and thousands of them, and the buildings outlined with Christmas lights and Chase and me holding hands as we wove through the crowds, him leading me, me stumbling behind. Suddenly, I never wanted this night to end. But then, just as suddenly, Chase was hailing me a cab outside the massive Spanish Interior Department building. And I knew I would never forget this night of holding hands. I don't give a damn how old I am.

Chase hugged me, and into the cab I happily jumped. When I looked back to find him, he had already been swallowed by the pulsing crowds. My euphoria only increased on the journey back home through the most beautiful streets I have ever seen in my life. The cabbie was driving north toward Calle Bravo Murillo along the Calle Paseo de la Castellana, a huge, six- to eight-lane thoroughfare running from the Puerta Del Sol out to the northern city limits. Every major intersection is a roundabout. Every roundabout has a lit water fountain spewing iridescent colored water into ornate sculpture-bedecked pools. The city is magnificent. I felt a surge of utter joy jolt through my inebriated heart. I am in love with this city!

I am head over heels something with this man!

If it isn't love, what is it? It doesn't matter. It's wonderful, and I'm just going to sit back and enjoy it. I am on an adventure, that much is sure, Paco.

Another thing that is sure is that Chase is in complete control. He is behaving and doing exactly what *he* wants to do—he's a very clever man— I always feel like there's a hidden intelligence inside of him that is fully aware of all things at all times. He has that "cop sense"—his eye scans every environment in full detail—I've noted it often. I feel like he is the safest man in the world.

Utterly reliable.

Utterly safe.

Utterly moral (in spite of personal lapses).

Utterly honorable.

I decided to let Chase lead in all future dealings. He knows and lives his own code. One thing I know I can count on.

Chapter 10

Dear Sean,

It's Sunday, and I am moving slowly. The lack of sleep, smoke toxins everywhere, and the alcohol are beginning to slow me down. But when I look in the mirror, I look *fantastic*!

My cheeks are naturally rosy. I am glowing. I look younger and very happy. Even though I feel as if I'm going to die.

This is love—I am sure. It is a powerful force—it's a *life* force. I can feel it breathing life into me.

I've been thinking there are many different forms of love. I have great knowledge of yours and my kind, but very little knowledge of any other male-female kind. I am impressed by the power I feel. It is rocking me by my new foundation. It is opening my eyes to new possibilities.

Paco, it is opening my heart to the future. I feel it happening. It doesn't matter about Chase per se, whether or not he loves me, whether his feelings are reciprocal or whether I am imagining all of this—he is an agent of change for me.

I am so happy inside. My heart is *singing*!

I know and feel all of these contradictory things all at the same time. It feels like opposing forces on a plane of serenity.

∞

Monday
December 14, 1998

Sean,

It's Monday, and I've gotten so much work done. I have done half of one paper, four-fifths of another, one whole paper, and my lesson plan for today. I feel good about that, but I have nothing for my 75-minute presentation tomorrow. I am very uptight about that.

I went to Pan's before school where we meet each morning for coffee. Cindy and Chase were there and Christopher. What a shock. They were all busy working—quick, am I dreaming?

Cindy told me about her trip to Segovia. It was gorgeous; she was in ecstasy.

Chase interrupted to tell me he went to Toledo the day before—

That news took the wind out of my sails—he did *no* homework this weekend? After carrying on and on about Group A? I just know he will be in a panic to get three papers and two lessons done in two days. Not to mention his 75-minute presentation tonight.

I am so disappointed. Chase left us—I knew he couldn't concentrate, especially with my censoring scowl, and was going to find a quiet room up in the ELA. Later when we arrived in school, I went looking for him. I found him in our planning room, his back to the door. He didn't look around when I opened the door, so I closed the door and retreated to give him the space he needed.

I am so pissed at him. Here he bitched and moaned about the other group screwing off and not doing their work, and then he went and did exactly the same thing.

I decided to stay away from Chase today.

During class, it's not hard to stay away from Chase. He and Ethan are always together—they are an inseparable team. In fact, on more than one occasion I've marveled that they've only known each other three weeks— they are close like brothers, anticipating one another's responses and needs as if they're connected.

At lunch, I stayed at the ELA with Christopher. We sat in the empty lobby and talked. He's even wearing a suit coat to teach in today. It's an olive-green hounds tooth tailored affair, a really fine garment, and he looks fantastic—he's clear eyed and sober. This is the Christopher I enjoy talking to. I've missed his camaraderie the past week.

He talks about how fucked up his life is and how much he wants to change it—it's a pile of bull shit—it's the addict's dance of whining "poor me." I've heard it before. I point out his inconsistencies—we argue amicably—Christopher loves to argue, just like you, Paco—he'd argue the sun was shining on a rainy day, just to hear himself present his case. He wants to be challenged. He wants someone to point the way. It makes me so sad. I wish I could show him. But he has to find it himself.

In TP, Chase was in a panic—he had so much work to do, his head was swimming. The tension was affecting the entire team. I offered to help. He turned me down—he had two hours to go before he had to do his shorter forty-minute presentation, and he hadn't written his lesson plan yet. Good grief.

I am feeling pretty confident. I have a reading I'm to do with the students today. I've not yet successfully finished a lesson, so I'm anxious, but all my materials are prepared.

Chase is reluctant to accept help; I'm not sure what that is about. I help everyone all the time, the mother force thing I guess—I get people food, I run errands, I cut poster board, whatever needs doing—pep talks, everything to support each person's teaching in our whole class. I've even given Dylan pep talks, telling him his strengths. Wherever I go in the halls, when I come upon a fellow classmate, I ask if there's anything they need help with. I love this feeling of togetherness, the group effort. I love supporting my friends because back home I'm a teacher and most of my classmates here are not—I know more than they do, and I can anticipate how they are feeling and what they need. Such a good feeling to help.

But Chase is reluctant. I'm a little hurt. It feels like a rejection, and I'm not sure why.

Then it occurs to me it's nothing of the kind. It's possible that Chase is so self-immersed right now, so focused on survival, and so independent, he wouldn't know how to accept help. Ethan is the same way. The two of them work silently side by side. It's an impervious and impenetrable duo is what it is. I've been the odd girl out in a male duo just like this with my two brothers Eddie and Andy shutting me out. The dejection feels familiar.

I left the group to work on my own, as I have been doing lately to get my own focus—I am so "other" directed, I have to isolate myself in order to focus on my own lessons.

Today's lessons actually went pretty well by outside measures. I finished my first lesson and got all the teaching elements in this time—I am very happy!

I thought Chase did a good job on his lesson as well. He did this cool thing—once again, he incorporated music into the actual lesson. He played a song called Wonderwall for the class. He wrote down all the lyrics, the individual words to the song, on white poster board and cut them into pieces, which he then scattered on the floor. The students had to individually choose a piece, like a puzzle piece, and attach it to the blackboard in the order of the lyrics and identify its part of speech, the song playing in the background. It was so much fun.

But he only completed one out of four of his language elements in the lesson—he spent too much time on the grammar of the songs and never got to the other elements: reading, oral speaking and pronunciation, or writing—he was *not* happy. It was his first real failure as a teacher, and he was upset. He kept saying, "It's good enough to pass. No time to lose focus." What a crock of shit—he was smarting, and I knew it. It hurt like hell, and he's not used to the feeling.

And then later to me, Chase lamented that he had three papers to do plus his 75-minute lesson for tomorrow.

"Do you need help?" I asked.

"No," he said again.

"What are you doing for your lesson tomorrow?" I persisted.

Chase raked his fingers through his now-shaggy blond hair—"I have no idea," he lamented, his voice a tad unsteady. He was worried.

I think this is about as undone as Chase gets, but then I think of Sophie and whatever went wrong there, and suddenly I could envision a much more impassioned Chase.

"What are you doing now?" he asked me.

"Going to study. But first I have to record Félipe." Félipe is another one of my students, a business student preparing for his English exams. I have to do a comparative analysis of spoken English for three students in a paper, so Félipe is my second of three student interview.

"How much do you have finished on the student analysis paper?" he asked suddenly. I told him about my papers and added that I was in a panic about my 75-minute lesson. "Don't worry about that; I told you we'll all help with that." Chase dismissed my worry. "Would you come to dinner with me?" He was asking in a hesitant manner that was unfamiliar to me. "Do you have time?"

"Chase, I don't have any lesson at all tomorrow. Of course I have time. Maybe we could talk over your lesson at dinner—"

"Yes," he agreed absently.

"How about if I meet you at the bar after Félipe and I finish?"

"No, I'm going to stay in the planning room and work," he said.

This new, tentative Chase shakes me up. He isn't accustomed to this kind of uncertainty and pressure, I think. But never fear. My specialty is talking through academic snafus. Half an hour later, we were heading around the plaza, past the stairs leading down to the Metro and the leaning Puerta de Europa towers, toward Prêt A Manger for some dinner. He is tentative even in the way he walks. His normal confident swagger is missing. It's unsettling.

We ate sandwiches in Prêt A Manger and chatted. During dinner, we talked about his lesson. I asked him how he would like to handle it. With his normal confidence, he said without hesitation, "Playing games. But I can't think of any that would be good."

Games. That reminds me. "Chase, heLLOOOO—have you forgotten the game book you left in my apartment?" The book was sitting off to the side on my desk. I could picture it clearly. It was labeled "Teaching Games". Chase was taken aback. Of course he had forgotten. "Why don't we go get it after dinner," I suggested.

For the first time, he seemed to calm down. He was still tense and tentative, but he had a small plan. We talked about Toledo during dinner. He relaxed as he recounted his trip. He had a great time with his friends. I was just a tidge jealous he went without me—he had invited me to go just a day ago. But I just couldn't leave with all this work to do.

On the way to my apartment, Chase asked what I was going to do this evening. Study, I told him. He asked if I would consider studying with him up in the ELA. That's what I love about him—he knows what he wants at any given moment, and he directly goes for it. It's so natural for him, a birthright. It's very sexy. I thought he was asking for company, that he's not used to being alone. But I knew I could offer more than that—I could help him climb out of this hole he'd dug himself into.

Is this enabling? Chase probably has female enablers all over the globe. Women must love helping him. … I do.

We take the rickety elevator to the fourth floor and walk to the far wing of the school to find a planning room. It's very late, and we are alone in the building. Chase finds suitable games right away that fire his imagination, of course he does. His natural ebullient energy starts to return.

While Chase works on his lesson, I work on the textbook analysis. He is asking me a lot of questions about how I did it and when I will be done.

I had decided, of course, that I would let him have it when I finished. I didn't feel good about it, but I wouldn't withhold it from him, either. I knew without a doubt he wouldn't copy it—his keen sense of honor would prevent that. I knew he would use mine as a template and it would shave a good three hours off his workload tonight. He has brought so much joy into my heart, I was willing to help him even if I heard warning bells pealing loudly in my ears. Warning bells about giving and not setting up any expectations in return.

When we returned to the ELA, everyone else had gone home for the evening. The halls were eerily silent. Christopher had taken off with Dylan and Hal to a bar somewhere. Cindy and Emma had gone home to study, and I have no idea where Michael had gone. Ethan left promptly upon the completion of his lesson. We're used to him quietly disappearing in the evenings. He doesn't socialize with us at bars. Sometimes he will tip a few at the bar after school and then go home to his wife, a warm dinner, and a computer for his homework assignments.

This all fits in with the religious persona I now believe him to have. I looked up suddenly and said, "Did you know Ethan is a religious man?"

Chase stopped his lesson writing with an offended knitting of his brow. "Oh, really? What makes you think so, Darcy?"

"He said so on my lottery tape."

"Exactly what did he say on the tape?"

"He said if he won the lottery he would go to Africa and become a missionary—" before I finished my sentence, I remembered the first tape and how it had been a lie. I looked up, and there was Chase with a broad smile on his face, his eyes twinkling brightly.

"HellOOOOOO!" he cried out. "He said it on the tape, did he? Helloooo, Darcy." He said my name with his deep Scottish voice in the soft recesses of the back of his throat, a soft sexy timbre that I so love the sound of.

We both burst into paroxysms of laughter. I took brutal kidding for my gullibility, and of course I know it will come up repeatedly for the rest of the course.

Then we settled in and worked for a good two hours together. Suddenly, the secretary turned out the lights on us! She told us in Spanish that we could move to another wing for another hour, but then we must leave. We moved to our old planning room next to the lobby.

Once there, I finished my paper. I told Chase, "You can take it with you tonight if you want."

Chase was tempted but hesitant.

"I know you won't copy it, Chase, but you can see the logic of it—look." And we went through it step by step. Chase had never done a textbook analysis, whereas I have just completed several in my education classes back home and am very familiar with the format. He asked me a lot of questions.

Reluctantly, he took my paper—neither of us is accustomed to asking others for help. I recognize this quality in Chase. He is accustomed to being a winner without struggle; I am accustomed to winning after great struggle—neither of us asks for help.

"Thanks," he said, uncomfortably, as if he'd just broken the law.

We started talking. I don't remember how, but he started talking about his grandfather and how much he admires him. It seems Chase's grandfather was an accomplished military figure, a man who was strong and fearless but honest and scrupulously fair. Chase spoke of him with reverence and loving adoration. I felt honored he would share this part of himself with me. I don't care about his lineage or the importance of his family—it doesn't mean a damn thing to me. I'm just a middle-class, Midwestern American girl; pedigree means nothing to me. What means something to me is Chase's values, what shines a light in Chase's eyes, Chase's caring. Now that's important stuff.

After a long monologue, Chase apologized for monopolizing the conversation—it was time to go. He said he'd like to hear about my family, too—I would like to share that with him some time, but at the same time, I suspect it will never happen. Time is short. We are down to our last four days together. The clock is ticking loudly in my ear.

When we parted tonight, Chase thanked me for everything and took off for a long, sleepless night of homework. He had let me see the softer, more vulnerable side of himself by inviting me to work with him. I don't imagine Chase has many occasions of such uncertainty and fear as he's experienced tonight. He is pretty fearless. As you know from your teaching days, Paco, nothing instills stark terror like the prospect of facing a class the next day with nothing prepared. But he has also shown me the valiant, strong side of himself through tales of his grandfather.

Those qualities of kindness and fair play that he told me about are the very cornerstone qualities of Chase's character as well. I know I have met and become friends with an exceptional man, an extraordinary man. I feel as if I am being touched by greatness of some sort in this experience with him. And I think that we were destined to meet at this point in time. He is putting me in touch with my own strengths of character in contrast to his, in my admiration of his strengths, and in his admiring mine. I have returned to my small room tonight feeling awestruck and humbled.

And I am feeling contented. Haven't felt content, Paco, since the hour before losing you.

⚘

Tuesday
December 15, 1998

My dearest Sean,

I couldn't sleep well last night—tossed and turned with Chase's essence all night long. I would rather have been with you, you know. I feel lucky to be having this experience, but I didn't ask for it. I'd rather be back home worrying about what to make for dinner, worrying about the budget, worrying about sweet you. I'd even rather be fighting with you. Anything, as long as you were with me again. I love you, Paco. I miss you so much, so very *mucho*.

⚘

When we met this morning, Chase was exhausted, pale, and preoccupied. I asked if I could help once again. Again, he said no—again, I felt rejected. Discreetly, he returned my paper before class. We did not discuss how he'd done.

In TP, Chase was a wreck—he was working furiously on his homemade materials. I offered help, and he wouldn't take it. I was perplexed. It was a team effort, was it not? I was trying to be a good team member, and he was thwarting my purest of efforts.

Ethan was working silently by his side. That is Ethan, always quietly going about his business. Very hard working. Very unassuming and modest. I like that.

At one point, Chase went to put his work in the photocopying tray, where the secretary would retrieve the pages and copy them; but it was ten minutes past 2:00 p.m. He had missed the copying deadline. He was distraught.

It was absolutely ridiculous. "Chase, listen to me!" I ordered him. His eyes snapped up to mine. "I will go down to the subway and get it done for you," I declared. There is a copying vendor down on the third sub-floor of the subway, of all places.

"No," he said, pulling away from the desk to stand. "I'll go do it."

"What is the matter with you?" I demanded. "You don't have time to leave this room—look at all this work!"

He looked at the work sprawled all over the desk with this hopeless expression on his face—books and papers, whiteboard marker, poster board, magazines, notebooks, teaching supplies piled on every surface.

"I do not have a lesson today; I can go down there." It was going to take twenty to thirty minutes, and he only had 1-1/2 hours and no lesson plan written yet. The lesson plans have to be clean and perfect; they are turned in for grading.

Reluctantly, he sat down and agreed.

"Thanks, Darcy," he said over and over. He was simultaneously grateful and hesitant. I did not understand this reluctance. Could he be that rigidly macho that he cannot accept a helping hand?

When I returned, I asked if there was anything else I could do. He said no—Cindy asked me if I wanted to go to lunch. I accepted her invitation. But immediately, Chase asked if I could help cut his poster board, which they all refer to as "card"—Chase uses more "card" than all of us combined; he uses it on every lesson to write his grammar on. I turned Cindy down to help Chase. Of course. Team effort.

Chase asked what he owed for the copying. "Nothing, Chase, forget it," I said offhandedly. He was too frantic to argue.

Chase's lesson went swimmingly. He got through two games and a lot of vocabulary—most of all, the students had a blast.

But Chase didn't feel that way—he thought it *bombed* but was relieved to have it over.

"I'm done!" he exclaimed with sudden joy. "Darcy, are you coming?" he asked about my coming to the bar.

"No, remember I have to interview Guillermo tonight, Chase. See you down there." I have my 75-minute lesson tomorrow, and I felt a frisson of disappointment he hadn't yet offered to help me.

The interview with Guillermo went well. He is a law student and a basketball fanatic! He wants to talk about Madrid Real, the Madrid basketball team. He spoke with great animation even when searching for the right English words to express sports terms and athletic maneuvers. He plays on an amateur team with friends as often as he can. He knows about the NBA lockout happening this year and asks my opinion about how long it will last. He watches American basketball! He's very sad for us that this will be the first year without Michael Jordan. It's very dear. I love these students, Paco. They are so excited to be learning English, so enthusiastic about their futures. And they are grateful for our lessons. It's so different from teaching in an American high school!

When I got down to the bar, it was Chase and Dylan of all people. Ethan had gone home. I told them I was frantic about my lesson—Chase told me not to worry, he'd help. He invited me to go to Chinese—okay I thought, just when is he going to help?

I told Chase, no, I was returning to the ELA to work—knock, knock. Anybody home? Hadn't we just gone through this last night? Didn't he recognize the panic in my eyes?

He hesitated, and I could see the realization register on his face, the way he had felt last night and the way I had stepped in to help him. He turned away.

I knew then.

Chase was going to party tonight because Chase was done. And that's all that matters to Chase, really. What ever is important to him at the moment, whatever is *fun* is what matters.

So young. So male—

I was *disgusted*. I felt sick to my stomach. And I was scared.

I grabbed up my things and said, "I'm leaving."

I heard Dylan saying, "You're leaving now?" as I beat it out of that filthy, stupid bar.

In my heart, I was hoping the kind Chase, the Chase of integrity would come to join me in a little while. He knew where I would be.

In my head, I knew I was on my own.

Still, I was so furious, I could spit. I understood I had to calm down and focus myself if I was going to survive this absolute mess—Chase had managed to single-handedly screw me *royal*.

He took my subjects away at the planning meeting and gave them to Michael.

He put me off for four days about figuring out what I was supposed to do.

Now he has abandoned me the night before my lesson.

I am livid. I put on Elton John and began to concentrate on my work. Before I left the ELA at 10:00 p.m., I was finished with my student analysis paper on Marta, Félipe, and Guillermo. Now all I had to do was figure out my 75-minute *non*-lesson.

By 2:00 a.m., I had made my homemade materials and I had half of my lesson plan (LP) done. But I still don't know what the actual grammar elements will be or the order or the LP logic—I need to talk to my teammates for that. And my teammates have abandoned me. We need to coordinate our elements to create one smooth lesson of which we are each one part. I don't think I will get any sleep tonight. I can't see my way around this lesson. It's clear as mud. How can I create a lesson plan when I don't know what my grammar elements are?

Chapter 11

Sean,

I did go to sleep last night, believe it or not. For four hours. Getting up after only four hours of sleep is sheer hell. I am exhausted. My head hurts and is spinning. My stomach is roiling. And I am filled with dread. The only saving grace is that this is my last stressful lesson of the course. My last time to get up without proper sleep.

I went to Pan's first thing this morning, and can you believe it? Chase is cool to *me*. I glared at him. He asks if I am ready, and I say, "NOOOO," and glare back at him. "You said you would help."

"Well don't worry. We will at TP." He was defensive and withdrawn, not kind, gentle, and caring.

Is he *crazy*? I wondered what kind of help that was going to be. I also thought to myself, he isn't going to help in TP because he isn't finished with his papers—he stayed out last night with Dylan, and he is wrecked.

I have never seen him look this physically bad. And he is not the least bit interested in my problems.

I am so angry!!!!

In class this morning, our alternate teacher, Gareth, was doing three hours of role plays. I thought, I am going to *die*—not today of all days. Too hard; too taxing. I am exhausted, stressed to the max.

At some point during the role plays, I realized I was completely and utterly on my own. It was sink or swim time for me. I didn't have a lesson plan, an algorithm, or even a theme, and Chase was not going to help me as he had promised.

If I don't do well teaching today, I will not pass the course. There is still a part of me that wants Chase to help, needs Chase to help on a basic male-female level. But my *only* concern today has to be for myself. I resolve to get the job done on my own. I've gotten this far in my life without Chase's help, and by god, I will do it today.

But hold on, another problem emerged. Michael hadn't come to school yet. As I found my own resolve in TP, we are told she might not show, and we have to be prepared to fill in. I turned to Ethan and Chase and said, "What are we going to do?"

Chase shot back, "You'll just have to cover the extra 75 minutes, Darcy. It's your day."

The irony of the situation, the fact that Chase had stolen my lesson and given it to Michael and now Michael wouldn't be there to use the material, loomed up and smacked me between the eyes. "The HELL I will!" I shot back.

Chase and Ethan huddled—Ethan said with confidence, "We have more than enough material. We're covered."

With relief, I turned back to my LP. I am as tight as a drum with anger at Chase. We are in TP, and he is not offering me help. Then he has the unmitigated gall to tell me I have to cover an extra 75 minutes when he knows damn well I am crazed over the one 75-minute slot. This is turning into a nightmare. What I get for associating with children.

Chase passed by and offhandedly asked, "Need help?"

"Yes!" I spat shrilly.

He walked away and did something else. Then he walked up again and said, "Do you need help?"

"Yes," I repeated, this time with gritted teeth.

He left and did something else.

I am the space shuttle revving up during countdown! The gases are billowing around me in huge clouds.

He passes by again and looks at me. Our eyes meet, and I implore him silently—he broke the gaze *again*.

I know he is fucking playing with me!!!! He has the power in his hands, and he is making me *squirm*. I fucking can *not* believe it!!! Him of all people. I would never have suspected this kind of behavior from him.

Ethan watched from the side. It was far more than I could bear.

I had warned myself all day to keep cool. Not to let him get me, not to do *anything* I was going to regret the next day.

Chase said again, "Need help, Darcy?"

And I *blew*!!!!! *Sky* high!!!!!

"NOOOOO!!!!" I bellowed. "I don't need your help. Not anymore I don't!!!" Then I shut my mouth, clamped it shut so the swears wouldn't get out.

I looked down at my papers and refused him eye contact.

There was *dead* silence in the room. I felt both their eyes on me—boring into me. They are *stunned*. Blimey, the American has wigged out. They didn't know *what* to do.

But I am not finished.

I stare down at my work and speak with frighteningly quiet intensity through my gritted teeth, "I have heard a lot about teamwork around here, and I have been a part of the team. I've done my part, but I'm not seeing a lot of teamwork coming my way."

"Darcy, what do you need help on?" Chase asked quietly.

"Nothing; I can do it myself," I said defiantly.

Then I looked up at him and I said, "I *asked* you for help repeatedly, and you wouldn't help—"

"What can I do?" he repeated quietly.

"I asked you for help three times, and now I'm not going to—" I stopped because I was going to say "beg," and both of the men in that room knew what I had stopped myself from saying.

I stared at Chase, speechless. I opened my mouth to cover it over, and he beseeched, "Tell me." It was a genuine request. No games. Now.

A voice inside said, *tell him. Take the help and move on. It's too late to save face. It's too late for anything.*

In one second flat, my brain analyzed exactly what I needed and organized it into three questions I heretofore hadn't even known existed.

Boom: "What language elements are you using?"

Boom: "What grammar are you using?"

Boom: "How can I integrate your elements with my vocabulary subject?"

I rattled the questions off in a row.

Boom.

Boom.

Boom.

He rattled back the answers, including a perfectly ordered integration of subjects and elements.

Chase is an organizational genius.

I turned to Ethan, who was staring at this scene speechless. "If I have any other questions, will you help me?"

"Aye," he responded.

I have only two hours to put this whole thing together with the materials I had already developed. The room is eerily quiet. I feel bad. I've blown it with Chase. How could I have yelled at him like that? I feel totally *ashamed*.

I couldn't bear to look at him. I focus on the work.

Chase and Ethan left the room.

My fingers are shaking uncontrollably as I try to write my LP. Inside, I am feeling humiliated.

Ethan returned, talking about something else.

I interrupted, "Ethan, I'm very sorry about that—I'm just so stressed."

"Not at all, Darcy."

The British reserve. The stalwart British politeness. The forgiveness of the devout.

I felt so ashamed. "No, I'm so sorry."

"Cheers, Darcy," he replied, eyes searching mine. Ethan was okay. He understood. All was forgiven. Oh, thank god. I was grateful.

Chase returned, and I looked down at my work.

I'd be damned if I would apologize to him. I would *not*—I would rather die than *ever* apologize to this man. He played with me—he fucking played mind games with me.

No one plays mind games on me and survives in a relationship with me. No one, not since the father of my first son, has fucked with me that way. And no one is so important, no one is so royal they can fuck with me—

Not negotiable. Period.

I was so revved up right then, my insides were just reverberating.

Ethan left the room again—he and Chase were madly preparing for Michael's slot—Michael was not coming for sure.

Once Ethan was gone and we were alone, Chase said immediately to me, "What do I owe you for the copying yesterday?"

His voice was low and calm and guarded.

I, on the other hand, am high strung, stressed out, and *humiliated*.

"Chase, it was pennies! It's meaningless. Can't I pay for something that small?" They are always paying for me. Always.

There was a moment of silence between us. Then, nervously, he said, "I just don't want you to think I forgot. I don't want you to think I'm that kind of person."

I looked up at him and melt. I just fucking melt. Now he chooses to show me a vulnerability?

Okay, I'll apologize. I'll get down on my knees and beg his forgiveness—anything—I love this man.

I am so completely schizophrenic with him. Who the hell is this woman? She is in no way related to me. No one, absolutely no one, at home would believe I am this woman.

If only I weren't so damned angry with him.

If only he weren't such a shit.

"Okay," I said. "It's fifty cents, I think. But please, don't pay me. It's silly."

Chase repeated, "I just want you to know I didn't forget." He wasn't just talking about the bloody money.

"Okay." I looked back down at my work. He is relentlessly staring at me.

Where is the air in this room? My lungs are going to fucking explode. There is no time for all this. No more fucking time!

I knew I had to move. I can not concentrate around this man; I can not work in his presence. And now I have only one hour. As difficult as it was to leave him, I gathered up my things and moved away to an empty room. Self-preservation at least still lives within me. Otherwise, I don't know who the hell I am anymore.

☙

My lesson went *fantastically*!!!

I was so pissed off at them that I made an executive decision to disregard all the stuff I didn't like (that Gareth, our teacher, had told me to do). I decided to concentrate on the stuff I liked—the difference between British English and American English. I estimated my tasks (homemade) were enough to take up the whole 75-minute slot—for the first time in four and a half weeks, I was right on target!!! Furthermore, I made my lesson funny (do you *believe* this? Under such dire circumstances? My passing is at risk here.) And during the lesson, I could see that Ethan and Chase were *killing* themselves laughing along with all my students. So was the teacher, Gareth. I had them all in the palm of my hands.

It feels soooo sweet. My last lesson was a total success!

And Chase loved it. Most of all, Chase loved it. I am thrilled. Thank god—what a total relief—I know without a doubt, I will pass the course. So sweet. I've done it, Paco, I've done it. And all on my own, to boot. I've done it in front of the only person in the whole wide world besides myself and you that I would want to impress. He has become my role model, my mentor. I adore Chase. I completely and utterly adore him. Even if he is a shit. Even if he let me down. Even if he hurt me. Even if he is just as human as everyone else on the planet.

Now I *am* ready to party!!! And so, apparently, is every one else in the course. Michael, of course, wasn't there. Her absence was noticeable as we toasted in Te & Me at 7:30 tonight. We'd all made it for sure but her—whether Michael would pass the course depended on whether she showed up tomorrow I guess, though I can't imagine how they could pass her under the circumstances. She has been terrified, too—I knew it because in spite of everything, I had tried to help her last night at the ELA while Chase was downstairs with Dylan. She had come to me while I struggled with my lesson in the planning room. She'd been hysterical—really hysterical, crying and sobbing and shaking—and I had tried to comfort her, tried to bolster her nonexistent self-confidence. Getting up in front of a class of students is not as easy as it looks. So ironic that Chase had given her the good material, the global music material I wanted to do so badly, and she was so scared she never showed up to do it. The material never got used. I had done better winging it, making up my own material, than I ever would have done have with the music. What do I know about global music?

Because of Michael's absence, Cindy was there celebrating with us, though she was drinking *agua* (since her drunk two weeks ago, she has been subdued and absent from our socializing). She watched Chase and me like a hawk—her jealousy was unmistakable—she has been upstaged by me. Though Cindy is never far from center stage—it's the best part she knows how to play. And that part was no longer attracting Chase the way it once had. Though I thought it still attracted him far too much.

The seating arrangement in Te & Me was thus:

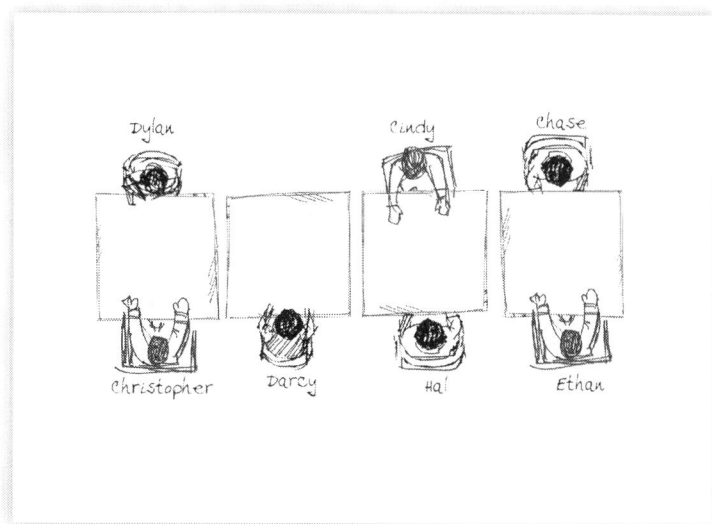

SEATING AT TE AND ME

Christopher was animatedly describing his last 75-minute lesson, which he said was a "bore"—of course that prompted Chase to tell everyone about my lesson—he pulled out my homemade Brit vs. Yank slang questionnaire, and the entire class roared as he recited each question out loud. Chase summed up my performance by saying it was a vast improvement over my earlier mood in the planning room—

Of course that incited everyone on Team A to speculate over what had happened in *our* room.

I couldn't look at Chase; my cheeks were, of course, burning with embarrassment. When Christopher insisted I tell all, I said, "We had a little tension on our team today."

"Tension!" roared Chase. "Ooo, I as much as thought I was going to be punched in the face! Isn't that right, Ethan?" Ethan nodded, expressionlessly searching my face.

With that, the others went wild, laughing and catcalling and prying all three of us for more.

"He would have deserved it," I thought to myself. Out loud I said, "Yeah, like I'm gonna punch someone."

"Never!" exclaimed Hal next to me. "Never you, Darcy," he comforted me in his melodious Welsh accent. Hal is such a dear. Hal is always there, supporting me, telling me how wonderful I am. It was Hal who encouraged me before class today, telling me what a brilliant teacher I am, telling me it is my brilliance in class that has inspired him to persevere all these days. I've given him the will to surpass himself. I give him hope. Hal is just the sweetest person to me. Always. I smiled at him appreciatively.

Chase indicated the end of the discussion with, "One *hell* of a lesson, though." His approving eyes met mine over the tables. That went down well. There was no one else in the world I wanted more to impress. We'd been neck-and-neck competitors, even while being neck-and-neck collaborators. At the end of the day, it turned out that Chase was pretty much my equal in the class, the person to beat in the academic wars. And make no mistake, in academia, there is always someone in a class one needs to identify and beat. Whether the Brits want to acknowledge it or not, school is a competition playing field. Though there is plenty of collaborating, the bottom line, and that would be the grade line, is the winning score. I realized at this moment that the person to beat had been Chase all along and that I had identified him unconsciously very early on.

Chase changed the mood with, "Dahrceee, what are underpants? Knickers? No, they're shorts! Of course they are short; they are knickers! Wha hey!" Everyone laughed in diversion and demanded more! "What is a dummy? An oral device to pacify a baby, silly, not a stupid person!" Everyone roared. "But wait! Darcy, what is a flasher? One who engages in indecent exposure? Noooo, it's a bloody turn signal!" Chase shook his hand as if it were on fire. He turned to Ethan. "They are so sadly confused, our Yankee cousins." He returned to me, "And what is in your purse, Darcy? Would there be an eraser in there?" He asked with an arch of his teasing Scottish brow.

"No, Chase, that would be a condom. A c-o-n-d-o-m," I retorted with a grin. The bar echoed with gales of laughter. I held up my glass. "To getting pissed!" I toasted them all.

"Cheers!" They retorted in unison as they clinked their glasses round the table. We were well on our way to getting pissed. And not a one of us was angry.

The subject of British vs. American slang kept everyone chattering for at least a quarter of an hour. Chase caught my eye and smiled over the others at me with just the slightest lift of a soft Scottish brow.

I smiled wanly back—if he thought by bringing up our problem in front of the group, it would be resolved, he was very mistaken—he didn't know much about rowing with an American—he didn't know anything about rowing with the likes of me.

Hal and Christopher kept me preoccupied with jokes about American English. They think *we* are funny, Paco! So cute. Cindy was doing her best to get center stage with Chase or Dylan or whoever could be enticed. She and Dylan had been chummy this week. I think they had made an alliance to keep Group A on track. Really there had to have been an alliance to keep Christopher on track. And Emma was there in body only—she couldn't care less about what happened to her group. It seemed as if Cindy had a major chip on her shoulder toward the rest of us. I thought it must have been very hard on her to be separated into Group A. And to think, I went home that night and cried because I was stuck in Group B instead of in A with Christopher, Emma, Cindy and Hal.

❧

Last night, when I was so angry with Chase, I stopped at the pay phone out on the street downstairs and called Cindy on her cell phone. I told her how mad I was at him.

"Is he gay?" I asked her at one point in the conversation.

"Chase? Definitely not!" she'd answered. "What made you ask that?"

"I don't know—I just can't believe he slept with a beautiful girl without touching her. It doesn't seem natural, that's all. I shouldn't have asked, sorry."

"I think he's mad at me," Cindy said suddenly.

That was an understatement. "Why?"

"He's just acting different. We used to be very tight. But now there's tension between us. We don't talk anymore."

No one talks to Cindy. One simply witnesses her performances.

She continued, "I think he doesn't like me. It started the day I met his obnoxious German friend. One of his friends told Lauren about me."

"Really?" That perked me right up.

"Yeah, and she got really jealous. I think she gave him an ultimatum to move out from my place. That's when he went to your place."

Hmmm, this was interesting. Chase had called Lauren that first night at my place. He'd left me suddenly, too—perhaps it had been Lauren calling the shots all the way from Greece.

Then Lauren has a lot of power over fearless Chase.

I've been having trouble understanding why Chase would stay with friends who only had floor space and no desk space and a party atmosphere. He complained several times about doing homework in the middle of the night in the bathroom because of the parties. That's insane.

"All the men are crazy about you, Cindy. What are you talking about? These guys are nuts about you!" Most women would *kill* for the kind of adoration Cindy gets from these men. It is pathetic, and their fascination with her never ceases to amaze me. Just because she is skinny, wears glamorous clothes, and has big lips, they are all gaga over her. It is so unfair—my whole life it seemed so unfair that the beautiful airheads got all the men. Of course, my whole life I did okay, even with the most handsome men. Steve had been extremely handsome. But in the end, I had gotten the real prize, er, that would be you, Paco, the most handsome man of all. Even so, it is still an irritant to see them panting after such a fluff ball.

"Really?" she preened with the idea.

"You're the one who's been distancing yourself from us. You haven't gone out once in two weeks." This was entirely true. And it had started with the night she'd refused to come out with us when we were going to study. The night Chase had taken off on her and been so angry with her.

"Really, has it been that long? I don't know what I've been doing—I just didn't feel like going out."

I pressed her, and she agreed to go out with everyone tomorrow night, our second-to-last night together.

&

Chase wanted us to go eat at the big Italian restaurant at Alonzo Martínez. Dylan, as usual, declined and left. We stayed on for "one for the road!" Amazing convention. Not to mention the endless rounds that precede any actual British bar departure, one wouldn't think of leaving without one for the road. Hal will even call for "one for the road" after we're on the road! And then everyone piles into yet another bar along the way to the next bar. Absolutely amazing lifestyle. Incomprehensible from where I've come from. In my family, anyone who even has one drink a night would be considered an alcoholic. Yet I have discovered that after I go home each night, it is rarely the end of the evening for Hal, Chase, and even Cindy—so it never ceases to amaze me. How can people drink this much and function in the morning?

Anyway, after "one for the road" we did, indeed, take off for the Metro. Once we arrived at the restaurant, Chase left the group to go the men's room. Christopher was wowed by the restaurant—he loved the atmosphere—Christopher has an appreciation for the finer things, despite his rebellion against them. We were ushered to a large, round table, which sat on a pedestal platform in the rear of the dining room, near the cozy table we had dined at last time.

Here is the seating:

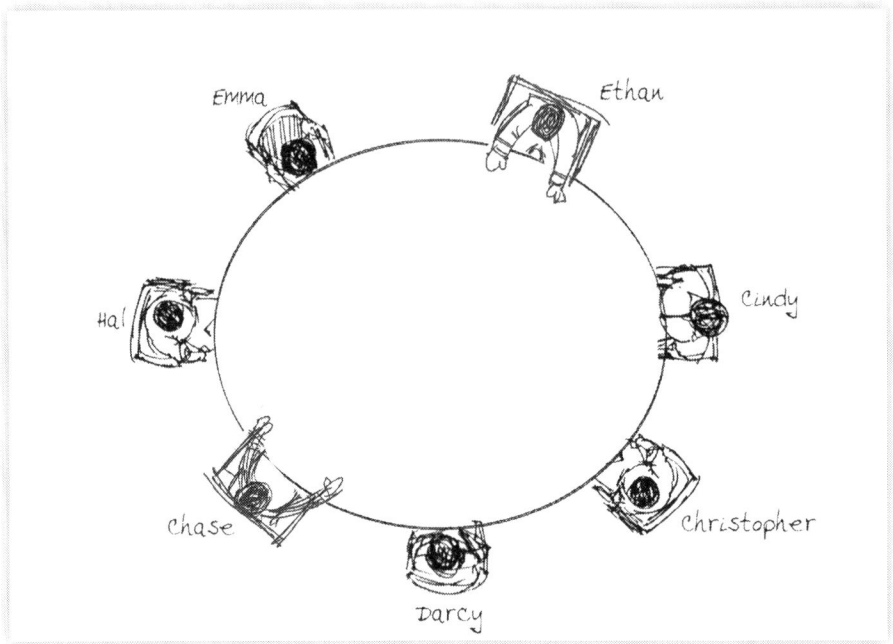

SEATING AT THE ITALIAN

I hung back and watched people seating themselves because I was determined to sit by Chase tonight. I needed to speak with him, so I had to make the opportunity to do so. Cindy tried to hang back, too, but Christopher motioned her forward and it would have been rude not to go. I followed Christopher and took the seat closest to the platform staircase. I didn't mind being next to Christopher at all; of course I knew Christopher's behavior would probably be a problem for the group before the end. There was one empty chair to my left, but the table was quite large and the chair was quite a distance from mine over by Hal. Whatever. It's very difficult to control seating at an event. Chase arrived and, to my relief, pulled his chair closer to mine.

Christopher and I were talking about something, and I was ignoring Chase. I was leaning toward Christopher.

"Darcy, where's your hat?" Chase had, indeed, bought Santa hats for all of us and had insisted everyone wear their Santa hats all day long.

I looked over my shoulder with a scowl. "I don't like it; it flattens my hair."

"Come here," he ordered and motioned me over. I sat up warily, and Chase inspected my hair. "Your hair looks beautiful tonight."

I knew it looked like shit. "It's all flat because of that hat—it's horrible."

Chase dropped his voice and leaned in toward me—he reached up and touched my hair. "I like it flat—it looks nicer." His voice was quite proprietary. He looked into my eyes.

Be still, my heart. Where was the air in this restaurant? I could feel my cheeks flushing beneath his gaze. I wish I had some self-control. Who's in charge of this body, anyway?

"But it's ugly," I whined.

"Much better than that poufy thing you usually have."

I caught my breath. "What are you talking about?"

"All the American girls, they wear their hair all poufy. I like it much better like this." He scanned it with satisfaction.

Chase had an uncanny ability to make a wild woman melt. I was still wild with anger inside, yet he was making me forget. Or decide to put it on the back burner for just a moment. Maybe it was I who didn't know what it was like to row with a Scot.

He put my hat back on, and I acquiesced under Cindy's watchful eye.

I was now drinking sangria after having a *vino tinto* in the last bar. The world was beginning to feel very mellow. As was custom, the Brits "started" the meal with a round of gin and tonics (never mind how many rounds actually preceded the start of a meal). Chase also ordered a pitcher of sangria. For me.

I raised my glass and toasted everyone, "Congratulations on finishing!"

"Cheers, Darcy!" The boys all saluted with a cheer and drink from their glasses.

Later, Chase and I huddled over the menu, shoulder to shoulder again. God, I love being close to this man. It's intoxicating. So much more than the sangria.

Chase and I ordered the same appetizer, the one we'd ordered last week when we were here with Ethan and Mary. Chase ordered the pasta carbonara, and I had a four-cheese pasta. Christopher ordered *saltimbocca* and refused a salad, so it came while we all had salad—he was distressed. I had told him to order a salad (he's always so hungry), but he'd refused. Once he tasted his entrée, though, he loved it and he wolfed it down like a starving urchin. By now I was leaning over and telling him what to do—when to order, how he's too loud—this is always how it is with me and Christopher. I have no compunction about telling him point-blank what he's doing wrong. At one point, I put my hand on his arm when he had spontaneously shrieked and disturbed the whole restaurant and told him he needed to lower his voice because this was a very nice restaurant and this was Ethan's neighborhood—we can't humiliate Ethan, it wouldn't be right. Christopher calmed down, and people resumed conversing.

Chase leaned into me and said softly into my ear, "You mother him."

I thought he was criticizing me and turned to object.

"No, that's good," he exclaimed immediately upon seeing the objection in my eyes. "Christopher needs a mother," he said.

Then he told me about a conversation he'd had with Christopher trying to help him straighten out. In his own way, I think Chase was trying to "father" Christopher—I'd noticed it in the Chinese when he was giving Christopher hell about being late to class. In the same way I mother Christopher, Chase fathers him. We are the helpers; we serve very complimentary leadership roles in this group, he the male version, me the female, the yin and the yang. The attraction of those two natural poles is strong.

There was a pause in our conversation, and we listened to the others. Suddenly Chase said, "Ethan, Darcy says you're quite a religious man."

Ethan's lips immediately turned up, and his eyes sparkled. "Aye, 'tis true," he said. "Cheers, Darcy." He lifted his glass and everyone lifted theirs to me as well.

Ethan was absolutely delighted by the news that I had believed him and used his religiousness as an excuse for all kinds of aberrant, antisocial behavior at the table, which caused the others to all talk and laugh at once.

I knew this was a good opportunity to start with Chase.

"So you thought you were going to get punched today. ..." I said softly.

"It was pretty dicey," he joked without missing a beat. He'd been waiting for it.

I will not apologize. I will not apologize!

"I shouldn't have—"

He cut me off, "No, Darcy it was all my fault. I didn't help you, and I knew it, and I still didn't help." His face was full of emotion and penitence.

"And god, I felt so bad. I promised you and I let you down *completely*." His body language was so dejected, so completely conciliatory.

"I shouldn't have yelled that way."

"Darcy." He put his hand on my arm. "I let you down completely. I wasn't there for you. I'll feel bad about that forever."

He was accepting total responsibility.

It took a moment for it to register. I was geared up for the typical male weasel slip-sliding around an issue. But Chase looked me in the eye and accepted the blame.

No excuses.

No rationalizations.

No stories to make him look good.

Oh my god, now *that* was fearless. And brave. And so very virile.

It might sound strange, but I think that was the strongest thing I have ever seen a man do. Once again I am completely wowed.

Of course, he followed the admission with a tease. "You really let me hear about it though. Ooooh," he intoned while circling his right hand in the air. "I didn't help, I abandoned you, I wasn't a team player—" he recited the litany, none of which I had actually said.

"I didn't say any of those things!" I instantly objected loudly and saw all eyes at the table turn to us. "Here's exactly what I said." I didn't care if everyone heard; I repeated it verbatim. "I worked very hard to say those 'I' messages about how it felt to me."

"Whoa, Darcy, 'I' messages? Who else but an American would say such a thing? It's *incredible*—such nonsense! Who talks that way? No one else in the wooorld."

Then he was off! And the group was laughing their heads off with him. No one could lampoon the Americans with quite as much inner angst as our Scottish Chase. He ranted and raved about Americans. He tugged at my Santa hat, all the while his leg touching the full length of mine and his warm eyes speaking smiles to mine.

Chapter 12

He had not said the words, "I'm sorry"; he'd done better. Anyone can be sorry—but it's very rare to take the blame squarely on the chin and admit it. That's what Chase had just done. In our relationship, Paco, I was always looking for the words, "I'm sorry," but now I realize they are meaningless in a relationship—the thing of substance is the recognizing of responsibility because that's where the change lies. If you don't accept complete responsibility for your actions and how they affect the other person, you will never change them. The words, "I'm sorry," are pretty hollow and meaningless. Chase had just taken the responsibility dead on.

It was the sweetest thing.

And I accepted his admission silently. He understood when I said I shouldn't have yelled—totally chivalrous.

We were okay again. No, we were better than ever. We'd just survived a very tense conflict.

And as implausible as it may seem on the face of it, or from the outside, I trusted Chase now more than ever before. Even though I knew he would probably do it again, given similar circumstances. Didn't matter.

Anyone could have a flaw—but to face it dead-on and own it, now that was something unusual. Extremely impressive.

Tonight after this exchange, I abandoned myself to the moment, to laughing and talking and drinking sangria. But mostly playing with Chase. We were a pair, a duo, and I could tell by the wistful look on Cindy's face, it was formidable.

We drank seven pitchers of sangria (I had four or five glasses), beers, gin and tonics, and then after-dinner drinks—Irish coffee—Chase had one; I declined. I was very happy by the end of the meal. It was a great time together for all of us. All seven of us, all foreign students sharing good company, our successes—an event, and the accomplishment of a lifetime, really.

Christopher was, of course, blotto. But he only embarrassed us a couple of times. He really was pretty good. Except when we all stood up to leave. I was the farthest from the table, at the foot of the stairs leading from the pedestal, when I heard him bellow, absolutely *bellow* from his diaphragm, "You BAHSTARDS!!!"

I turned back and saw him drunkenly swaying in his seat, staring fixedly at the now-empty table.

"You BAHSTARDS!" he repeated. "You left me in the bar all alone. ..."

I knew immediately he was referring to last week when Chase, Ethan, and I had left him to come here to this very restaurant. Somehow in his drunken state he has put the two events together. I ran back up to the table.

Chase was already trying to calm him down.

When Christopher saw me, his expression got soft and his voice got gurgly. "How could you do that to me?" he implored.

"But, Christopher, you were on the phone. You left *us*. You refused to come."

He paused and considered. "No. You-left-me!"

"Only after you wouldn't come—you told me to get away—"

"No, I would never do that to you, Darcy. I love you!"

With that, he got up and swayed step by step over to where I stood and hugged me.

"I love you, too. I'm sorry if we left you."

"It's okay." He was instantly docile and became cuddly as we walked outside together, everyone in the restaurant staring at us as we left. He was very affectionate then, and we walked behind the others arm in arm.

Christopher said to me, "You're so nice to me; I love you, Darcy."

"Yes, yes, and I love you to," I said in a soothing voice. We went around and around how much we loved each other.

It is amazing to me how attracted I still am to him even though I am now emotionally removed from him in a much more comfortable way. Maybe this is who I really am, Paco. Maybe I am not so lost; maybe I am just beginning to find myself.

Cindy and Ethan and Chase were up ahead, and Hal was directly in front of us. It was 2:00 a.m., and we had class the next day, lessons to give, though they would be unobserved on this last day, which meant we could be spontaneous and not do lesson plans. We caught up with the others who had stopped at a stoplight one block before Alonzo Martínez. The rest were huddling about where the next stop would be. I asked Chase to get me a cab; instantly he took one long stride out into the middle of the street, arm outstretched over his handsome blond head, and hailed one for me. My every need immediately seen to … oh my, a girl could get so used to this.

I said goodnight to everyone. Chase opened the cab door, and I said to him, "Will you look out for Christopher tonight?" Wordlessly he took me by the shoulders with reassuring affection and kissed me on both cheeks. I reached up and kissed him on both cheeks in return.

I couldn't look into his eyes, though. The parting would have been too awkward, too hard, as it always was now.

And I didn't particularly want him to see the adoration shining in my eyes.

We only had two more days and nights together. Then we would probably never see each other ever again. I let that thought spin through my brain and exit like a summer's tornado.

Still, the city made me high all the way home. This beautiful *ciudad* and Chase. Who could ask for more? I am such a very happy woman! I can't believe it's me.

❧

Thursday
December 17, 1998

The next morning, the crew was *wiped out*. Chase et al. had moved on to another bar after I'd left. That morning in TP, Chase said to me, begged me, "Can we have a night off tonight? I'm so tired. Do we have to go out?"

My heart sunk. We only had two more nights together. To spend one of them without Chase in the same room would have been unthinkable.

"But Chase, tonight is flamenco!" He had promised me flamenco, and it hadn't happened yet. Tonight was the last opportunity. The chances were slim to none, though, that it was going to happen. Chase wouldn't get his rest. And I wouldn't get my flamenco. I had a feeling the group was going to want to be together.

"Flamenco is it, then?" Chase looked hopeless.

"My last chance," I said with a nod. Chase put his head on the resource table and groaned.

He was completely done in, and I was raring to go. At last, age before youth. I have more stamina. Of course, I have been pacing myself. Actually, I am gaining energy with every passing day. The glow has intensified. I am thriving under the care and attention of five British men. I love every single minute—even the bad ones—they are all "ours." I am *living*, really living my own life for the first time in more years than I can remember. I am experiencing rebirth—I am *alive*!!! And life is so damned beautiful I can hardly stand it.

I don't want to go home. The thought is such a downer.

Chase and Ethan took over the plans for today's classes—I was out of the loop and could have cared less. Gareth wasn't there but showed up at 1:00 p.m.—so all we had to worry about was 75 minutes, half of which was a test—Chase turned the test into a game (of course), a grammar auction, and that left 35 minutes for more games. Chase asked at the end of TP if there was something I wanted to do, and I put my hands in the air and exclaimed, "No, it's all yours." Chase was eager to get before the class again. But he was completely out of steam.

Somehow during TP he got sidetracked onto sports (as usual!), and he was talking cricket—which of course I know nothing about. That annoyed the hell out of him—especially since cricket was the origin of our baseball (according to him, of course), which he considers an inferior game. And then we Americans call our playoffs "world championships." Oh, how that fries him. He goes on and on about it.

"Darcy, world champions! Dahrcy, world champions. Dahhhrcee! World champions? RUBBISH!" He's up and out of his seat now. Over to the map of the world. "Where is the world? Playing CRICKET!!!!!" He uses a pointer to show all the countries on the globe that play cricket.

"Darcy, what's a bowler?" Chase begins quizzing me on cricket terms, and of course I don't know any of the words.

"Someone who knocks down pins?" It's Greek to me.

"No! NOOOO!" He starts revving up—he wipes the white board off and draws a wicket and a post (????), then he starts explaining the gist of the game—before I know it he's diagramming the whole game on the board and acting out different parts of the game in the room. He's appointed a seat for me from where I am to "watch and learn."

"You will be tested," he warns—of course I can't remember a thing, because I could care less. And I am laughing so hard I can hardly even hear his rantings and ravings any more.

"Darcy, this is the pitch," he begins.

I respond through paroxysms of laughter, "Is that a field, Chase?"

"Oh Darcy, Darcy! Listen, it's a pitch." He turns to Ethan, "She's hopelessly uneducated, isn't she?" Ethan nods with a grin.

But Chase is determined—he spends the better part of an hour explaining and demonstrating.

I am laughing and laughing, doubled over laughing the whole time! He is *insane* about sports. Absolutely INSANE.

And so outraged at America.

The teachers come in and listen periodically—word has spread throughout the faculty, and they *love* it. Chase is their darling. He can do no wrong. Anyone else would have been reprimanded, but for Chase it was "Excuse me, Chase, just one question please." Business conducted, then "Carry on, then." Carry on for Chase!

And Chase would carry on. Unfuckingbelievable!

❧

By the way, yesterday, in addition to our problem, Chase was reamed by our teacher, Gareth, in "feedback" for his 75-minute teaching slot. Gareth took exception to what he did (all games, no substantive language segments) and really went after him. He wasn't telling Chase anything Chase didn't already know, but for some reason Chase's face went completely red with rage and he argued with Gareth. No one would dare argue with one of our teachers—that would be considered the height of disrespect. It was inconceivable that Chase would do this. Moreover, Gareth was not to be dissuaded by argument. Gareth argued back, which made Chase even more combative. They argued on and on.

I couldn't believe Chase didn't just let it go—that's what he had advised all of us to do when we had gotten bad feedback or ratings. But when it came his time, he fought back. What a hypocrite.

Chase got his second less-than-perfect grade for the course, and it didn't sit well with him. He couldn't take it calmly. It rankled him and made him mad. Welcome to the club, Chase. Tables are turned, and it isn't very palatable, is it?

I could empathize with him, but he deserved it. He had chosen to play games instead of doing academics. I told him, "Anyone else would have gotten an "ineffective." Even in spite of his criticisms, Gareth had given Chase an "effective."

He didn't argue. He knew I was right.

❧

I failed the cricket test miserably. Chase decided I must come to England to attend a cricket match with him and Ethan. *They take up to five days*!!!! I am hysterical with laughter. What a ridiculous game!!!! He says cricket will soon be a recognized sport in the Olympics once again—the last time it was played in the Olympics was in 1900. No wonder they booted it out of the Olympics—it takes days, days! Complete insanity. Of course my levity only spurs him on.

That is what it's always like with Chase. Impassioned and laughing, one of us taunting the other, the other responding with a further taunt. Such energy. Such fun. Between Chase and Christopher, I have never laughed so long and hard in my life. Really, it's been close to four weeks of nonstop laughing my ass off.

I think constantly of how little time we have left. Every second is becoming precious, to be savored and memorized. I take out my camera and begin to take shots of Chase wherever I can do so without embarrassment. Chase relents and allows pictures (he resisted two weeks earlier on the balcony). He understands now. He knows what is in my heart. It is communicated silently between us and in his capitulation.

Chase hears me say different things to different people about going home—to my class, I define the English term, "looking forward to," as the feeling of seeing my son again. To my classmates, I say, "I never want to go home." He is significantly quiet when I talk about moving to Spain. I don't know if it's disapproval or the inner belief I will never do it. He *never* encourages me to move. I am acutely aware of that. I just keep thinking to myself, I can do anything I want to do. There are no limits! For the first time in forever, I see no limits. Oh my god, Paco, how I am changing.

After the cricket lesson, Ethan went shopping for Christmas party supplies for our last class. Chase was completely spent. He put his head down on the table and took a nap. I have never seen him like this in all the four weeks.

I, on the other hand, am full of energy. The energy of the doomed. This is our last TP together. I memorized Chase's hair, his hands, his nose, his mouth while he sleeps. Then I left to socialize in the lobby. I found a Canadian from another class named Roger and talked to him, saying our goodbyes. Chase stumbled out, not to *ever* be left alone, and socialized too. He asked me if I wanted to go to lunch. It was Chase, Cindy, and me. Cindy is very quiet these days, not the exuberant person she was. But she has not found a way back to center stage with us and has lost her edge.

At lunch she asked if either of us has ever had a near-death experience. She related a time she almost died in a boating accident. She and a friend had gone out in a row boat on a lake in the Poconos and capsized. Her friend panicked, grabbing her for dear life. They both nearly drowned. It was a harrowing story, truly.

Chase told a story about mountain climbing and getting stuck on a ridge he couldn't get down from. He told about his last thoughts when he thought he would die, how he realized he would have liked to spend more time with children and how he resolved to do so if he should survive. There is more "realness" in Chase's little finger than in most people in a whole city. It occurred to me that his teenage experience with the classmate who committed suicide could have also influenced his desire to help others. Especially children or teens. When I think about it, Chase is always kind, even when he's pissed off. In fact, I can't imagine him ever being truly mean. I think the boy's suicide was a major turning point in Chase's life. Perhaps he would be a completely different person today if that hadn't happened. He could so easily be living the unexamined life. Instead, he has become a man of caring and kindness, a teacher who is working to help young people. I think there are profound moments in life when everything is altered forever. Losing you, Paco, is one of those moments for me.

෧༙ර

After Gareth finished his lesson for the day, we had our Christmas party with the students. It was a lot of fun. Chase and Ethan had found a store in Madrid that had British Christmas treasures like Christmas puddings and crackers. Chase was as excited as a five-year-old child to share these with the entire class. He conducted a class on the Scottish Christian customs of his church at home, The Church of England—they weren't so different from Catholic traditions. We ended with a lesson on a song by Lou Reed, "Perfect Day," with "card" of the lyrics that the class had to tape up on the board according to grammatical position. There must have been fifty to sixty cards. We all participated. It was great fun and fast paced. The other class had let out, and Team A and their students entered our room and watched, including Liam. I knew this would be the last time I saw Liam, and it filled me with sadness as I studied his face, his voice, and his beautiful Irish accent so I could remember them forever—he will leave for Ireland with his wife and baby on Friday when we are to be having our last class with Gareth.

After my 75-minute lesson yesterday, Liam sought me out and asked how it had gone. I told him, "Great"—I was glowing and happy. "Gooyd, gooyd!" he kept saying in his beautiful Irish accent. He was genuinely pleased for my success.

On Thursday, Gareth had given me my feedback on the slot, and it was glowing. Chase was the only one to criticize something I did. It was small—I let it go—who *cares?* Passing was the real goal. But Chase got the grade; I'm sure of it. And wild horses couldn't change my belief it was set in stone by week two. He was the golden boy, of course. Even when he got reamed, he got an "effective," which was my highest grade. I got quite a few of these, but never a solid "very effective," which Chase has become accustomed to.

扳

After class, we took all the students to a new bar recommended by the students—one down the street we had never gone to before.

I was feeling so *sad*—there was a lack of energy in Chase at the bar— he was completely spent. He socialized with us but moved over to a large group of the students and stayed there. Once he moved, I knew he was gone for good. I knew this was the beginning of the end for us. Everything would be colored by "the end" emotionally. And he was pulling away.

But I was mad at him for it. At one point he looked over the heads of the girls he was socializing with and found my eyes. We always seek each other out in a room with our eyes, locate one another, and it feels securely anchored when we find each other, as if all is right with the world; we have become a security for one another. I looked at him sadly, madly. He smiled and waved. I did not respond. He was wasting our last minutes together. So sad.

But not for long.

I decided to focus on the students, too—Cindy and I were with most of the guy students, and Chase and Christopher were with the girls.

I'd had two *vinos*, and was sailing high. I was speaking Spanish to my students. They could not believe how silly I was and were laughing at everything I said. We had a blast together.

Chase was continually seeking me out with his eyes. I knew he had separated on purpose—just about everything he does is purposeful, I think. I was pissed at him for it. We would have a forever separation in 24 hours. I didn't get this one. Nothing will make Saturday easier for me. There is no real preparation for total loss. In this, I am experienced.

But in the end, Cindy made this moment easier for me. Early in the evening she spotted a cute Spaniard in the bar. He noticed her, too, and they flirted in passing. She was swooning over him (remember, she is engaged to Vincenzo, who is in Italy, whom she is going to meet in twenty hours!). When this stranger left the bar, she was distraught.

"Go find him, Darcy, *please*!" Yeah right, me go search.

But later, I happened to go outside to get some fresh air from the smoky bar and I sat on the bench in front of my apartment along the busy *calle* Bravo Murillo. I looked into the coffee shop in front of me, and lo and behold, there he was. The gorgeous Spaniard. Sitting at a table in the shop. I went back into the bar and told Cindy. She was ecstatic.

We went out to find him—I was thinking, this is just a lark, for fun, a game—he is adorable, but it's a game. After all, she's engaged.

Much to Cindy's profound disappointment, he was not in the shop when we returned. So we sat on the bench to talk. We were in a good mood now, laughing and joking and retelling funny ELA stories. Suddenly I saw the Spaniard emerge from behind a counter in the shop.

"Cindy, look. There he is!" Cindy was once more elated. She wanted to go in.

But the Spaniard spied us outside and rushed out to greet us. He was bubbly and energetic and very funny. He spoke English very well. He was ecstatic now.

We had a blast, laughing and talking, and it turned out he owned this coffee shop. He was gaga over Cindy (of course). But she was gaga over him. She was *crazy* for him—insane over him—she wanted this man! It was obvious. I was simply *amazed*. All we have heard about for the past four weeks is Vincenzo this, Vincenzo that—we've had to listen to their love calls on the mobile phone, we've even had to stand still on city streets so she could hang back and talk to him. One day this week, we were on a cold windy street waiting while she gushed the love talk with him on the cell phone. The men were imitating her "love voice," and I said to Chase, "I cannot believe the whole group is standing in the street waiting for Cindy to talk to her lover!"

Only Cindy.

But the group honored her relationship with Vincenzo. It was pure and sexual—it was love on the bloom. It was what everyone dreamed of having (and having with Cindy). The love itself became like a group mascot. There was reverence and group patriotism around it. It was understood to be a sacred thing in the group culture.

So when Cindy brought Eduardo into our bar and had drinks with him exclusively, every single Brit noticed it immediately. It was as if time stood still and no one else existed in the world—just Cindy and Eduardo leaning over the bar, huddled against one another, drinking and laughing—and Eduardo had his hands all over her! He held her hand, put his arm around her shoulder, touched her derriere, smoldering.

Chase's eyes were glued to the scene. He came directly over to me.

"Hello? What have we here?"

Within seconds, all the men had gathered around me.

"Who is he?"

"What is she doing?"

"His hands are all over her!"

Hal said, "I'm going to *kill* him! Let me at him!" His hands were balled into fists. Sweet, nonviolent Hal was instantly driven to violence with the emotions he felt. Chase stopped him.

Christopher gurgled, "Cindy, Cindy, Cindy," as if she was wounding him grievously.

It was as if an earthquake were happening. Each and every man was thunderstruck and crushed by this new development, by her behavior.

Yet they couldn't keep their eyes off them—her—they couldn't stop looking at *her*. There was a strange excitement creeping into their faces—

I thought, *Cindy is cheating on her fiancé, and they are all turned on by it.* This is *outrageous*—this is *disgusting*. I thought this was some strange twisted and perverse form of sexism. I was furious with the men.

Chase said to me, "What is she DOING?"

I replied with a shrug, "I dunno, she likes this guy."

"She's got Vincenzo. How can she DO this?"

He was upset, but his eyes never left the pair even as he spoke, and his eyes were lit with a strange light.

I walked off in despair. I am *disgusted*.

Disgusted with this night.

Disgusted with Cindy.

And most of all, disgusted with all the Brits.

All I wanted was a quiet evening, an evening of flamenco, all of us together for the last time, and this was turning into quite a show—the Brits were a bunch of voyeurs. They couldn't stop leering at Cindy and Eduardo who were, well, quite honestly, on the way to devouring each other in public.

Chase followed after me and said, "Let's get out of here."

We had planned on going to the little Alps restaurant past the Chinese for dinner. But now Cindy refused to come. She was staying with her new Eduardo. Everyone knew precisely what this meant. It was tawdry. It was really ugly.

"Leave her, then!" Chase exclaimed with his own disgust.

As we left, I felt so sad—everything was in ruins.

Christopher took my hand and led me across the Bravo Murillo with almost disastrous results—he ran out in front of oncoming traffic, which nearly couldn't avoid us. He almost got us killed in the heat of this situation. I was left panting with the exertion of racing out of harm's way and raw fear.

Here is how we paired off as we walked up the street.

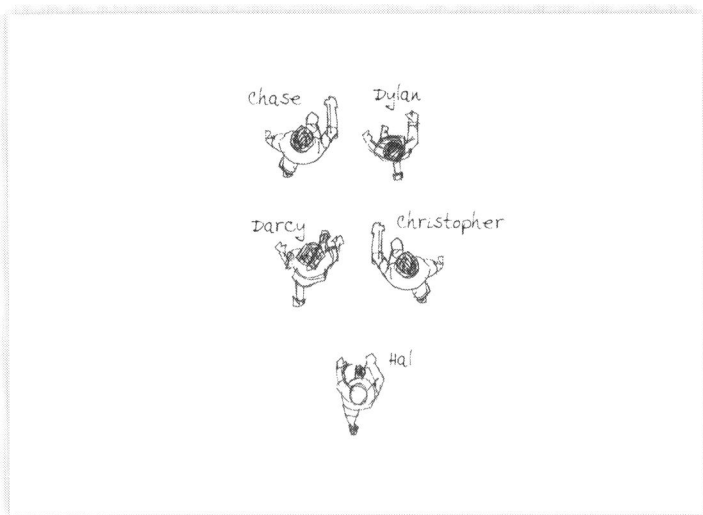

WALKING DOWN THE STREET

Suddenly, Christopher *howled*, "CINdy!!!!!" into the air. Then Hal started! They began to wail and buzz over Cindy and Eduardo.

I was fuming.

"But look at you. You love it!"

"What?" They asked in unison. "You are hot after Cindy, and now that she's gone off with a stranger, it's making you hotter!"

"No!" denied Christopher. Hal was shocked and speechless.

"This makes me sick," I said and continued walking on.

I looked back, and they were standing dead still in the middle of the street. Stunned. Speechless and motionless. I heard Hal talking to Christopher. He called after me, "No, Darcy, it's not that way!"

But I didn't turn back. I proceeded after Chase and Dylan, who had disappeared across a small fountain square and around the corner. What was I going to say? I was suddenly overtaken with guilt over my outburst, shame at my feelings. I'd been petty and taken out the emotions of the night on them. I didn't want Chase to know. How was I going to cover over my outburst with Chase and Dylan? Christopher and Hal were not following. They must have been mad at me. I was suddenly frightened—I was not going to pretend—if they came, surely they'd tell Chase and Dylan.

I rounded the corner and spied Chase and Dylan—they were all the way across the square, almost a block away.

Chase turned back and saw me alone. He gestured a question. I gestured a question back—Dylan broke off from Chase and backtracked toward me.

"Where are the others?"

"I don't know. We had a fight and they won't come."

"A fight?" Dylan was incredulous. "What did you fight about, then?"

"I yelled at them about Cindy." I wasn't going to try and whitewash it in the least. I'd been impetuous and unthinking.

Without a word, Dylan took off toward them.

I proceeded toward Chase, who is coming back for me.

I have single-handedly ruined the evening!

Chase approached—god, I would have liked to die and didn't want to tell him. He hates these kinds of scenes.

"Where are the others?"

"I don't know. I yelled at them and they won't come."

"You yelled?" Chase was equally incredulous—the only conflict I'd had the entire four weeks was with him after great provocation, and he knew it. "What's happened?" He looked at me in disbelief. "What did they do?"

"It was *me*. I got angry and I yelled at them. I'm sorry. I couldn't stop myself."

"What about? Tell me," he demanded. "Oh my god, are you tearing up?" He reached up to my cheek and touched the wetness. Then he stroked my hair with his other hand.

"I'm so sorry. I must be drunk. I lost my temper. The only thing left is for me to go home—they'll tell you what happened, I'm sure." I am so overcome with shame, I can hardly stand it in front of Chase.

I turned to leave, but Chase grabbed me and said, "No, you tell me. It's okay. Stay. Don't go home. It's okay. What has made you so upset?" I can see the boys coming across the square now. "What has driven you to tears? You must tell me, Darcy, and we'll sort it all out. We'll make it right! What is it?"

He was soothing me, consoling me, for by now my shoulders were shaking with sobs. "It's about Cindy. I just can't stand the way you are all reacting, that's all."

Had I stabbed him with a dagger, he couldn't have been more stunned. He literally took a step back and placed his hand over his heart (no lie).

"Then you're mad at me as well?"

So I blurted the whole thing out. "... and you're hot over her—she takes off with a stranger, and it makes her MORE attractive to you."

"No!" he shouted repeatedly. "No, Darcy, no!"

"I'm sorry, I can't stand it. And it's ruining everything. We only have one more night. Now I will have to go home and hate all of you forever. I know I've ruined everything—but I can't help it. I can't stand it."

I was drunk. But I am totally distraught with myself for losing it. And I am so inebriated I can not control the words that are coming out of my mouth.

"Listen to me." He grabbed my arm again and came very close. "I hate her for what she's done. Dylan and I were just discussing that very thing. You have to believe me, Darcy. We are disgusted. What she has done is the worst to us. It does not attract us. You've got it all wrong. It's the opposite. No, no you have to listen. You don't *believe* me, do you?" He saw it on my face. He saw it in my eyes. I think they are dogs in heat. That's what I think. I'm not proud of how I feel, but it is real.

"Dylan, tell her what we were talking about before." Chase was hopping back and forth around me like a basketball player guarding his basket.

Dylan, Christopher, and Hal arrived, and they all concurred. Dylan was very matter-of-fact and esoterically British in his speech.

"She has violated a fundamental rule of decency," he explained very precisely as we headed for the restaurant.

Chase cried out, "She went off on a one night's stand with a street creep, for gawd's sake! And she's engaged to married. It's the lowest!"

They were now all carrying on about how horrible her behavior was. Hal and Christopher entered the restaurant with Chase. I followed with Dylan, who was explaining "the code" that had been violated. "No, that is IT for her," he said adamantly. "I want nothing more to do with her. This is despicable behavior. We do not condone this behavior."

I had called their honor into question, and they were defending themselves against my verbal attack. They were hurt and bewildered. But even more than that, they wanted me to believe them. They wanted to convince me. Reluctantly, I told Chase I believed him when he came back and asked.

But I didn't. And he knew it. They would forgive her behavior in an instant, I just know it. Cindy can break any damn code she wants and get away with it because she's beautiful. I tell Chase that, and he says, "No—not this one. That's it for Cindy. I'm done with her."

We were ushered upstairs for dinner. Christopher joined us a few minutes late—I didn't know where he'd gone off to. Here is the seating arrangement:

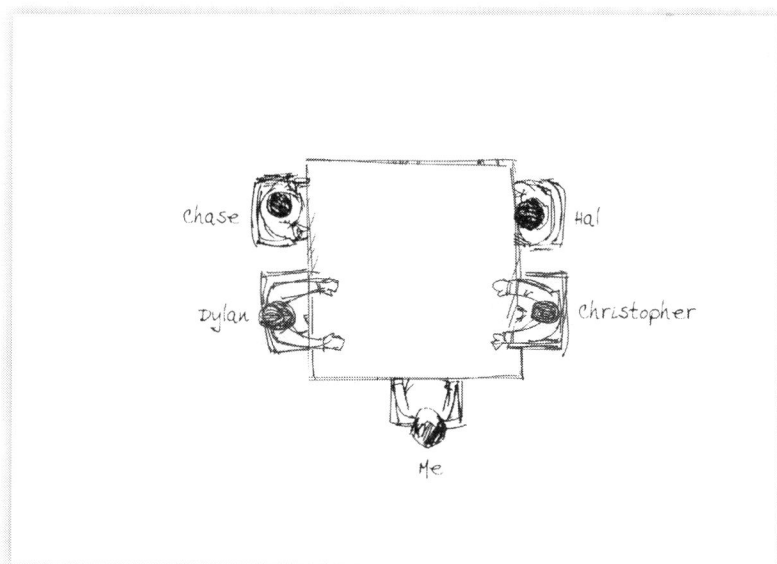

DINNER SEATING AT THE ALPS

I didn't like the seating arrangement because I was not next to Chase but figured it was part of our separating.

Dylan was very solicitous to me. He was not offended, as was Chase. ("How could you think so poorly of me?" was in his eyes.)

Someone brought up a general sex topic as usual, and Dylan leaned over to me and said, "You know, from the very beginning I looked on you as a mother figoor to the group, yet it feels completely natural to be talking about sex with you." He was mystified.

I looked at Chase with a smile. "Go figure." Chase's face lit up.

Dylan continued, "I would never talk about these things with my own mother, but you are different." I decided to take that as a compliment, which I had never heard Dylan give before.

The boys discussed what attracts them to a woman—actually Christopher discussed what turns him on about men! Much to Chase's disgust—he was rolling his eyes. I'm pretty sure that the bond between Christopher and Dylan is an affair. They are very loyal to one another. Neither of them will participate in any bad talk about the other. It's kind of sweet, really. (And still I find Christopher sexy—what is that? I will never understand my feelings for him.)

Chase brings up this bond between Christopher and Dylan repeatedly. I believe he knows and wants me to say it out loud. But I never do—I'm not gossiping about Christopher—I care too much about him to hurt him if it got back to him. And Chase is just too decent to say it, either. But he asks the question, and each time I see the answer in his eyes.

Christopher was talking about bums, and Dylan was talking about ankles (they are both bisexual, methinks). Hal and Chase were silent on the subject. Hal is way too sweet and modest to engage in this kind of conversation—I cannot imagine having a bawdy conversation in front of Hal—he is way too decent, way too gentlemanly for that.

Not being modest at all, and feeling raw about this general subject (I am not a siren for Chase), I told them they'd gotten it all wrong.

"It's not about body parts. It's about people. It's a whole package—if you just look for body parts you'll be missing what's important, and that's where the good sex is."

Chase's eyes lit up, and he was nodding his agreement.

"Am I right?" I said to him.

"Right, Darcy!"

"If you want good sex, go for the spiritual, the physical, and the personality. It's not just one element."

Chase gave me one of those all-knowing, sharing looks. We've had part of this discussion before, but not the personality part. The bonding part. I'm glad he agrees in principle—it takes some of the sting out of tomorrow. I know we have reached our end.

Here's the thing. Chase is taken. I know that. I respect that. I honor that because that is part of the very man who arrived in Madrid in the first place. If he weren't committed to two other women, I never would have seen how seriously he takes his commitments—one of the qualities that I find so attractive. And even though he is in the middle of a mess of his own doing, it's his own values that make it a mess for him. Otherwise he wouldn't care.

Though I dream of Chase every night, I would hate to play any part in the unraveling of his commitments. On one level I am grateful I don't have the ability to even tempt him.

Moreover, as I told Sarah the other night in a phone call from the plaza, Chase is this magnificent creature from another generation. He needs to find an equally magnificent woman to mate with and have a family. It would be a crime against nature not to. We can never belong to one another in that way. I know this completely. I understand this from my own position in my life. Still, what we are sharing is special. And I treasure it.

Chase began to talk to Dylan about Sophie. He was distraught about his upcoming divorce. He was distraught about losing his son. He told the whole group, "There is not a day that goes by I don't think about him, not a day that goes by that I don't miss him. There's not a day that goes by that I don't ask myself, 'What am I doing? Have I made a mistake? Should I go back?'"

I listened silently. I offered no pearls.

Dylan jumped in. "It's not a mistake! You don't love her. Sure, you could stay but you'd be miserable. You deserve better. Like I told you the other night, you deserve to be happy. And you cannot control what happens to Nicholas. He will hate you. Your wife will see to that. There's nothing you can do but hope he understands later when he's an adult."

I was *horrified*, totally disagreed, but kept my mouth shut. Chase was hurting right now. It was no time for public arguments about his lost son.

I also realized why he went off with Dylan instead of helping me the other night—he wanted to confide in Dylan (of all people). He wanted to talk about Nicholas—sometimes you need to just talk about the ones you've lost and miss. It's a burning, pressing, urgent need that Chase felt that night. To know that softens the hurt a bit. A pretty compelling emotional need next to my academic need. I am feeling pretty selfish myself at this point.

For dinner, I ordered pasta—everyone else ordered pizzas. I was feeding Christopher my garlic bread—such a starving, ravenous boy. But I feel sick—the emotional tumult of this day has gotten to me. I eat half of my dinner and give the rest to Christopher.

"Oh I couldn't," he objected. But he did. "You're always feeding me, Darcy. Thank you. Thank you!"

No amount of food will ever fill his voids. But still I try. Mother Earth.

The boys are drinking like there is no tomorrow. Chase has switched to *water*. Only the second time ever. He is very melancholy tonight.

At midnight, it was Dylan's birthday. The entire staff, at Christopher's behest, turned off the lights, brought in a cake with candles, and sang to him. It was very nice. And Dylan was so pleased. He said there were no people he would rather celebrate with more than us.

Then a waitress came with free rounds of some clear liqueur. It seemed it was the owner's birthday too—he said he was 58—but he looked 85. It was frightening.

Everyone saluted Dylan, tapped the shot glasses on the table, and tipped the glasses up—everyone but Chase and me. There was no way I was drinking that stuff. Chase had stopped drinking, but under the relentless insistence of the others, he slammed one back—

I thought he was going to die. His face turned bright red, and he lost his breath—he began to cough and put his hands to his throat as if he were choking. It was the most amazing display. I was riveted—scared for him— he seemed so fragile tonight.

Finally he opened his eyes, and I said, "Are you okay?"

He nodded mutely. He could not speak.

Later on the street, he told me it was the vilest liquor he had ever tasted. It immediately made him ill and drunk. He knew it would be so.

I said, "What's the matter with you? Why did you drink it, then?

He looked over with a macho grin. "Had to, Darcy. A male thing."

This macho drinking thing is unbelievable to me. You know something's going to make you sick and you do it anyway to save face? That's middle ages. It's barbarian!

But Chase is very invested in this bravo, macho culture.

Chase is a man's man.

A team player.

A man's man—a woman's man—well he's attractive to and attracted by, but he's not really got that together yet.

I've never been attracted to a man like this before. He is nothing like the men I usually fall for.

"Let's go," he said to me after we paid. The others were haggling over the bill. We both hate this incessant haggling over paying.

Chase and I left the restaurant first.

On the street, I said to him, "I'm worried about Nicholas." Chase looked at me askance. He didn't want to hear it, so I gave him the short version. "Chase, you are such a wonderful man, a unique man. And your son deserves his father. No one else can do that for him—be his father. I don't know about you and your wife or Lauren. You have to work that out. But Nicholas is different. Nicholas is your son, and he needs you."

Chase was silent.

I shut up.

I'd been pretty offensive to him tonight. But I'm feeling urgent; time is so short.

We walked to my apartment in silence.

I tried to fit my key in the lock, but it kept landing off-center.

I handed it to Chase.

He easily opened the lock. You would *never* know he'd had too much to drink. Awkwardly, we said good night. He was not there tonight. I watched him leave from the doorway. He sprinted across Bravo Murillo in the opposite direction from the Metro stairs. He headed down Calle Paseo de la Castellana on foot.

I realized he was walking home. It was at least a five-mile walk, and it was 1:00 a.m.

He needed the solitude. Chase had so much to think about.

I am not sleeping much tonight. I've been tossing and turning Chase all night long.

Chapter 13

Friday
December 18, 1998

When I arrived at school this morning, Ethan was the only one there. He is *wrecked*, can barely speak. The others straggled in late. Christopher was a half-hour late. We are a motley crew on the last day. I can smile but could barely speak. I stumbled to my seat and flopped into it. Poor Gareth had to conduct a four-hour class with the likes of us.

He turned to me for answers, and I just blankly said, "Huh?"

Everyone laughed!

Sitting down next to me, Cindy whispered that she was with Eduardo 'til 5:00 a.m. at a pool hall. Right. She was very happy—too happy—she was wracking up the balls, all right!

Chase told me he had indeed walked home last night and had been accosted by hordes of prostitutes on every block. He told me how they grabbed him and he had to fend them off, of course dramatizing the tale with glee. I imagined this and was horrified. He told me how he found a phone at 2:00 a.m. and called Lauren. She had just arrived home herself from going out with friends in Athens (3:00 a.m. Greek time). This life-style is completely strange.

I feel sorry for our teacher. We are worthless today. Every one of us is unable to participate. It is pathetic.

Of course, Christopher is the *worst*. He keeps drifting off to sleep at his desk. And he is seated right next to the teacher. I was watching him with concern. If only I had been sitting next to him I could have jabbed him with an elbow.

Suddenly he began to snore in Gareth's face! A huge snort-snore rang out in the classroom! And Gareth said, "All right Christopher, that is it for you."

Christopher was up with a "Huh? Huh?" And we were all laughing our heads off.

I was pissing myself I laughed so uncontrollably. I have absolutely no self-control this morning.

"Mr. St. George, you may leave," said Gareth. "Go to the conference room and think about how rude you are!"

He'd been kicked out of class! I could not believe this final commotion he was causing.

When we went on break, we found him, not in the conference room as he had been instructed, but down in Pan's sipping *café con leche*. We joined him and had a great laugh.

I will never meet as outrageous a person as Christopher ever again. Of this I am completely sure because in all my years, I have never met anyone like him 'til now.

But get this—when we returned for our final lesson, it was a review of the entire five-week class. The lesson was a game for which we paired off. Chase and I got to play as a team.

Chase and I stunk—we got minus points. It was Christopher who re-membered everything from the very beginning of the course to this very morning when he had been in and out of sleep. Christopher got every single question right. It's as I have told him repeatedly over the last four weeks— he is brilliant—or at the least very, very smart. He can even learn through sleepy osmosis.

Finally the lesson was over. We had all passed. Michael had arrived, and I asked her if everything was okay. She answered, "Yes." That's all. And I didn't pursue it. But the message was she had passed the course. Further proof to me that it had all been decided long ago.

We were to meet our teacher, Gareth, at the Chinese. We were all very subdued on the way over. This is our last outing together.

When we reached the ornate golden door, Cindy pulled back and said, "I'm not coming in."

"Why?" everyone asked in unison.

"I have a stomach ache, and I have shopping to do before I leave tonight," is all she would say. She hugged each one of us and said her final goodbyes. And then she turned away and left.

Chase had been angry for two weeks at Cindy for making reservations to leave town on our last day. It didn't matter that she was meeting Vincenzo in Italy. To him, it represents a lack of loyalty to the group. It's unthinkable to him not to spend the last night with the group. He ranted and raved about it, saw it as further proof of her shallowness. He did hug her, but he was so offended and disappointed. He had cared about her deeply. He was taking her defection very personally.

Emma begged off too, saying she was too tired to go out tonight. We were all beyond tired at this point. Chase tried to cajole her into staying, even used team guilt to coerce her, but Emma was not swayed. Having used most of his angst up on Cindy, he just waved Emma on in disgust.

When we chose seats, Chase went around to the far side where we had twice before sat together. I held back. I chose to sit opposite him. Michael sat next to me. The seating looked like this:

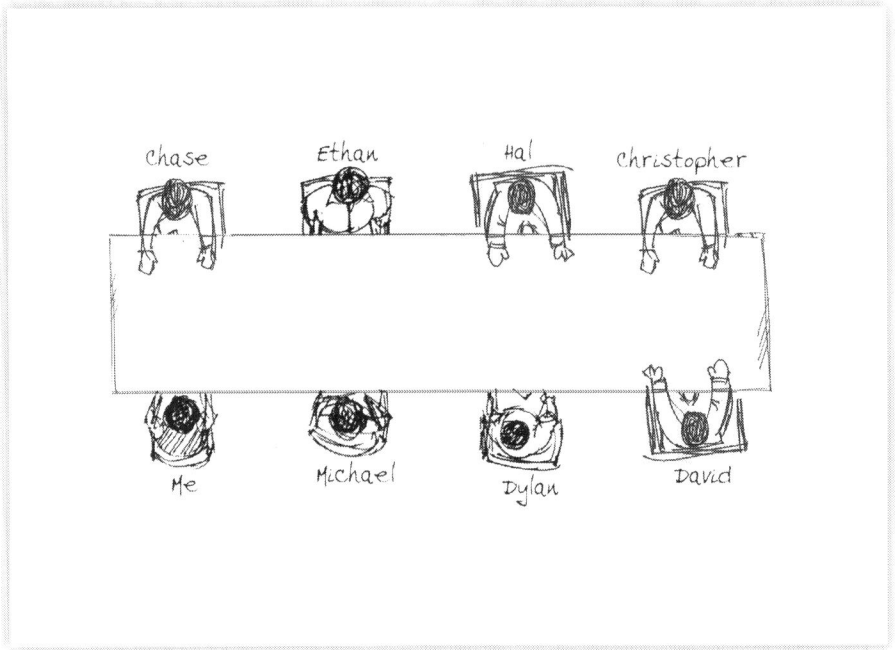

SEATING FOR OUR LAST MEAL

Chase is silent and very serious.

I am thinking, it's almost over and we have nothing to say to one another. We *never really* had anything in common but the course.

I am troubled by this thought. It would invalidate everything we've been through together—everything I've felt for the last four weeks.

Or would it?

Perhaps it had all been an illusion brought about by severe adversity, stress, and fear. I have hallucinated my attachment to all five Brits.

I do have a great imagination.

Chase became very impatient with the slow service. He organized the table to order (always our leader, and he does it so well—I have learned so much from him).

Finally, the waitress brought *vino tinto y vino blanco*. Chase took my glass first and poured for me. As I was about to pick it up, he reached across the table and placed his hand on the glass, saying, "No, there's something wrong with it. Don't drink it."

He looked at it. He smelled it. He tasted it, and he called the waitress—
"This is bad. *Muy malo*," he stated authoritatively.

I just feel warm all over—Chase has watched out for me again. I feel
protected and cared for by these small civilities. I haven't had this luxury
since the day you walked out the door, Paco. And you know? When someone looks out for you, underneath it all, at the end of the day, it means that
to someone, you are worth being looked out for. And it's not a matter of
self-sufficiency or independence or believing in yourself. It's a matter of
feeling cared for on this whole wide planet. It's a matter of connection to
any other living soul in this life on an equal plane. I haven't felt this kind
of connection in such a long time. It feels so good. It may sound superficial, but this is what has brought the roses to my cheeks. It makes me feel
truly alive. I think when you don't have this kind of caring in your life,
whether you are married, single, or widowed, you wither on the vine and
you just die.

I have missed you so much, Paco. But at this moment, I realize that
I can still feel cared for. At this moment I realize that it is possible for
me to feel cared for by more than just you. At this moment I realize for
the second time on this trip that I could have a future. My life may not
be over.

I have just spent five years without the protection of my man. It's these
little things that a man does for a woman that make her feel cared for and
loved, make her feel special. They are a man's way of laying a claim for the
world to see—I value this woman. I will watch out for her.

All of the Brits have done this for me—every single one, but especially
Chase. As a result, I feel important and valued for the first time in years.
That's what the glow is on my face, a reflection of being cherished.

If I never see these boys again I will never forget this feeling. Whenever
I am down, I will remind myself: I have been loved. I have been loved
by Britain's best! For they are that. Each and every one of them. For
all their very human weaknesses or prejudices and frailties, they have
been brought up well and they are each caring and sensitive boys. Some
see the British reserve and politeness as a mask against dishonesty and
deception—I am fortunate to have been the recipient of their generosity
and caring natures.

They treasured me. They revered me for who I am. And I them.

And of course, Chase most of all. Chase even cleans my glasses for me—I am so bad at taking the time to clean them, and so I love that most of all. He would notice my glasses were dirty, and after teasing me about the dirt, "Darcy, what is this?" He would hold up his finger. "How many fingers am I holding up? HeLLOOO, how can you see?"

He would take the glasses off my face and clean them with a little smirk on his lips. Then he would reach over and place them carefully on my face.

"There, how's that?"

"Oh Chase, it's you!" I would reply. "Thank god, I thought a mugger had stolen my glasses!"

So dear. So very dear to me. No one *ever* cleaned my glasses before. Not even you, Paco. Not even you.

And no one ever protected me from bad wine before. Of course, I never needed to worry about bad wine before. ...

I looked at Chase as he poured wine from the new bottle, and thought I would miss him very much, indeed. What a treasure. How lucky I have been to have met him.

This will change my life. I know it in my heart. After being loved so well for these five weeks, how could I return home the same person? I won't. I know it.

These were the thoughts racing through my mind and touching my heart as I watch Chase across the table.

Everyone helped Hal order now. He is so sensitive about meat, everyone wanted to spare him a bad experience. Chase and I looked at each other with smiles. We had discussed Hal and vegetarianism so often:

"Darcy, what is the top of the food chain?"

"Chase, who has a free will?"

"We are the top—we eat meat! What is so hard to understand?"

"We can choose not to if we figure it out. Some of us use our intellects!"

We go around and around. The dance of the carnivores. The dance of acceptance.

꧁

We shut down the Chinese that day—it was about 5:00 or 6:00 p.m., way past time for *siesta*, and it was so sad. As we drank, Chase and Ethan and I talked. Chase asked us what we would do for Christmas, which was only six days away. We talked about the holidays—bittersweet—Chase was so excited about going home to Lauren.

Ethan asked me questions about Jaime.

We had at least four rounds of *vinos*, and then the brandy appeared!

Afterwards, we went on to the new bar near my apartment. Dylan said his goodbyes—he was having another birthday party later this evening. The rest of us sat at the empty bar. I pulled up a barstool next to Hal. Here was the seating:

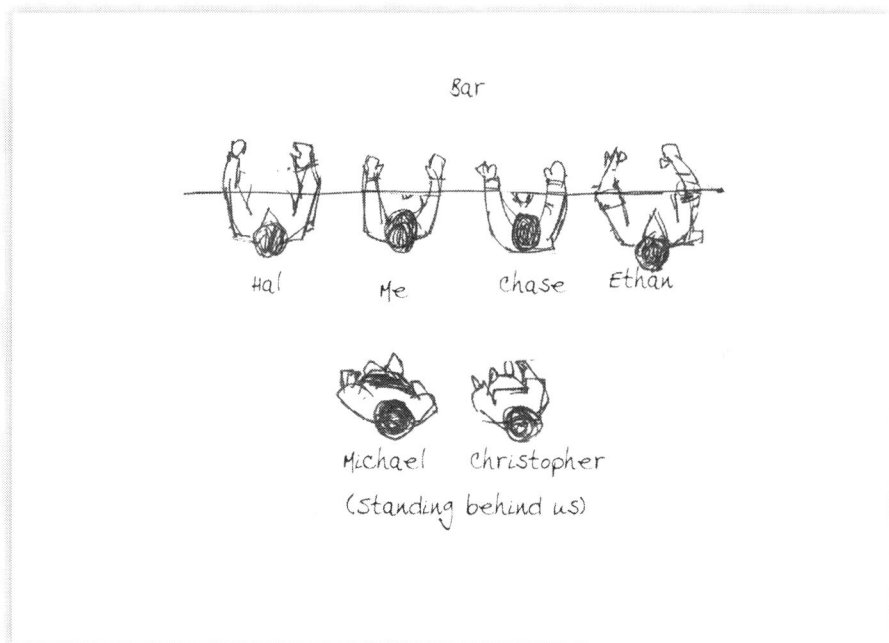

STANDING AT THE LAST BAR

I was no longer looking to be near Chase, but I longed for it. I socialized with Christopher, Michael, and Hal for a long time. I was drinking *vino tinto* and feeling very good. The class was over. There was no longer any reason not to let loose and just have fun.

I needed to use the bathroom, which was in the basement. When I returned, Chase motioned me over to where he and Ethan stood. They pulled up a chair for me.

"What would you like?" asked Chase.

"A bloody Mary."

"All RIGHT!" They both loved that and eagerly negotiated with the bartender for this drink. The bloody Mary was very strange tasting and strong, not like any bloody Mary I'd ever had before.

I still thought the conversation was awkward and stilted. Everyone knew our time was now measured in empty drink glasses.

Then, in walked Eduardo. He greeted us all as old friends! The boys asked him how Cindy was—he said she was at the train station by now.

I turned to Chase and said, "Oh my god, he knows exactly where Cindy is!"

"Stomach ache, indeed," Chase sneered.

He jumped up and begged Michael for her cell phone. Michael handed it over, and Chase called Cindy. He had to—he couldn't *not* do it.

That was exactly what I had meant. She was forgiven enough that everyone there wanted to say goodbye to her. Including me.

Chase said his goodbyes quickly and handed me the phone; she was still talking.

"I'm going to miss you!" she was saying so sweetly and sexily.

"Hi Cindy! It's me, Darcy."

"Darcy, hi! I'm just arriving at the train station. You know why I left before don't you?"

"No."

"Oh, I can't do goodbyes. They're too hard for me. I thought you knew."

Now, how would I know? And as if goodbyes aren't hard for everybody. As if we weren't all suffering right now—

I passed the phone to Christopher, who yelled out, "Cindy, Cindy! You are my favorite of EVERYONE! I'm so sad you're leaving!"

I looked at Chase. Unacceptable behavior, indeed! She was completely forgiven by Christopher, who is the king of unforgivable acts.

Chase sidled up to me. "I was never attracted to her, you know."

I looked at him quizzically. "You weren't?"

"You don't get it, do you? She is not my type. I knew it the first time I met her, and it never changed for me. I am not attracted to her in the least."

He was still defending his honor to me.

"And I was right. She has no morals. She is shallow and totally self-centered. In fact, I don't think I have ever met a woman as self-centered and selfish as she."

I was mollified. Now I believe him. He could see it in my face and re-laxed for the first time since last night.

Meanwhile, Eduardo decided he must see Cindy off at the train station and he rushed out to get there before the train left. This set the boys off once again—oh! The slurs on her character—they were merciless. I think they were condemning her because she had hurt them. They had really cared for her, and her actions had showed no caring for them in return. Because at the end of the day, they would have forgiven her any transgres-sion of any code. I just believe that is the way it was.

Suddenly I realized I must talk to Christopher. Now. If I don't talk to him now, there will never be another time.

I stood between him and Michael, who had not left his side all evening. "You hurt me last week," I began.

Poor Christopher was so drunk by now, he simply began to gurgle at me.

"When? Me? No, Darcy, not me!"

"You called me Mrs. Robinson."

"I'm SORRY! I didn't mean it! You must forgive me!" He was holding me now, hugging me and squeezing me, and he was scared.

"You know, Christopher, I am not Mrs. Robinson."

"No, of course not, you're nothing like her!"

"But I do think you're the sexiest thing I ever laid eyes on!"

Christopher's eyes grew wide and horrified. "No, Darcy, no!"

He grabbed me and hugged me. He was *wild*! He was kissing my neck and hugging me like a crazed wild man. In my ear, he said, "But it will always be unrequited," in a horrible whisper of regret.

"I know that, Christopher," I replied seriously. "But I want you to know how much you have affected me. You woke me up, dear man. I am very happy. You have changed my life. And I want to thank you."

"No, this can't be true!" He was alternately kissing me wildly and hug-ging me in great big bear hugs, and then he moaned, "It can never be!"

"It's okay, Christopher. It's okay," I soothed him. My feelings for Christopher are so intense, so raw, physical, primitive—so complex. Yet I'm okay with it just the way it is.

At this moment, I thought nothing could surpass the emotion I was feeling—I was wrong. Eventually Christopher calmed down, and I returned to my seat by Chase and Ethan. Chase was inviting Ethan to play on his Olympics field hockey team for Greece. I was on my seat, Michael standing behind me with Christopher to her side. ...

Michael put *her* hands on my waist, which made me jump. Before I could turn, she put her hand clear under my butt and pushed her hand up into the crevice of my derriere!

I *screamed* bloody murder! And jumped right off my barstool into Chase's arms.

"Darcy, what! What! What's happened?" he demanded at full attention.

I looked over at Michael, who was pretending nothing at all happened. I calmed myself but I was shaking, and I said, "Chase, would you please take my seat?"

"Why? I don't need a seat."

"Because Michael just goosed me, and I can't be near him right now."

Chase's eyes got wide, and he immediately sat down. "Let him try it," he said fiercely into my ear.

We were of the same mind about scenes. Unspoken. No need. I was relieved.

But I was *staggered* that this person I had trusted as a woman could goose me! She had made innuendoes at me for four weeks, which I had ignored. I had gone off with her alone—I was completely stunned. I mean, I thought she identified herself as a woman and I was safe with her.

Apparently I was wrong. I wasn't safe from the HIM part, I thought. Or perhaps it was the HER part! Ay, yi, yi. One of the great mysteries. I have lived a sheltered life, I think. An American life. A sheltered, suburban American life. I am innocent of whatever Michael's life and emotions are about. A life of incomprehensible poverty and violence, I think. But I have always accepted Michael for whoever she was. I knew she was different, but I related to whomever she presented to me each day. I do not regret this. The rest is none of my business. It's personal. It's private.

Later, at about 10:00 p.m., Christopher and Michael were saying goodbye—they were going over to Dylan's birthday party. Christopher said to me in front of everyone, "You are the nicest person I have ever met. You have said the nicest things to me every single day. And I will miss you sorely."

"I will miss you too, Christopher. You have changed me, and I love you for it."

We embrace. I have meant every word.

Michael joined in on the chorus of how nice I am.

"You only saw my good qualities. You always built up my confidence and supported me. Thank you." She hugged me—how *utterly confusing*. "You did that for every single person in the course. I watched you."

"I only said what I saw."

"No, you have a gift. You make people feel good."

She spoke from her heart. I was touched by her gratitude, for I had really reached out to her when no one else would. It's not that I did it to receive acknowledgement, it's that I made an effort on her behalf and then I took the heat for that with the teachers and in the end, she had caused me trouble.

And then there was Hal, who was leaving, too. Dear, sweet, innocent Hal.

"You'd better write to me," he said in an emotion-choked voice. "Or I will be very annoyed. I'm not kidding now. I'll be very *annoyed*."

"I *promise*. I love writing. I'm the one who writes copiously. Remember?"

At that moment, Christopher collapsed on the floor—he was so drunk, he simply slithered down to the ground, his body as fluid as a waterfall.

Michael and Hal got him on his feet and helped him out to the street— it took a good few minutes—I couldn't imagine how they would get him onto the Metro and then to yet another bar. The fact that this was their intention was beyond the beyond. Beyond all reasonable thought. If I live to be a hundred, I will never understand this mindset, this way of living. It has its charm, but it is also completely irrational. And completely beyond my control. I have walked through some sort of time portal into their lives, and out will I go in just a few short, precious hours.

Once they left, Ethan, Chase, and I went back to the bar. It felt like a great load had been lifted. It was the three of us again ... the Three Musketeers.

And we settled in to relaxing, recapping, and having our typical brand of fun together.

Ethan was completely *wrecked*. I have never seen him this bad before. His face and neck are streaked with scary red missile streaks. Chase's solution is to put him on beer. And water. But he was keeping an eye on him and asked him regularly how he was. Once his face returned to its normal color, Chase allowed him to resume his bloody Mary. ...

I thought to myself, this is lunacy. Utter, British lunacy.

Chase asked if I would send him something from America.

"Sure, what do you want?"

"A sweatshirt. From the University of California! Can you do that, Darcy?"

"Sure, I'd be glad to, but what size?"

"What size do you think?" His voice was sexy, his eyes daring me to find out.

"May I?" I asked.

"I'm all yours."

Don't I just wish?

I turned Chase around and began to Braille his back, up from his waist to his shoulders and out. "Turn," I said, while coaxing his tall body. He was grinning from ear to ear. Then I did the same to his chest.

I was touching him like a lover, not a seamstress. It was a natural way for me to touch Chase, as if I'd touched him this way a thousand times before. It felt heavenly.

His eyes were smoky, his grin sumptuous.

"Whoa girl, have you got the lay of the land?"

"I guess that will just have to do," I said smartly.

Ethan looked on with a smile. Dr. Eckleburg approved.

"I was afraid you'd have to pry her off," he said to Ethan, but he still held my hands in his.

And that was how the last half of the evening was. Hot, sexy, fun like the contact sports Chase loved so well. I just wanted to touch him so badly. And I did, his arms, his legs, his hands, whatever I could get away with. And he was touching me back.

Chase was repeating his invitation to Jaime and me to come to Greece. He said very seriously that he was not joking. I said, that's what he says to all the girls he meets. Very seriously, he said I was the first. The only. We must come. I accepted. We shook on it.

Then he asked, "May we come and visit you in America, Darcy?"

I said with delight, "Sure, come and visit!"

"No, I'm not kidding, now. I want to come."

"That would be wonderful."

"Are you serious?" He seemed uncertain.

"Chase, I would love you to come and stay with me. I'm not just saying it—I want you to come. We'll have so much fun together." Chase has only ever been to California. "Chicago has jazz and blues and *baseball*."

Chase's eyes lit up. "Baseball? Can we go?"

"Of course—which team do you want to see?"

"Cubs! We have to see the Cubs," he said instantly. I couldn't believe he knew about the Cubs! "Ethan, can you and Mare come?"

"Sure. Mary wants to see America."

Chase's eyes were on mine as he spoke to Ethan. "When do you get your first vacation?"

"Spring 2000."

"Spring 2000. Is that okay, Darcy?"

"Yeah."

We were all yipping and cheering now.

"It's a pact," Chase said seriously. We all put our hands together. "We will meet in Chicago in 2000!"

"But we can't just stay in Chicago," I protested. "You have to see Yellowstone and Colorado."

"We can hire a car and do a road trip!" Chase was ecstatic! "Ethan, how does that sound?"

Ethan loved it.

"I have a car. We can use my car," I offered.

"Did you hear that, Ethan? We have a free car! Wa HEYYYY!"

We had two pacts.

Chicago in spring 2000 and Greece in summer 2004, if not sooner. We were all jubilant!

"And we have to do bungee jumping," Chase exclaimed.

"No. No bungee jumping," I declared firmly.

"But Darcy, you have to do! You must do! You can come with me. We'll go in the same harness together. I'll keep you safe."

I was laughing my head off! "No one is safe doing a bungee jump, silly. It's insane. It's the one thing I will *never*, ever do!"

Chase looked me in the eye. He is suddenly serious. "Not even with me? Wouldn't you trust me, Darcy?"

I gazed up into Chase's eyes silently for one long moment.

"Yes," I breathed quietly. "I would go with you, Chase." I would do anything with him if he said it was safe.

Chase let out a cheer. "She'll go! Ethan, she'll go! Will you go, too?"

Ethan was laughing hard as he nodded yes.

"Then we'll do naked bungee jumping!"

Chase had gone beyond the beyond. ...

"I'm not doing any naked anything."

Then he started lobbying for naked bungee jumping.

To shut him up, I said yes.

"Wa HEYYYY!" He was hollering and hooting!

We are all three laughing so hard it hurts.

We talked about so many things—Jaime, oh! He made me call Jaime— he wanted to say hello to Jaime, and he came with me to the phone. Jaime wasn't home, so I put a message on the machine:

"Hi, honey, it's Momma. I'm just calling to see how you are today and to say I'm leaving in the morning. Hope your flight was good, and I can't wait to see you. Love you!"

When I finished, Chase was standing right behind me and he said, "That was the nicest mum call I have EVER heard." He was reverent again.

"Really? What kind of message would your mom leave?"

"Where the fuck are you? Call me!"

"That's outrageous!"

"That's Mum. That's why I don't call her. ..."

We talked about Eddie—he wanted to know everything about my brothers and sisters. I tell him I have a cop brother—he wants to know what position he has—hesitantly I said, "Well, he's not a cop on the street anymore."

"Did he get a new job, then?"

"Kind of. He's the chief."

"Chief?" Chase's eyes lit up—god, I love it when his eyes light up! "Like, as in chief of police?"

"Uh huh."

You would have thought he'd hit the lottery jackpot. He was *so* excited. He wanted to call Eddie now. So we did, but it was Friday evening rush hour in Chicago and he couldn't talk—he was annoyed with me, and I felt bad. But Chase was not swayed. I told him my brother collects police paraphernalia from around the world.

"Then I will send him a patch and a Scottish police hat. Would he like that?"

Now my eyes lit up. Chase pulled out some paper from his wallet. "Write your address and phone number. I'll keep it in my wallet," he said.

I had seen all the contents of his wallet before while he was staying with me and I knew that was where he kept memorabilia—I had objected when he earlier gave away his class address sheet. But he kept my address in his special place. I was mollified once more.

When I was done, he said, "Can I send the police things to you? Will you make sure he gets them?"

"Of course."

He was so satisfied with himself and with me.

Before we knew it, the bar was closing. It was time to leave, time to say our final goodbyes.

I am so sad.

We make our way to the street. Chase is coming up to my room to get the remainder of his things. So, Ethan shook his hand and hugged him.

He turned to me, and I reached up on tip-toes and hugged him. I don't think I realized 'til that moment just how tall Ethan is. He held me very tightly. I was surprised at how solid he was. He wouldn't let me go. He told me how glad he was we met and how great I am, etc. I told him he was the best. We kissed on both cheeks, and then he hugged me once again. I am overwhelmed with emotions—

As Ethan retreated up Bravo Murillo toward the Metro, Chase took my hand and said, "See? Ethan never gets emotional—that was beautiful. Did you see that?"

We walked the few steps up to my door. It feels like a gallows walk. So restrained—I know I have to be so restrained or I will lose all control and blubber all over the place. That would never do.

Chase took my key and opened the front door.

Once in the lobby, he put his hands on my shoulders to steady me.

"What? Aren't I walking straight?"

"You're fine, girl, fine."

There is no air in the tiny metal elevator. It takes forever. Chase is standing on one side, and I am on the other. That leaves one foot of space between us. I can barely breathe.

Chase opened the apartment locks. I didn't have to retell him which keys went in which locks. He remembered from days and days ago. It's amazing.

Inés was inside watching TV in the living room.

"Come in," I said to him as he shrank back.

We went directly to my room—the tension *so thick* between us.

"Is that the acrobat?" he whispered incredulously.

I paused and thought—oh! I had told him about my landlady's night-time paramours, the exploits I regularly heard through the bedroom wall. "The sexual Olympics!" I giggle. "Yes, that's her!" We laugh and laugh silently in the little bedroom.

Chase retrieved his stuff, changed his shoes while standing up (I told him he could sit down, but he wouldn't).

It is *excruciating*.

When he was ready, he came to me and kissed me on each cheek. Properly. With restraint.

I returned the proper kisses. Such formality. Such a *need* for formality.

He moved to go. I led him back through the apartment to the front door, which I closed behind me.

In the pitch dark hall, I whisper in choked voice, "Goodbye, Chase."

And Chase reached for me. I turned my cheek to him, thinking he wanted to kiss my cheeks again.

Suddenly I felt his lips upon mine, his soft luscious lips brushing ever so softly against mine. The same soft lips in my dream.

It was over in a heartbeat.

"Goodbye, Darcy," he said in that smoky, Scottish voice that I will never forget for the rest of my days.

"Goodbye, Chase, goodbye. ..."

I turned and retreated through the door.

I don't know how I got to the bedroom, but I dropped down on the bed and I began to cry. And cry. And cry. Great sobbing cries into my pillow.

In the moment, I had thought the kiss was a mistake in the dark. I turned, and he missed my cheek.

But as I rerun the kiss in my mind, the reality was I had turned away from him and he had found my lips!

It was the most exquisitely beautiful kiss. His lips were so soft, so pliant, they melded perfectly with mine.

I am *devastated*. I will never see Chase again. I have felt his soft lips on mine and I will never see him again.

I am so much more devastated than I thought I could be. My heart is breaking. It hurts so much.

It was the kiss—the kiss, that couldn't ever be. ...

Chase! Oh my sweet, sweet Chase!
I will never forget your soft lips.
Your lips will haunt me in the night.
Every night, your soft, tantalizing lips will come to mine in the dark.
Every night I will reach for you. And you will be gone.

I know about the empty nights, Paco. I already know about the gone.

December 19, 1998

Dearest Sean,

I'm on my way home. We took off from Madrid Barajas Airport about five hours ago, and now, after a layover at Heathrow, I am over the Atlantic again. Looking out the double-paned airplane window, I can see the teeny, tiny whitecaps below. It's so vast out there. The whitecaps are blurry through the moisture inside the window and in my eyes. I feel numb with the sadness. If I allow it to engulf me in its entirety, I may never extricate myself. We are both airborne right now, Chase and me—me heading west, he heading east; I am feeling the miles between us grow. Tears are flowing down my cheeks uncontrollably. Quiet tears. Streams that effortlessly run their own course. I hope the lady next to me can't tell. Yet, I don't really care. I'm beyond caring what others think of me. So far beyond.

In the cab this morning, as we sped on the A-10 toward the airport, I gazed out the window at the white houses speckled along rolling Iberian sunlit hillsides and wanted to press my forehead to the window and scream, "Nooooo!" to the driver. It wouldn't have helped.

I want to go home. But I don't want to leave this magical, wonderful new world. I can't wait to see our Jaime. Paco, it's been three months now. Can you believe it? My first three months of being separated from our son. Agony. How ironic I am now pulled away from returning to him.

I know I will never be the same. But where will it lead? I feel as if I will be starting over. It feels as if this is the beginning of something new. Funny. It's kind of come full circle, Paco. Kind of like I'm the pioneer now, crossing the seas to a strange new land. A land completely foreign to me, my new life without you.

It's over. This incredible experience has come to an end.

Adios, España.

Love you forever and ever.

Your forever,
Darcy

P.S. What will happen to me, Paco? I'm still scared.

Epilogue

Dearest Sean,

I'm writing again. Oh my god! I'm so excited. It's been five years since I've written ... well, since losing sweet you. But all of a sudden, since I've returned home from Madrid, I'm absolutely inspired. I finished a first draft of a new book. I wrote it in pencil. Paco, it was like automatic writing; I put the pencil to paper and just started writing, and it simply poured out of me as if it wasn't even voluntary. It's the most amazing thing I've ever experienced. Like it was just waiting to be put down on paper. Now I need to start editing what I have—it's really a mess. Lots of work left to do to make it into something readable. And I start my new semester next week.

So I gotta go, want to get back to it before the day is gone. But first, I have to write to this stranger who wrote me an email today.

Sean! You'll never believe it—I went on the Internet to look up this Scottish singer that Chase played during his lessons 'cause I want to hear the music playing in the background while I'm writing—you know how I love to write to music? Well, anyway, for the life of me, I can't remember the singer's name. I know he's British, 'cause the Brits were so wild about him and they all knew every lyric of this song, every single note! But I can't remember the name of the song, either; wish I had written it down. ... So, I went online to this place called Yahoo! Funny, this Website is what they call a kind of search engine. It searches the Internet for you, like an automatic card catalog; you can find information and Websites with it—so much has happened since you've left, Paco. The world is changing so fast. I wish you could be here to see it. Wish we could share it together. ...

Anyway, I surfed over—they call it surfing the Web, like surfing the card catalog—to Yahoo, UK, and I found this Website for a record store chain in the Northwest of England called Townhouse Records. And so, I called them up to ask about this song. Can you believe it? I called England. A transcontinental call! Remember when we went to England on our honeymoon? Paco, it was so wild actually talking to someone there. And he sounded as if he were right next door! Incredible.

The manager of the store answered the phone; his name is Will, and he said he would help me locate the song. Isn't that too cool? He's a very nice man; I like his voice very much—he sounds like Cary Grant.

But anyway, he sent me a CD of this Scottish singer named James Grant with a song called Walk the Last Mile. But, get this, after all that, it's not the right song. So I noticed an email address on the Website and wrote him an email thanking him for his help, telling him I love this James Grant (very sexy voice). But it's not the right singer he's found for me. I asked him, could he think of any other singers it could be? I mean, I love this new guy named James Grant—his music is fantastic! But it's not the right song for my inspiration—I need to find this other Scottish singer. I just really need to hear that particular song to set the right mood while I do my editing. I need to hear it so I can remember Chase singing it in class. I need to hear it so I can remember that feeling of Spain.

Paco, I got an answer email from Townhouse Records within 15 minutes! I could not believe it. That Will guy is really there. But, wouldn't you know, it wasn't Will who signed the email. It was some other guy who answered my email. I'm so confused. Some guy named Rob answered my personal email to Will. It's kind of creepy, really. To write to someone and get a response from someone else entirely.

Who the hell is Rob? I don't know anyone named Rob in England. And he didn't say a thing about Will. Just talked about the song. Said he'd "have a think about it," whatever that means.

Paco, it's kind of scary having a strange man write an email to me; I mean, this whole email thing is so new—I'm just not sure about it. It's odd. You don't know who's at the other end of the words. Can't see a thing. Kind of spooky.

But mostly it's really annoying; actually, it's disappointing—I like this person Will, and now some stranger has written to me instead.

He said, he'd have a *think* about it … the phrase is so cute … that is the most adorable thing!

Okay, talk to you later, Paco. I gotta go find out who this weirdo Rob is.

Love you!

Love You Forever, and Ever, and EVER,
Darcy

P.S. Where **ARE** YOU????

Made in the USA
Charleston, SC
20 July 2012